D0482064

THE SECRET OF A HEART NOTE

THE SECRET OF A HEART NOTE

Stacey Lee

KATHERINE TEGEN BOOKS
An Imprint of HarperCollins Publishers

Katherine Tegen Books is an imprint of HarperCollins Publishers.

The Secret of a Heart Note
Copyright © 2016 by Stacey Lee
www.epicreads.com

Library of Congress Control Number: 2016938951
ISBN 978-0-06-242832-5

Typography by Ellice M. Lee
16 17 18 19 20 PC/RRDH 10 9 8 7 6 5 4 3 2 1
❖
First Edition

To Jonathan

ONE

"Beware, ye aromateur; lay your traps of love,
but do not yourself get caught."
—*Larkspur, Aromateur, 1698*

MOST PEOPLE DON'T know that heartache smells like blueberries. It's not the only scent, but it's the main one, and if someone comes to us smelling like blueberry pie, Mother and I turn them away. The heartbroken need time to heal before we can work our magic.

According to Mother, today's client does not smell like blueberries, which is why I'm in our workshop, crushing cinnamon for the client's elixir—what the rest of the world calls a love potion—instead of doing my algebra homework. Under our new arrangement, I get to attend public high school instead of being homeschooled, as long as my duties as an aromateur don't suffer. Unlike the mothers of most fifteen-year-old girls, mine doesn't give a Turkish fig about homework.

The blue door of our workshop heaves open and Mother steps in, all five feet of her, looking like a blue fairy with her pixie cut, and her gardening uniform of denim shirt, jeans, and visor. She wears only blue, not because she's sad, but because any other color distracts her nose. "Our three thirty just drove up. You ready?"

"Uh, sure." Why wouldn't I be ready?

With a sigh, she rolls her SPF sleeves down her skinny arms. "Mimosa, we talked about this. You do the secondaries for the men from now on."

"Oh, right." So today's client is male. Mother always does the initial intake but wants me to handle the secondary sniffs for the men, since their scentprints are not as complex as the women's. I don't share that I haven't read the client's application yet. Juggling seven periods of classes and my work as an aromateur is proving trickier than I thought. If Mother knew I was falling behind, I could kiss high school good-bye, and I haven't even made it to two months.

"Meet you in the courtyard in ten." The door closes with a thud.

After a few more grinds with my mortar and pestle, cinnamon sings over all other scents in our perfumery. The only one the spicy aphrodisiac can't muscle out is our crown jewel, the orchid Layla's Sacrifice. As its bud unravels into three perfect petals, its marmalade scent becomes so strong, it drowns out everything else, even from behind its glass terrarium.

I drop my pulverized bark into a jar of ethanol, then shelve the tincture between cloves and cardamom on one of our apothecary shelves. Cardamom's running low. I should do a complete inventory so Mother can plan her buying trip, but later. It's already waited a month. It can sit tight for a little while longer.

Just outside the workshop lies a small courtyard shaded by a banana-sweet ylang-ylang tree and its buddy, an eggnog-scented nutmeg. Even plants that ordinarily wouldn't grow in Northern California flourish in our garden, a three-acre parcel shaped like a painter's palette. Our workshop sits where the thumbhole would be.

I plop down on one of our teakwood benches. The scent of our client tickles my nose, even before I see him. I close my eyes. It's not a complete scentprint, more a slight change in the ambient notes that intensifies the closer he comes. The top notes whiz by first, grub lichen, caper, and pepita—an earthy, spice-filled scentprint that is oddly familiar.

My eyes pop open. Mr. Frederics, my *algebra* teacher?

I jump to my feet. Of the two million single eligible people who inhabit the Bay Area, population nearly seven and a half million, did it have to be him?

Mr. Frederics's black and balding figure glides alongside Mother down the path that connects our house to the workshop. He's wearing the same argyle cardigan he wore in class today, and his face is remarkably wrinkle-free like his pants, despite his fifty plus years.

By the time the pair step into the shade of the courtyard, I manage to stop gaping, though Mother can smell my shock. Her amber eyes become slits. She knows I didn't read his application.

"Hi, Mr. Frederics," I say brightly. "Won't you sit down?"

"Hullo there." His voice has a rich timbre that makes it hard to dislike him.

He settles down on one of the benches. Mother and I share the one opposite him. He squeezes his finger joints, one at a time, the same way he did last week when he explained factoring polynomials. "Now, Mimosa, I don't want this to be awkward, so if you're not okay with it, I'll understand."

"Not at all, Mr. Frederics," Mother answers before I can. My toes curl against the leather soles of my sandals. "We are delighted to have you as a client. And let me reassure you, Mimosa will not be taking advantage of the situation. You know we adhere to the highest standard of conduct."

I scowl. Rule One of our ancient code of ethics states that "an aromateur's nose shall never be employed in the creation of elixirs for personal gain, but for the betterment of society," meaning we don't charge for our services. However, the rule is vague, leaving the aromateur to decide what *personal gain* means in gray areas.

"We've decided Mimosa will be dropping algebra until the end of the semester."

"Wh—?" I get out before Mother shoots me a look that could cause my hair to catch fire. Three years I spent teaching myself enough math to qualify for algebra. Not to mention, Mr. Frederics is the only teacher who doesn't jump every time he sees me.

I clamp my lips, but the scent of my anger, like burnt rubber tires, blackens the space around me.

Mr. Frederics pulls at his collar. "Oh, I wouldn't feel right about that."

"I assure you, Mimosa is as committed to our work as I am. Isn't that right, Mim?" Mother places a hand on my knee, which has started to bounce. "Mim has a very packed schedule, and she's bright. I'm sure she can pick up with algebra next semester."

Mr. Frederics casts me a worried gaze, and my smile starts to hurt. If Mother loses face because of me, there will definitely be no algebra. Better to play along for now. "It won't be a problem."

"Let's move forward, shall we?" Mother pans her face to me. "Mim?"

"We're happy you chose Sweetbriar Perfumes to be your relationship intermediaries." I recite the spiel Mother wants us to use for all clients, never mind that we're the only aromateurs on the planet, not including Aunt Bryony, who lost her nose when she was nineteen. "Everything we use in our elixirs is botanical, no synthetics. We grow what we can here in our garden. The rest comes from organic or wild sources."

He nods. "Good, wonderful. You know I'm a big proponent of reducing our carbon footprint. I drive a Prius."

"You're not currently in a relationship, is that correct?" I ask.

"No. I haven't dated in seven years."

Mother's petite nose wiggles. This is a key part of the interview. A lie smells like pewter and sour grass with stale yellow undertones, rather like a sweaty palm that has been clutching dirty coins. Mother can detect a lie as easily as most people smell dead fish. My own nose—which looks like someone took pliers to Mother's, tweaked it longer and a pinched a bump on the bridge to be funny—doesn't detect a single wayward molecule, though Mother's the expert.

She could have waited until *next* summer to take him on as a client. It's not like we don't have enough people on the waiting list—six hundred or so lonely hearts last time I checked.

Mother raises her thin eyebrows at me and ticks her head toward Mr. Frederics. Get on with the program.

"Could you tell us a little about, er—" I don't know the target's name.

"Sofia," says Mother.

He beams. "I'd be happy to." The grassy sweet smell of the flower heartsease drifts from under his collar, the telltale sign of a crush. He's got it bad.

"As you probably know, she's a bit of a neat freak, but I love her for it."

But why would *I* know she's a neat freak?

"She's smart, as is obvious." He looks at me, waiting for confirmation. A chill passes through me, the way the temperature drops when a cloud passes over the sun. I really should have reviewed the application. "Read all the books in our library, which, as you know, is considerable."

Our library means the Santa Guadalupe High School library. "Ms. DiCarlo?"

Mr. Frederics coughs and straightens his sweater cuffs. "Er, yes."

I would never have put Mr. Frederics and the school librarian together. The math whiz listens to ethno jazz and his breath smacks of oats and honey. There's a laidback vibe to him, despite his snazzy outfits. Ms. DiCarlo, a petite redhead, buys hand sanitizer in bulk, and probably goes to bed in business casual. But, it could work. Both are middle-aged, use words like *juxtaposed*, and have good posture. Most important, their scents don't clash.

Mr. Frederics's eyes shift to Mother's. "Oh dear, I'm sorry, I thought—"

Mother's cheeks flash pink, and her eyes become pestles, grinding into me. "There is absolutely nothing to be sorry about. Mim has not had time to read the file." The smell of burnt tires drifts from under her collar, stinging my nostrils. The teakwood plank suddenly feels too hard under my bottom and I shift from side to side.

If the librarian is the target, what's next? Is Mother going to ban me from checking out library books? Ridiculous.

"She is single, yes?" Mother gets the interview back on track.

"Absolutely. Never married." Mother taps my sandaled foot with the toe of her clog and discreetly points to her nose as she inhales. The vein across her forehead has begun to throb. She's as annoyed with me as I am with her, but I have more to lose by showing it. So I focus on the task at hand: decoding Mr. Frederics's scentprint. Mother can do it in one quick sniff—she's that good—but I'm still learning. I take a deep inhale and unravel his unique combination of scents, layer by layer.

Besides the top notes of lichen, caper, and pepita I already detected, Mr. Frederics smells like candelabra and Guinea millet, not surprising given his African roots. All in all, at least eighty more notes play to my nose like a complicated chord.

Aromateurs perceive smells like most people see faces. A single glance can take in a thousand pieces of information, from the curve of the cheek to the exact shade of skin. It's the same with our noses, only it's easier to remember smells, since the olfactory bulb neighbors the limbic system, the area closely associated with memory and emotions in the brain.

"So what seems to be the problem?" Mother takes charge.

Mr. Frederics blows out a breath and his chest collapses. "Thought everything was on the up and up. She let me buy her a granola bar at the vending machine. When I told her I'm the president of the Latin Hustle Club, she said she'd think about joining. Then over the summer, her rabbit died and she shut down."

Still no lies. Mother nods empathetically, chin tilted to encourage him to go on.

"My mother wants to see me knotted up before the chariot swings lo for her." Mr. Frederics adjusts his necktie. "She's ninety-two. Thought Ms. DiCarlo would be the one. She favored me, too; I could tell by how she always processed my requests before the other teachers'. Polished my books nice and shiny."

Probably deciding I am no longer fit to conduct this interview, Mother launches into a final set of questions about his background and criminal history. Unlike in the classroom where Mr. Frederics speaks with an easy confidence, now he stammers and sometimes blushes, though his answers are honest. The lovelorn are often self-conscious. Clients come to us when they've tried everything to woo the target but can't get the fire going, whether due to shyness, insecurity, or even prejudice. Elixirs free the inhibitions. Coax the spark into a flame.

"Mim, the rules." Both Mother and Mr. Frederics are looking at me.

"Right." I clear my throat. "Our elixirs don't guarantee a love match. They only breathe on the embers. No embers, no fire. If a fire comes to life, you must maintain it. We never rekindle."

We can reignite love that has died as long an elixir was never used to form the original bond. Only one shot at the love apple. It's in the Rulebook.

"Sure, I understand. How soon can it be ready? I'm in a bit of a hurry. My mother's heart's been acting up. Think it's the stress of me not being married."

"We'll have to do some due diligence on Ms. DiCarlo," says Mother, "but if everything checks out, we could have something for you by tomorrow."

Great, a rush order.

"I appreciate what you're doing here. I just hope I'm worthy of her." Even in full shade, Mr. Frederics's scalp is dotted with sweat. He tugs out a handkerchief from his sweater pocket and swabs his scalp.

"We wouldn't be doing this if you weren't," says Mother smoothly. "Mim, I need you to get grub lichen from Arastradero. Go now before dinner while we finish up here."

I groan. Arastradero Park is a good hour round trip on my bike. "I smelled some grub lichen growing on Parrot Hill Road. Can't we use—"

"No." Mother pastes on a smile.

She hates using roadside plants because of car pollution, but I wish she would make an exception just this once. I haven't completed a homework assignment in days—not just algebra—and now with Mr. Frederics's rush order, it looks like the truancy will continue.

Mother arches an eyebrow. We trade the annoyed smells of molded lemons for a moment, but I give in, as I always do.

"See you tomorrow, Mr. Frederics." Hopefully from the third row of your classroom, if I can help it.

Clouds of crepe myrtle petals billow around my ankles as I trudge toward the courtyard with the wishing well just outside our kitchen. The aspens are getting ready to dump their fall plumage on me, too. At least my best and only friend, Kali, all six feet of her, will be helping me sweep this weekend. I collect my bike from the courtyard, then pedal down our long driveway.

Such is the lot of an aromateur, sacrificing our needs for the common good. We're not even supposed to have needs. Our noses are like nun's habits, cloistering us to a life colored by chlorophyll. We can't afford the luxury of letting our hearts slip. Mother would faint if she knew I wasn't going to high school just for the academics. That I had interests beyond the briar. That I wanted friends, more than just Kali. And that looking at boys was a nice change of scenery. Mother would lose her leaves over that one, for sure.

While there's no explicit rule against romantic relationships, our colonial ancestor jinxed them in her Last Word: "Beware ye aromateur; lay your traps of love, but do not yourself get caught." Fall in love and, like Aunt Bryony, lose your supersniffer. It's why Mother chose my father from a list of donors she got in the mail like a Christmas catalogue. And why she named me after the flower mimosa, better known as touch-me-nots because their leaflets fold inward at the heat of a human hand.

Love witches can't fall in love.

T W O

"Listen with your nose.
The flowers sing to us in all their complex glory,
swaying to the strains of a whimsical wind."
—Posey, *Aromateur, 1809*

THE TOOLS IN my bike basket rattle as I bump past the sweet-briar hedge our ancestors planted to deter the curious. Hooked prickles and dense foliage form the perfect screen for our peculiar lives.

I pull my bucket hat lower down on my head and steer toward Arastradero Park, the biggest patch of green in quiet Santa Guadalupe. Sometimes I think Mother goes out of her way to make work for me. It's as if she wants me to fail, so she can be right about school being a distraction.

I pedal hard, sweating away some of the black pepper notes of my irritation. It can't be easy for Mother, either. With me in school, she's doing some of the heavier chores by herself now, resoiling, digging up dying roots. I help her during workshop hours from three to six, but it's not the same as having me beside her all day. She rarely complains.

After locking up my bike, I hike down a running trail toward the scent of grub lichen, an invasive species Mother won't allow in our garden. I bypass car-size lemonade bushes, zingy with a hint of gym socks, toward a patch of lichen flourishing at the base of a eucalyptus. I put my nose right up to the musty scent, even though it smells like raccoon urine. Aromateurs are trained from an early age to view each scent with objectivity.

"You lose something?"

I flinch and glance behind me.

Court "Warrior" Sawyer jogs in place with those feet fleet enough to net a spot in Sports Illustrated Kids' *The Top 20 Under 20*. A sweat-soaked T-shirt with his number ten hugs his lean soccer physique, and a hoodie droops from his hips. I scramble to my feet, heart thumping.

"You scared me." I didn't even smell him approaching, with my head stuck in grub lichen and my bum in the air. Now that he's right in front of me, he's all I can smell. Driftwood, tonka bean, and something smoky, like the air after a campfire. I don't usually pay attention to a person's scentprint unless there's a need, but sometimes, like staring, you can't help it.

"Sorry. Thought you might have lost something." Even when he's not smiling, his brown eyes appear to be crinkled into half moons.

A clump of damp hair flops into his eyes.

Stop staring. Talk. "Oh no, I didn't lose anything." Only my dignity. "Just harvesting lichen." Does that sound weird? Yes.

A pair of dimples materializes on either side of his mouth. "Hm, okay."

"Okay." I begin to turn away. I'm a comet that briefly passed into his solar system but now must return to deep space where I belong.

"I'm Court Sawyer."

I suppress a laugh. No kidding. Our eyes connect. Sure, he's cute, even up close, but overrated-cute. His eyes squint and he has one of those Count Dracula hairlines that, like the economy, is one day headed for a recession. That said, I can see why he's a photographer's dream, with dark features against a naturally pale complexion, and a sweet curve to his lips.

"It's Mimosa, right?"

"Just Mim."

"I've seen you here before. You're the famous love witch."

"Infamous, you mean."

"Is it true you can smell a person five miles away?"

People love to exaggerate. "No. Four miles, max, and only if the wind is right."

He smiles. "How do you do that? I can barely smell my own sweat."

Magic? Mutant genes that grew billions more scent receptors than the average person? Probably a bit of both. I give him the short answer. "Genetics. It's no big deal."

"Genetics, huh." The trouty odor of doubt floats away from

him. "People say your mother locked you away in a tower. No one ever saw you until you started school." He shakes out one leg, then the other, seeming uncomfortable with standing still.

"My mother wanted to homeschool me."

"What changed her mind?"

A year of begging. A couple of all-expense-paid guilt trips. "The math got too complicated."

He laughs, though I wasn't kidding. I fumble around my messenger bag for my plastic jar and collection tools, hoping he gets the hint. As good as he smells, I can't be late.

His face grows serious. "Can you really make people fall in love?"

"We open their eyes to the possibility of love. But the decision is theirs." Every few years, some journalist writes about us, giving logical explanations for our singular sniffers, like the journalist in *Scientific American*, who said our genes hail from the Paleozoic era when humans still walked on all fours. Others call us frauds. Grandmother Narcissa, an anomaly even among aromateurs, put most fraud claims to rest when she scented out a rare prickly pear growing in Arizona, used to treat diabetes. She smelled it all the way from our home on Parrot Hill.

But still, we have our skeptics.

Court rubs the back of his neck. "So I've been wanting to ask, do you make potions to help people get over each other?"

I cough to cover my embarrassment. *Him*, needing our services? "We don't work with minors."

15

He flashes a smile, and my adrenaline spikes. "It's not for me."

"Oh."

He doesn't explain. Perhaps he's talking about his mother. Last year, pictures of Court's tech-millionaire father cavorting with scantily clad "models" surfaced on the internet. Even Mother knew about it, and she hates gossip.

I finally say, "It's unethical." It's mostly true. We do make Potions to Undo Feelings, or PUFs, in extreme cases like aromateur error. Mother has never made a mistake, but she did make a PUF once before I was born.

"Making people fall in love isn't unethical? I mean, opening their eyes to the *possibility*."

I square my hat. "We have rules. The client and the target—I mean, the love interest—must be of sound mind, impeccable personal history, an adult over eighteen; the list is long." Some of my hair gets in my mouth and I blow it out. "Anyway, Mother says falling in love is the easy part. Things get complicated after that."

"I see." He touches the peeling bark of a eucalyptus and looks up at the leaves.

The bluesy scent of friar plums drifts toward me, the subtle note of despair, and my annoyance fades. "My mother tells people who are heartbroken to plant roses. They require a lot of attention, and when they finally bloom, you'll be ready to give them to someone else."

"Roses, huh?" He's looking at me.

"Yes. Only heirlooms. Hybrids don't smell as sweet. April Love. Distant Thunder's nice. They have a peppery finish over a dusky center." I'm babbling.

"You'd be an intimidating person to buy flowers for."

"Me? Oh, I don't really need flowers."

He grins. Pinching his shirt, he wafts it a few times then stops. "Sorry."

"It's okay. It's nothing I haven't smelled before." That didn't come out right. Hastily, I add, "I mean, everyone sweats."

He scratches the back of his head. "So what do I smell like?"

My turtleneck feels like it's choking me. "You smell like a campfire, with heart notes of fir needle, and nutmeg, plus a ton of cinnamon—" I stop. He might know cinnamon is an aphrodisiac. "And other stuff."

He blows out an amused breath. "You want to know what I smell in you?"

Me?

He takes a step closer and sniffs, stopping my heart in its tracks. "Butterscotch pudding." He keeps a straight face.

A flush migrates all the way to my scalp. "You're making fun of me!"

"I'm sorry, all I meant was you're not chocolate, vanilla, or strawberry. You dare to be yourself." His eyes sweep up my five-foot-eight-inch frame, from my prairie skirt to my bucket hat, which hides most of my messy bob. "You've got style."

Actually, what I have is a concerned mother, who makes me cover up as much skin as possible. I try to hold on to my anger, but it slips away. "I just wear whatever fits me from Twice Loved."

"You hold your head up, even when people say you eat silkworms."

"They taste heavenly with a bit of butter." I press a hand to my heart and affect an expression of bliss, a look that must be too convincing, as his forehead crinkles in uncertainty. Cheeks burning, I add, "Also, I make humans fall in love with their shoes." That's the latest rumor. I freak a lot of people out. One girl at school even screamed when she looked up from her sandwich and saw me standing beside her. Kali said people are afraid I'll put a spell on them, I just need to give them time—though I doubt time will make a difference.

He chuckles, and dimples once again light up his face.

I force myself to think about lichen. Black and scratchy like pirate whiskers. "I should finish up here." Mother will start to worry.

"Right. See you at school." He gives me a lopsided smile, then lithely jogs away. The word *lifeguard* is emblazoned across the hoodie wrapped around his hips.

I shave the lichen into my jar with a metal scraper, but my heart is still racing. At least I managed to keep the weird to a minimum. I shake thoughts of Court's dreamy smile from my head, lid my jar, and stuff it in my bag. Job done; time to clock out.

Two bees follow me back to the running trail. I'm like an ice cream truck to them. Only instead of Popsicles, I peddle pollen, which is impossible to rid myself of without constant showering. Once they realize I'm no flower, they usually leave.

Four girls on rollerblades whiz toward me in a cloud of sunscreen and hairspray. The predinner rush is in full swing. Arastradero gets especially crowded when the school year starts—it's a prime running spot for the athletes and more interesting than the hamster wheel of our school track. I step off the path to let them pass, and recognize the head roller as Vicky Valdez, Court's ex-girlfriend.

Coincidence? Or not. Kali told me that when Vicky and Court broke up, she became known as Exxed-Valdez. She's still not over him.

The girls trailing her veer as far away from me as the paved path allows, casting suspicious glances my way. Vicky, though, stays her course, black hair flowing like seaweed and unencumbered by a helmet. Her gaze lingers on mine for a moment, cool and appraising, and the scent of disdain, like rancid kumquat, invades my nose. Without missing a beat, she muscles forward with her short but well-formed legs. She's never spoken a word to me, but I don't need words to tell me she doesn't like me.

As they roll away, I catch a whiff of habañero peppers, so faint that if it were not for the breeze, I would've missed it. It's coming from the direction Court ran. I inhale. Sifting through the plant smells, I find it again, the hot scent of panic. I run toward the source.

Just around a bend, Court's lying curled up on the ground, his lifeguard sweatshirt a few feet away. The hot, honey aroma of bee toxin pricks my nose. He got stung?

Panting, I drop down beside him. "Court? Are you okay?"

He struggles to breathe. He must be allergic to bee stings. Those can be fatal.

"Do you have an EpiPen?" Frantically, I search his pockets, noticing the silver MedicAlert bracelet beside his watchband. I don't find the EpiPen, but I do find his cell phone. I dial nine one one.

It rings once, twice, three times. Why doesn't anyone answer?

As the phone continues to ring, my nose guides me to the sting, which is right under his bicep. There's a deep scratch mark where he failed to remove it. The black stinger sits just under the skin. Carefully, I dig it out with my fingernail.

Ring. Ring. "What is your emergency?"

"My friend got stung by a bee. He's allergic."

"What is your location?"

"Arastradero Park, about a hundred yards from the giant lemonade bushes."

"The *what?*"

I look wildly around me for another landmark. "We're in a grove of gum cannabis."

"Cannabis? Is this a crank call?"

"Oh no, not that variety . . . Er, east of the tennis courts? Hundred feet from a water fountain?"

She pauses for at least four seconds. "Okay. I've dispatched the ambulance."

After I answer more questions, we hang up.

"You're okay," I tell Court. "They'll be here soon. I need to fetch something."

Court's eyes are bloodshot and watering. I pillow his head with his sweatshirt. Dumping the lichen out of my specimen jar, I scurry off in search of plantain weed, which grows everywhere except when you're looking for it. I try to follow the scents but the lemonade bushes and buckwheats are interfering, and an uneven breeze stirs everything together.

I drop to my knees and sniff the ground. Got it. The zesty trail leads me to a strong patch just a few yards from where I harvested the lichen.

Court's nearly unconscious when I return. Fighting down panic, I stuff plantain leaves into the jar, add stones, then shake the whole thing to release their oils. I pull my sleeves down to cover my hands and lift his head onto my lap. Then I undo the jar and hold the opening to his mouth and nose, praying the anti-inflammatory weed will reduce the swelling.

At last, his chest moves a fraction, and soon he's breathing in short shallow breaths. I set the jar back down. Sweat trickles into my eyes and I wipe it away with my sleeve. His bicep is taut and curved, even at rest. I take a plantain leaf and hold it against his bee sting, being careful not to touch my skin to his, even though I already touched him to get out the stinger. I'll take care of that later.

I listen hard for the wailing of an ambulance. His head feels heavy and hot in my lap, and I shift around to get comfortable. It strikes me that this is the closest I have ever come to a boy, much less one so popular. His pheromones pelt my nose from all angles; it's like being hit by a confetti canon.

Court moans and turns his head to one side.

"Can you hear me? Court?" I should talk to him. But what about? I could ask him some questions.

Right. Poor guy can barely breathe, let alone answer questions.

I could do something to distract him from his pain until help arrives. Sing? Dance? Tell a joke? If I did any of those, I might make things worse. Maybe I could tell him a story, if only I could think of one. Well, I do know one.

My throat has gone dry and I swallow hard to get my voice working again. "My mother says we're related to the Queen of Sheba. You see, the queen gave King Solomon rare spices for the chance to pick his brain, which led to the world's first power couple. They had a son, and when he began to crawl, they discovered he could sniff out a single poppy seed stuck in a hundred-foot-long carpet."

A siren wails. The paramedics will be here soon. Time for the neutralizing mist, which Kali dubbed Boy-Be-Gone, or BBG for short. When you live and breathe flowers, it's not just the bees who are drawn to you. If I touch individuals predisposed to liking me—most often boys, but sometimes girls—residue from the thousands of elixirs Mother and I create transfers off my skin, like the dust from a moth's wing, causing attraction. It's why I always wear hats and long sleeves in public, though I draw the line at gloves, which would just make me look like a germaphobe. BBG nixes any mushy feelings that may arise from contamination by this "aromateur's pollen."

From my bag, I pull out a crystal atomizer that fits into my palm and is as small as a perfume bottle. My finger feels for the pump, and just as I'm about to spritz, Court's eyelids flutter open. I catch my reflection in his startled eyes, bewitched and bewildered, like I was the one bitten.

"I, I—" Closing the door on my doubts, I spray. One dose lasts a lifetime.

He watches the beads of mist float in the air. A gentle breeze carries some of them away. He turns his puzzled eyes to me.

"It's just something I, er, do. It's calming. I feel calm. Don't you feel calm?" Living with a human polygraph, my mother, means I lie as well as grass.

I hear the chatter of girls and raise my voice. "Hello?" Maybe someone can flag down the ambulance when it comes. "Can someone help me?"

A girl half skates and half walks into the grassy clearing, and I recognize her from the group of rollerbladers who passed me earlier. Her mouth drops when she sees us. One by one, her friends pile up behind her, including Vicky who cries out, "Court?"

Her blades kick up clumps of grass as she dashes to us. "What happened?"

Court squints at her, then his eyes close again.

"A bee stung his arm."

"He's allergic!" she says, as if I didn't already figure that out. "Oh my God, Court baby. Did you find his pen?"

Baby? Gross. "He doesn't have one on him."

She kneels beside me and elbows me out of the way, lifting his head and placing it on her own lap. "Move over."

I eye her long gold-painted nails, hoping she doesn't scratch his face. "Maybe you shouldn't move him."

"Are you a medical expert?" Vicky shoots back. The sharp, weedy odor of her hostility—stinging nettles—peels at the inside of my nose.

The other girls, now crowded around us, glare at me as if I'm the bee.

Sirens wail louder now and a truck rumbles up, the red visible through the screen of plants. A pair of medics rush to us, holding equipment. "Step aside, please," barks one of them. The girls back off.

"He's allergic to bees," Vicky tells the medic, her throaty voice tight and high.

Court opens his eyes again. "I'm, I—" he mumbles.

The first medic pulls out an EpiPen from his bag and sticks Court in the thigh. The medic's partner examines Court's arm, which is no longer angry and swollen.

"How are you feeling? Any trouble breathing?" asks the first medic.

"No, no, I'm fine." Court struggles to sit up, aided by Vicky who straps her arms around him from the back.

"Just rest against me, baby," she coos. "You're going to be fine. I'm so glad I found you in time."

I dig my arms into my stomach. Anyone else might be repulsed by her boldness, but I remind myself it's better this way. I am a mere comet.

The medic asks Court more questions, which he answers mostly through nods and monosyllables. Slowly, I get up. He's in good hands now.

Court catches me stealing away and says in a quiet voice, "Mim? Thanks."

Vicky cuts her gaze from him to me, and her eyes lose their anxious cast and harden. The unmistakable scent of jealousy, like sour milk, putrefies the air.

No good ever came of that scent.

"You're welcome."

I refill my jar with lichen, then hurry away, but the scent of jealousy stays in my nose long after I've left the park.

THREE

"Everything smells, especially emotion."
—*Mu Jin, Aromateur, 1621*

I LIFT A pair of poached eggs out of the pot, willing them not to break. They make it to the plate without incident, so I add a banana scone to my arrangement. Free and easy. I cannot coax Mother into a good mood if I'm giving off stress smells.

At our kitchen table, Mother looks up from Friday's crossword puzzle. The wagon-wheel lamp bathes her with warm light. She pulls off her reading glasses and lifts an eyebrow. "Confined."

I don't lose a beat. "Constrained." Mother and I used to do the crosswords together until I started school.

"Cramped."

"Caged."

"Cornered."

I set the plate before her. "I dub you Sir Synonym, but there will be a rematch," I say good-naturedly, even though I have another one up my sleeve: *curbed*.

Mother grins, and I return the smile despite the fact that I'm so tired, even my face droops. She was up even later than I was, but unlike me, there's no stoop to her shoulders, no circles under her eyes. Her hair is neatly combed in place, not tangled like brambles under a slouch hat.

She tucks her bookmark with the pressed flowers into the seam of her crossword book. "You should've slept in, though this is a nice treat. My favorites."

"I felt like banana scones, too." Their caramel goodness swirls like a halo of scent above each buttery wedge.

Smell and emotion are closely linked in the brain. Pleasant smells trigger positive emotions, which then give off more "feel-good" smells. I fed Mother banana scones before asking permission to attend high school. It worked, too. She let me go.

The earthy scents of vetiver and French sage warm the air. Good, she's relaxing.

"I haven't changed my mind about algebra."

Though I keep my expression neutral, the scowlish odor of molded lemons gives me away. I grasp the back of a chair and focus on a narcissus flower engraved on the window frame.

"You're already taking too many classes." She waves around a scone. "What is *so* urgent about that subject?"

"Math is useful. We might be able to formulate algebraic expressions for the elixirs using ratios of base notes to hearts and tops." Maybe there are even formulas for calculating attraction, maybe even love.

Her scone slips from her grasp and detonates the eggs. Yellow blood oozes forth, sulfury with a hint of sunflower seeds, which our chickens love to eat. "Why would we do that when we have our noses? It would be so cumbersome."

"For future generations." As the only two aromateurs left on the planet, the survival of our kind is hanging by a spider thread. "We could leave a roadmap behind after we're gone." Maybe the gene pool would spit up another aromateur.

The eggs seem to stop oozing, held in place by the sudden chill in the room. "Why? Are we planning to go somewhere?"

"No," I quickly say, regretting the turn in conversation.

Her eyes tighten. "Each client is unique and elixirs can't possibly be reduced to a formula. Our knowledge has been passed down from mother to daughter for thousands of years. That is all the formula we need."

I take a deep breath and let it out slowly. Arguing the point will not help my cause. "Fine. But how exactly does algebra break Rule One?"

"Mr. Frederics could unintentionally favor you in grading."

"I'm not going to college, so grades aren't important. I'm just there to learn." I hold my breath, hoping I didn't just send lie odors into the environment. It's mostly true.

"We have to avoid even the appearance of impropriety. Our business is built on reputation. If people don't trust us, they'll stop coming. Our skills, our *noses*, will go to waste. Don't you want to be an aromateur?"

"Of course." This is the third time she's asked me that since I brought up the issue of school. It's like asking me if I want to be Persian, Welsh, Inuit, Chinese, or any of the other seventy-two ethnicities in my genetic makeup. I didn't choose them, I just *am* them. "But people will never stop coming. We're the only love witches in the world besides Aunt Bryony—"

"*She* is no longer an aromateur," Mother says of her estranged twin, and the vetiver and sage drain away. When my aunt lost her sense of smell, she became, in Mother's opinion, "useless." The two lost contact twenty years ago when my aunt left. "Honestly, Mim, people don't go to high school to learn. They go there to suffer. Teenagers are a different species, angsty and hormonal with that canned apple juice smell. It's much nicer here." She gestures toward the window, which offers a glimpse into our ten-thousand-plant garden. "Plants are our books, and we have a full library."

I groan. It occurs to me that it isn't just dropping algebra that bothers me. It's also Mother's refusal to care about my interests. Of all people, she knows how multilayered people are. We spend our lives decoding people's complexity. For once, maybe she could decode *mine*. As hard as it sometimes is to believe, she was a teenager once. Didn't she ever wonder if there was more to life than mixing elixirs? "I have a whole life of weeding ahead of me. I just want to—"

She puts a hand on her hip. "You want to what?"

Take up a sport, like football, or crew, and limp away, flush from victory. Join the debate club, and say things like "That's a logical fallacy!" Scream over boy bands. I don't want to waste my teen years elbow-deep in soil and begonias. But if Mother knew I wanted to have a life outside the briar walls, she'd think I was planning to defect, maybe like Aunt Bryony. "Not weed."

I gather my books and my lunch into my messenger bag, almost knocking our chipped guacamole bowl off the counter. If I was the type to throw things, that ugly bowl would make a satisfying crack against the wood floors. The frustrated scent of loosestrife peels off me, a noxious weed that smells like garlic breath. "I'm late."

"Mim."

I pause in the doorway, but don't turn around.

"I'll think about algebra," she says.

In front of the library, a modern building with large glass windows, I remove the vial of elixir from my bag. A tiny fragment of Mr. Frederics's handkerchief with a sample of his saliva floats inside. Saliva's a key component of elixir.

I warm the vial in my palm, then shake it vigorously. Usually, we shoot the arrow by sprinkling the elixir directly on the target, or something we are certain the target and no one else will touch. Elixirs are clear, tasteless, and virtually undetectable by the regular human nose. They're also the same temperature as skin, and lighter than rain, making them nearly impossible to feel. The elixir affixes to the target and in a few days, the target starts subconsciously "noticing" the client's scent. Magic.

Through the windows, I spy Ms. DiCarlo at her desk, rubbing an alcohol-soaked cotton ball over a book cover with such vigor, she might erase the picture. Her red hair bounces around her shoulders, flipped up at the ends into a single fat curl.

I walk right up to the librarian's desk. "Hi, Ms. DiCarlo." Beside her keyboard lies a small Starbucks cup filled with a shot of espresso, still steaming, with a *D* marked on the side for what must mean "decaf." I could drop the elixir into the cup. Mom made it so concentrated, a single drop will work, even if Ms. DiCarlo doesn't finish her drink.

First thing's first. Our Rulebook requires us to verify that the target is not married and is not a sociopath. We learn about these things during the client interviews and a background check. I simply take a few whiffs of the target to confirm.

Windex and bran muffins with splashes of peaceful green notes, like holy basil, the scent of pensiveness. Decoding a person's scentprint—peeling away the outside package to see the person inside—is usually my favorite part of the job. But it's not what I came for today.

She blinks at me with her doll-like eyes. "Hello. Are you new?"

"Yes. I'm Mimosa," I say, feeling dumb at my lack of a last name. "Please call me Mim." Another sniff. I don't detect sour mash or black rot, which could indicate psychosis.

Ms. DiCarlo sits up so straight, her chair rolls back a few

inches. Even faculty isn't immune to the rumors about me. "Oh yes. I've heard you were here. May I help you?"

"So far, no one has signed up for the Puddle Jumpers' teachers' team." Kali put me in charge of recruiting for the charity event she leads every year, buddying troubled youth with SGHS teachers and students. She thought it would help people get over their hesitancy toward me by showing them that I can be fun, too. Plus, it's something we can do together outside of the garden. "Are you interested? You'd be perfect. Kids always love librarians." I sniff deeper. I don't detect any male odors on her whatsoever. No female ones, either, other than her own. Single for sure.

"Oh, well, yes, that's true." She tries to suppress a smile, but it doesn't work, so she waves my comment off. "Well, when is it?"

"Next Friday during homecoming week."

"Let me check my calendar." She opens a drawer and pulls out a bound stack of papers that looks like a manuscript. Under the manuscript, she finds her day planner, which is thick as a bible. As she replaces the manuscript in the drawer, I catch the words, *Avoiding the Torture Chamber of Medieval Library Collections, by Sofia DiCarlo*, on the cover page. She's a writer.

She flips through the mostly blank pages of her planner and finds the right day. "Looks like I'm free."

"Great. Is there anyone I might ask to be your faculty partner?" If she says Mr. Frederics, we definitely have a match.

Her traffic-light green eyes shift to the corner, while she thinks it over.

I help her along. "Mr. Frederics, maybe?"

She tilts her chin to the side. "Why not? He always makes the students laugh."

I catch a zing of anticipation, the one that smells of iced tea, followed by happy puffs of apple blossom, meaning compatibility. Check. Moving on. "One other thing, I'm searching for a book called *Women in Nineteenth Century America: Socialites to Spinsters.*"

At the word *spinster*, I detect a note of something salty spiking her natural scent. Something wistful. She's definitely open to love.

She types something on her computer, then frowns. "It's in special collections. I'll fetch it."

Standing, she smoothes her blouse into the waistband of her tailored skirt, then hurries toward a back room. When the door closes behind her, I dump in the contents of my vial. More than enough.

A minute later, she returns empty-handed. "I'm afraid the book is missing, but City Library has a copy if you want me to make the request."

"No, that's okay. Thanks, anyway."

The Rulebook requires me to witness Ms. DiCarlo take the bait. I exit the library and spy on her through the library windows. She goes back to polishing book covers, still not touching her espresso.

When I pick up the scent of a campfire, my heart jumps.

Court treads toward the library, his arms swinging easily,

eyes unfocused and relaxed. The school songbird, Cassandra Linney, bounces alongside him with her arm hooked through his. The two might have stepped out of the pages of a J.Crew catalogue. On him: cashmere V-neck in moss green, size medium. On her: the clambake skirt in seaport blue with cropped pinstripe jacket, size petite. Cassandra flips back her corkscrew hair with a snap of her wrist.

For reasons I don't understand, my secondhand sundress suddenly feels as shabby as it is. The Aromateur Trust Fund set up by our medieval benefactors only covers business expenses, meaning we live frugally. Still, did I have to choose *this* cable-knit scarf and *this* ratty hat? Looks like something out of a grandma's closet. I wish I didn't care so much. After all, once my stint here at Santa Guadalupe High has ended, I will disappear back into the briar, as always.

I shrink into the shadow of a building post as they approach, hoping Court's too distracted by the living mass of Cassandra's hair to notice me. The sound of her trilly laugh makes my teeth hurt.

I return to spying on the librarian. She still hasn't drunk her beverage. What's wrong with her? No one likes lukewarm espresso.

"Mim," comes Court's smooth voice.

I straighten back up. "Oh, hello," I say, as if I just noticed them.

Cassandra's blue eyes grow large at the sight of me, and her corkscrew hair seems to straighten momentarily in fright. Her unease wafts over me, the slightly molded smell of rained-on pavement. "You're Kali's friend."

"Yes."

"Well, if you see her, tell her I'm looking for her."

"Okay." I hope she's not still mad about the homecoming half-time show. Kali said Cassandra threw her sheet music when she learned Kali, a junior, would be sharing the stage with her.

"I'll catch up later," she tells Court. After a last look at me—the fruity rooibos smell of curiosity joins her unease—she sails off toward a group of seniors.

"H-how are you feeling?" My voice sounds unnaturally chipper.

"Good as new. Thanks again for saving my life." He touches his arm where the bee had stung him. His dimples appear, one on the left, and two on the . . . I shake myself free.

"You're welcome. You should really carry an EpiPen."

"I usually do, but I left it in the car. What was in that jar?"

"Crushed plantain weeds."

"You saved me with weeds? Wow. Someone could make a fortune."

"They have to be fresh." I shrug. "The power of the flower."

"So what happened to the kid?" When I don't say anything, he adds, "Queen of Sheba? King Solomon?"

"Oh." So he did hear my story. Curls of blushing bromeliad, smelling like sun-kissed pineapple, rise from under my scarf. "He became the emperor of Ethiopia. But I'm sure we had our share of dirtbags and pond scum, too."

He moves closer, and his shadow slips over me. "Maybe you can tell me about them over burgers sometime."

"B-b-burgers?" I stutter. "You mean like eating with you?"

He laughs. "That's generally what happens."

"Oh, I couldn't do that." I squeeze wrinkles into the worn cotton of my sundress.

"Why not?" His voice softens. There's a freckle on his neck right in the notch below his ear.

"I have dietary restrictions."

"You're vegetarian?"

"Yes. I can't eat refined sugar, vinegar, or salt." Our overdeveloped sense of smell requires us to follow a finicky diet. Nothing too pungent, like garlic or onions, and absolutely no salt. A single bite of a honey-baked ham almost did Mother in one Thanksgiving. She lost her sense of smell for a week and refused to eat anything but rice.

"But doesn't that get a little bland?"

"Actually, most of what people perceive as 'taste' comes from our sense of smell. So when we smell foods, we're getting the full flavor experience."

He grins, and I detect the amused vanilla scent of animal crackers. Maybe I don't need to be *so* truthful all the time.

"Well, maybe we could just go enjoy some dinner smells

together. It's the least I could do to thank you."

Of course. An appreciation dinner. The BBG would've neutralized any feelings he might have developed for me. "Thank you, but it's not necessary."

Disappointed notes of blue hydrangea weigh down the air like sad jazz music. He probably doesn't hear *no* often.

A woman in a sweat suit riddled with rhinestones steps out of the library with a shaggy pet under one arm, a stack of books in the other. A ukulele is slung against her back.

"Hi, honey. I stopped by to get more books." She pecks Court on the cheek. Court's mother could be mistaken for one of the seniors with her trim figure and hair done up in pigtails, with only a bit of gray to give her away. Her scentprint is a complicated mix of rare plants, lying under a thick fog of blueberries. You would never guess her heart was aching by looking at her.

Court relieves her of the books and the pet, which turns out to be a purse. She keeps her ukulele.

"Couldn't you leave it in the car?"

"Of course not." She bats at his arm. "The sun warps the wood. Who is this?"

Court tips his head toward me. "Mim. She's the one who saved me."

"Oh, you're Mim! I can't thank you enough, darling. I gave Court hell for forgetting his pen." She fishes keys from the purse Court is holding and hooks them onto his pinky. "Fetch the car for me, dear. I parked by the Cat in the Hat."

I must look stumped because she adds, "That's what we call the wind sock. Get it?"

"Oh, right." The red and white wind sock on the street fronting the school does look like a Dr. Seuss hat.

Court flashes me a smile that spreads a strange warmth throughout my body. As he jogs away, I avoid watching.

Mrs. Sawyer focuses her bright eyes on me. "You're the perfumer's daughter, right? Melanie mentioned you started school here."

"Yes." Court's younger sister, Melanie, has never spoken a word to me other than, "I sit there," when I chose the wrong desk on my first day of algebra.

The woman steps close enough to count my nose hairs. I know because I can count hers. Taking my chin, she steers my face from side to side. "Nice bone structure. What a sweet little bump." Her eyes almost cross. "And those amber eyes, like that cougar I saw on *Big Cats*. A little mascara and gloss, you could do runway. You've got the height and the lines."

"Thanks." I'm not sure what kind of lines she's talking about. Far as I know, models don't really speak at all.

"*Talofa*," Kali calls out a Samoan greeting as she rolls up from the parking lot on her Vintage Schwinn.

I gently extricate myself from Mrs. Sawyer. "Hey, K. Where you been?"

"Went for a ride. Trying to get healthy so I can be stealthy."

In one smooth motion, Kali hops off her bike and steers it into its usual spot at the library bike racks. Despite being the biggest girl in the junior class, limbs thick and large like the rest of her Samoan family, she moves as gracefully as a gazelle.

"Hello, Kali," says Mrs. Sawyer. "You've grown up since Girl Scouts."

"Haven't seen you here in a while, Mrs. Sawyer."

"Call me Alice, both of you. The divorce is final." She flashes us her beauty queen smile. She is a former Miss California, which makes her the most famous person in Santa Guadalupe. "Now I'm on a reading kick." She pushes a shoulder down toward her books. "Sofia, er, Ms. DiCarlo, orders the best romance novels. I never go to City anymore."

Ms. DiCarlo. With a start, I turn back to the library window. Ms. DiCarlo is no longer at her desk, though the Starbucks cup is still there. I groan. I'll be late to Cardio Fitness, waiting here for her to drink it.

"But enough about me. Congratulations on winning the half-time spot," Mrs. Sawyer—Alice—tells Kali.

I wasn't surprised when Kali was selected to recite a poem as part of the entertainment for next Friday's game. She wins every poetry contest she enters, and her monthly slams for the Puddle Jumpers are legendary. She could be the next Poet Laureate.

Kali beams. "Thanks."

Alice touches Kali's arm and leans closer. "I was on the committee. Your submission was very Gertrude Stein."

Kali stiffens and her face turns red. "It was?" The boggy note of anxiety trickles from her direction, even though the poet Gertrude Stein is one of Kali's heroes. Unlike Gertrude, Kali is not yet out, herself.

Alice nods with her whole body. "Absolutely." She doesn't seem to notice Kali's discomfort. "'Kite' was about individuality, about being yourself—"

Kali clears her throat. "Actually, I have another poem I was thinking about doing."

"Oh, here's Court." Alice waves toward a late-model BMW pulling up beside us. "Kali, if you prefer to do another piece, I'm sure that's fine, as long as it doesn't have any F-bombs. Are you girls coming to Melanie's birthday party tomorrow? The Bandits will be there. Melanie even hired bouncers."

Kali snorts too loudly, and Alice's smile wavers.

"I'm sorry, Mrs. Sawy—I mean, Alice," I say. "But we might be the riffraff your daughter hired the bouncers for."

"Of course not. It's my home. I'm paying for the party, and I'd love for you to come." Her voice takes on an edge. "I've been wanting Melanie to make friends with more sensible girls. See you girls later. Oops, I forgot something." She disappears into the library, then, moments later, her kitten heels clack toward the BMW. Court gets out, and his mom takes his place.

Kali's still frowning; I bump her arm with mine. "I like that poem. 'Kite' is more about being yourself even if it means you're flying solo. It's not about being gay. I think you should still do it."

"Right. And end up like Barry the Fairy."

Her freshman year, a kid named Barry had to move out of state after bullies spread rumors that he must be gay since he was a violinist, and Photoshopped pictures of him in a compromising position with a male quartet.

The door of the BMW closes with a *whump*. Court hops to the curb. Before Alice drives away, she lifts a cup to her lips, and drinks.

A Starbucks cup, with the letter *D* inked on the side. The car smoothly peels away.

Holy gladiola. I just fixed Court's mother.

FOUR

"BAD DEEDS, LIKE PESKY SEEDS,
GROW INTO MOST VICIOUS WEEDS."
—*Primrose, Aromateur, 1715*

MOTHER IS ONE of the gentlest human beings I know. Despite the tight rein she keeps on her emotions, she gets weepy whenever one of the soil engineers (earthworms) has a run-in with her shovel. Her fingers move light as mosquito legs as she nurtures the plants in our garden, hardly leaving a trace of her scent anywhere, unlike me, who tracks fingerprints all over everything I touch. But as sure as the hair standing up on my arm, she will kill me for fixing the wrong person.

Kali bumps my elbow with hers, jolting me from my frozen state. "Snap out of it, Nosey. We're late for Cardio."

"I—I just fixed Alice."

Her eyes bulge. She's the only one who knows the intricacies of what Mother and I do. When we were thirteen, Kali's father brought her to help him build our trellis and Mother hired her on the spot. She said Kali "smelled good"—despite all the loneliness wafting off her like the moss baby's tears.

In a few sentences, I tell Kali what happened.

"It was an honest mistake. Your mom will understand."

"I can't tell her. I screwed up a job." I should have watched to make sure I fixed the right person. I flouted one of our basic procedural rules, but I was distracted. "She's going to know it was because of a boy."

"How?"

"She'll figure it out. She'll question me, and I can't lie to her."

"At least Alice's elixir won't kick in for another few days."

A group of boys saunter toward us, pushing one another and laughing. I move out of their pathway so that I don't accidentally contaminate them, when the one in front slows, causing a traffic jam with the rest. The boy wipes his palms on his ripped jeans and shuffles up to me. He clears his throat, toggling his Adam's apple. "Um, hi, Mim. Remember me from Spanish?"

"Er, sure." I remember the smell at least, elementary moss, and a salty licorice from the Netherlands. The latter triggers the memory of the seed vendor in Amsterdam on whom I dumped my yogurt muesli shake when he tried to kiss Mother.

I realize I'm lingering and shake myself from the unpleasant memory.

The kid, blue eyes staring at me, blushes, and I detect the grassy sweet smell of heartsease. I contaminated him. Maybe I breathed on him in the hallway. I jam my hand into my bag, feeling for my Boy-Be-Gone.

Kali slides her eyes from me to them and sighs. I give her a slight nod.

"Well, would you look at that?" Kali says loudly, pointing behind them.

The boys' heads snap in the direction of her finger, toward Principal Swizinger in her dark suit and hose. The principal stoops and picks up an empty Doritos bag, which she deposits into a nearby trash can.

I depress the pump of my mister, disinfecting not only the kid with the blue eyes but the two closest to him in one pass. If nothing else, at least Mother will be happy at my economy.

Kali rests her chin in her fingers. "Someone should nominate the Swiz for a peace prize. A Greenpeace prize."

As Blue Eyes turns back around, his grin fades. His whole face droops like he's trying to remember the constant for pi. He stares at a cloud. Maybe the pi's in the sky. Before he can speak again, Kali pulls me away.

"Could've sworn you sprayed him before. They're all starting to look alike."

"Mother will pull me out of school," I hiss, back to worrying about Alice. "I haven't even made it through the first quarter!"

"How are you gonna fix it?"

"I'll have to make a Potion to Undo Feelings, though I've never done one before." I put my hands to my cheeks, which feel rubbery and cold. "Mother made one ages ago. I don't even remember what the Rulebook says about it."

"Maybe you should go home now."

"No way. Then she'll definitely know something's wrong."

"Tell her you're sick. It's not a lie. You do look a little green."

"Love witches don't get sick." Another side effect of growing up in a garden is the self-healing. I never had a wound that didn't disappear by the next day and I've had a cold only once. We just make others sick. Lovesick.

Twenty-five juniors follow me as I lead them through a Michael Jackson song in Cardio Fitness, though I'm really just copying Kali, who's at the far end of the room. She's on fire, jumping higher and squatting lower than anyone else, and she's not even breaking a sweat. This is certainly the kind of experience I would never get in the garden.

In our stuffy gym, the high school smells, which I thought I had habituated to, take turns slapping me around; the sharp tang of twenty-six sweating bodies, the tinny juice of appley angst, combined with the nose-curdling fumes of recent paint lifting off the white walls.

Our Czech instructor, Ms. Bobrov, stands in the back, clutching a clipboard and appraising the class. "Move forward everyone!" She makes sweeping motions at the students, most of whom seem to be shrinking toward the back wall away from me. At her order, they move forward, but by only a few inches.

Of all the days Ms. Bobrov could choose me to be dance leader, naturally it would be today, when I'm so unhinged, I can

45

barely stay on tempo. She must have smelled I was weak. Scientists say smell is our most complex sense, stirring people to act instinctually, often without us even realizing it.

Kali does a body roll, and I nearly injure myself trying to replicate it for the class. After I catch my balance again, I find the beat and shuffle from side to side, which I can do without hurting myself. I have to unfix Alice before the elixir begins to work its magic, or I'm toast. Lives are at stake here, *love* lives. Assuming I can figure out how to make the Potion to Undo Feelings, how am I going to do it without setting off Mother's nose alarm?

I stumble over my own feet despite the easy shuffle and Vicky, in the front row, snickers. The jealous scent from the previous day has ripened into something different, something calculating, like spiky holly. Beside her, Court's sister, Melanie, echoes the snicker, halfheartedly jogging in place like her batteries are dying. I do my best to ignore them.

Finally, the song ends, putting us all out of our misery.

"Very good, B plus," Ms. Bobrov announces in front of everyone.

On the way to the locker room, Kali and I pass through the courtyard formed by a main block of classrooms and two wings in the art-deco style. Panels of young pioneers adorn the upper walls, boys panning for gold, girls contentedly quilting. Bet they never had to worry about their mothers banishing them to the far Arctic Circle for one teeny little mistake.

The crisp Northern California air pecks at my skin but fails to cool my anxiety. Students shrink away as I stumble along, their expressions changing, their voices lowering. I try to ignore the mothball smell of their suspicion, like a closet that is rarely opened. But today, every wrong scent rattles my cage.

The only sign Kali exercised is a mustache of perspiration over her generous mouth. Even her braids are still tight as chocolate Twizzlers. She frowns at me, and I can smell her concern, but then she bumps my elbow. "You were killing me with boredom in there. It's the moonwalk, not the sleepwalk."

"Mimosa, could I talk to you?" says a raspy voice from behind me. I recognize the black elder of Vicky's scent, ripe like a skulking vagabond, before I turn around. It's joined by celery, creating a scent combination that's familiar in a way I can't put my finger on.

Vicky, flanked by Melanie, manages to rock even a polyester gym outfit. She stretched the neckline of her shirt to hang over one shoulder and rolled the shorts as high as they can go. Without her trademark heels, I can see the top of her head.

"Yes?"

Melanie frees a strand of blond hair from the trap of her lip gloss, and leans in toward Vicky like she wants to share a secret. Her face roughly approximates her mother's, but with bigger eyes and a spotty complexion spackled with foundation.

Vicky elbows her away. "I need you to make a love potion for me."

"They're called elixirs. And we don't work with people under eighteen."

Vicky laughs in the self-assured way of the very wealthy. When she flips back her thick black hair, her gold earrings nearly blind me and I detect the bitter reek of tobacco under a canopy of Poison Apple perfume.

"Well, see you later." I grab Kali's arm and steer her away.

"No, wait, *por favor*," Vicky says, working her accent. "Court and I were *meant* to be together."

I freeze in my tracks. Court? I should have known.

"I just need a little help unconfusing him." Her voice trembles. "For his own good." Any rookie aromateur could smell that their chords clash. Certain notes do that, just like music. Invisible airborne warfare.

Casually, I glance at the lunch tables a few paces to our right that form straight lines all the way down to the field. Court and his friends always eat lunch at the last table, but I don't see him there today.

"Pssh," says Kali. "No use crying over spilled oil. Probably found someone else who floats his boat."

The juniors' mouths form two O's of indignation. Melanie recovers first. She rubs Vicky's arm. "Of course not. He loves you." She overarticulates, making sure each word is perfectly formed before she sends it out into the world. "Your Christmas formal picture is still on our mantle."

"I want our homecoming picture to be on your mantle. He's the *one*." Vicky's eyes plead with me to see reason. "I love him so much it hurts. Don't you understand?" She clasps her hands as if praying.

Though I never had a boyfriend, or even a boy who was a friend, I do understand the washing machine nature of love: the hot churning, the hand wringing, the head spinning, the sometimes final rinse with cold water. Aromateur is my name, and love is my game. But rules are rules. No minors.

Plus, we would never take someone like Vicky for a client. She reeks of insincerity, like dirty bathwater and pond salt. "Sorry, can't help you."

Vicky crosses her arms over her chest, and her tone turns snappish. "Court's almost an adult. He'll be eighteen in six months. Can't you round up?"

At the nearest lunch table, a bunch of gamer nerds are playing video games on their phones. Drew Reaver squints at us through his thick-rimmed red glasses. The poor guy's got it bad over Vicky; I can smell the heartsease from here. She might have the personality of a wet porcupine, but the boys still go gaga over her. Must be the celery, whose stalks are known to induce lust.

I shake my head. "Again, sorry. You'll have to hook him the old-fashioned way."

"My brother is *not* a he-ho." Melanie flips back her blond hair and stomps one of her pink Nike sneakers.

I look at Kali for help, having no idea what a he-ho is. She snorts loudly.

"I'll pay you double." Vicky whips out a credit card from somewhere in her bra. "Platinum." She holds it out as if she actually expects me to swipe it through something.

Kali flicks her eyes to the sky and shakes her head. "Are we in a bad movie? *Attack of the Killer Bimbos? Close Encounters of the Turd Kind?*"

Vicky's sweat glands ooze the angry scent of rubber tires, and I quickly say, "Money's not the issue." Clients don't know our no-fee rule until we take them on, and then we swear them to secrecy. Aromateurs have always been obsessive about privacy.

Vicky's eyes harden. "I know all about how you work. You have ethical rules, blah, blah, blah." She waves her credit card. "But I bet you haven't splurged on yourself in a long time. I mean, your hair . . ."

My hand flies to my unruly bob, which I trimmed myself with hedge clippers when I couldn't find the scissors. A flash of heat passes over my face.

"Now, Mim, you're new, but you should know something about me." Vicky leans closer. "When I was two, a Rottweiler tried to take my binky. Guess who won?"

Kali replies. "I'd say whoever didn't have to suck your stinky binky. C'mon, we don't have to listen to this crap."

She begins to haul me off to the locker room, when Vicky says in a singsongy voice, "A lady walked along the beach, as lovely as a summer day. And when I asked her for a kiss, mermaid-like, she slipped away."

Kali's eyes snap to Vicky's. In one quick motion, Kali shrugs off her backpack and feels the front pocket. It's empty. "You stole my journal."

"I learned so much about you and your"—Vicky winks—"preferences."

I gasp at the same time Kali lets out a Samoan curse. Kali's hands bunch into fists, and she shifts her weight from one flip-flop to the other, glaring at Vicky hard enough to sear holes. "Give it back, or I'll make you into jam."

She could do it with one swipe of her tattooed knuckles. Kali used to eat girls like Vicky for lunch back when she hung out with her brother's friends. Her parents worked late hours—her mom as a nurse and her dad on construction—and left the upbringing of their youngest to their sons.

Vicky tilts her head, and her asphalt tresses cascade to one side. "You wouldn't dare. Unless you want everyone to *know*. Remember what happened to Barry the Fairy?"

"Blackmail is a crime," I huff.

"You mean, black female." Vicky winks at me and her spidery lashes nearly tangle. "You can have the journal back when Court falls back in love with me. Bring the elixir to Melanie's party tomorrow."

Melanie frowns, and Vicky's the only one left smiling.

"Elixirs take time. I can't just snap my fingers—"

"The homecoming dance is in two weeks. I'm in kind of a hurry." Her tweezed brows squeeze closer together, as if to invoke sympathy, but then she snaps her gum and the effect is lost. A moment later, she breezes toward the locker room. Melanie hurries after her.

Kali scratches at the black tattoo bands on her upper arm, then her neck and her shoulder blades. Hives have started popping up on her skin.

"Come on." Instead of continuing to the locker room, I pull her to a planter of aloe vera near the lunch tables. The plant grows wild in this area. "We'll think of something." I break off an aloe vera tip and hand it to her. "Rub this on the itchy spots."

Kali rubs the plant on the welts on her arms. "Nasty she-squirrels. Wish I could dump 'em."

According to Kali, squirrels are the most vicious animals, cute but dangerous. She eyes a rubber trash can at the end of Drew Reaver's table. The year I met her, Kali got suspended from the eighth grade for dumping a boy in the trash bin.

She clenches a fist and begins to get to her feet. "Maybe I *will* dump her."

I pull her back down by the arm. "No. You're always telling those Puddle Jumpers, 'If the puddles get too big to jump over, just step through them,' remember?" Kali said if her mom hadn't started bringing her to hip-hop classes at the Puddle Jumpers Center, she'd probably be in juvie by now.

She scowls, but doesn't get up. From Drew Reaver's table, someone yells, "Eat dust, baby!" Drew opens a carton of chocolate milk and guzzles it.

I take a long drink from my own water bottle, though it doesn't erase the bad taste in my mouth. Blackmail. If I don't make Vicky's potion, she'll out Kali. People love their traditional values here in Santa Guadalupe, where the grass even grows to the right. But I would never do something so wrong as fix Court.

I'll give *Vicky* a potion. A sprinkle of durian in her powder will make her olive skin turn orange for a day. "I could give her a fake elixir . . ."

"She'd know when Court doesn't ask her to the ball."

I cut my eyes back to Drew, sprawled over the table like a spider with his pale white arms poking out from a T-shirt with a picture of a succubus. His dark blond hair hangs in greasy ringlets below his ears, but his face is scrubbed. "What happened on that episode of *Animal Planet* when the tiger was chasing the gazelle, then another gazelle came along?"

Kali puts down her aloe stub. "The tiger went hungry. And?"

"Ask any predatory cat. It's virtually impossible to pursue two prey at once."

Kali follows my gaze to Drew. "You're going to fix her with Drew?"

"Shh!" I put my chin on my hand and chew on my lip. Vicky threw the first nut. It would be foolish to let her strike without polishing up a few of my own. Drew likes her anyway. It might be the perfect match.

Drew looks up at us. He lifts his chocolate milk at Kali. "Haven't seen you at Stan's lately."

"Been watching my weight," she yells back to him.

"Cool."

I strain for Drew's scent, and Kali waves a hand in front of me. "Earth to Cupid. Abort plan. If I'm standing in the light, you'd better stand there, too."

"So you don't mind if certain laundry is aired?"

"Of course I *mind*." Kali's lips squish together.

"Exactly." I catch Drew's scent. Horseradish, beavertail, potatoes . . .

Kali frowns at me.

"You don't like it because you're a good person, not a squirrel."

Her face tightens. "That's bonk—hooking someone up with a freak show like that."

"Drew's a nice guy."

"I was talking about Vicky."

I snort. "The elixir just opens the eyes. If there's no spark, nothing will happen. But if there is, that's two more passengers aboard the Goodlove blimp. She might thank me one day."

"Give her the fake elixir for Court if you want, but don't fix her with Drew for me. That must break a dozen rules." She chucks the aloe stub into a bush.

I clamp my lip. She's right. Aromateurs can't go fixing anyone we choose.

Not to mention, today's mistake is so big, you could probably see it from space.

FIVE

"Dandelion,
a yellow sun transforms into a white puff of moon,
then feels the breath of wishfulness, and scatters
its seeds, like stars into an empty space."
—Ixia, *Aromateur, 1771*

DESPITE THE DISQUIET I cause among the student body, I like school. I like raising my hand and answering questions during class. I revel in feeling smart on the few times I score A's. But this morning's lessons pass as slowly as glacial melt. At least I already had algebra today. The last thing I need is to see Mr. Frederics, whose love life I may have screwed up forever.

Finally, the lunch bell rings. On autopilot, I follow a balding path of grass toward a grove of trees. The sun pokes me in the eyes, and I keep my hand up to shade them. I stop at the second to last tree, a sprawling mulberry, where I always eat my lunch, since Kali works the hot lunch line "scooping the goop" as she calls it. I feel less alone there than in the cafeteria, surrounded by people who try not to sit by me.

Not to mention, being outdoors gives me a break from all the pent-up high school smells. The concentrated odor of teenagers, with their fickle natures, rivals even the smelliest crowds in the world. Not even the jam-packed trains in India, or the World Cup crowds Mother and I battled in Brazil on the hunt for a rare bakupari tree can cause such proboscine consternation.

I plop down on a dry spot and cradle my head in my arms, wilting at the thought of Mother's disappointment.

I won't be able to fix Ms. DiCarlo with Mr. Fredericss elixir until I make the PUF for Alice. The librarian will just have to wait. If I fix her now, I might end up with a messy love triangle, and a cartload of new problems.

Maybe a woman like Alice could fall for a man like Mr. Frederics, even though they sit on different ends of the salad bar. A graduate of Georgia Tech and a proponent of reducing our carbon footprint, he's crunchy granola, the healthy kind with organic seeds and nuts. She's crisp iceberg lettuce, a natural flare for dressing, and freshly plucked from the runway by her ex-husband at the tender age of nineteen. But, it could work; their scents are in alignment.

I shake my head. They could be Romeo and Juliet for all I care, but it wouldn't matter. My mission is to stamp out any embers, not blow them into a flame. Unfix Alice. Fix Ms. DiCarlo. And avoid the subject at all costs with Mother so I won't have to lie.

The rough bark of the mulberry feels warm against the back of my head. Closing my eyes, I inhale. Campfire smells fill my nose: charred cedar, roasted hickory, and fir needles.

Court ambles in my direction with his trademark casual stride, backpack slung over one shoulder.

I stop breathing as I watch him close the distance, wishing I didn't feel so giddy. Behind him, the school appears stately and calm, with clean blocks of blond stone rising behind columns of Italian cypress.

Moments later, he stands before me. "Hi, again. I'm not following you. This used to be *my* spot. I sat here all the time freshman year." He drops down beside me and straps his arms around his knees. On the right toe of his Converse All Stars, someone wrote in black marker, "Beware of Foot." "You get tired of people, too?"

"The other way around." His squint deepens, and I add, "People prefer I keep my distance."

"People can be idiots."

The undeserved sympathy jabs at me like goatheads, cough-syrupy creepers that grow through the smallest cracks and can puncture even tires with their sharp spines. I pray that he leaves now so I can continue panicking in peace.

He fiddles with his watchband as he stares off to the right, where the field extends toward the five-thousand-capacity soccer stadium. "You coming to the game?"

"Game? Oh, homecoming." Dummy. It's only the biggest event of the year, of which Court is the star. He chuckles.

"I'm sorry. I'm not sure if I can go." Because I might not be alive.

"It's okay. It'll probably be boring."

"I doubt all your screaming fans would agree."

His mouth hints at a smile, which quickly disappears. "The only fan I care about is my mom. This game means a lot to her. I don't want to disappoint her. She's had enough of that this year."

"I'm sorry." Sorrier than you know.

"It's okay." He glances at me. "My mom plays her ukulele in the key of B minor every night. Doesn't matter what the song is, it could be 'Happy Birthday' and it would still be in B minor. It's so damn depressing." When he shakes his head, his hair flops into his eyes. He doesn't brush it aside.

I rub my temples. "I smell protea in your mother's scent-print." Protea, also called sugarbush, is usually sweet, but hers is especially melon-like in the top notes.

"Protea. From Proteus?"

"Yes. You know the myth?"

Tapping his finger against his forehead, he says, "Greek god who told the future. He'd change his shape so people couldn't recognize him and bug him with questions."

"Nice."

He stretches his back. "See, I'm not all jock."

"They named protea after Proteus because it comes in a thousand varieties—pincushion, brown-beard, tooth-leafed, et cetera."

He snorts. "No dude wants a flower named after him. So why the protea?"

"People who smell like protea are resilient, survivors. Victory has the same sweet notes, like champagne sorbet."

"Wow. So, does defeat smell sour, like a bunch of stinky jocks crying for their mamas?" His grin teases one out of me.

"Actually, yes. Any emotion based on fear tends to be 'sour,' like helplessness, self-pity, rejection . . ."

A circlet of yellow flowers straight as candles grows near Court's foot, their florets arranged in perfect Fibonacci numbers. Court plucks the only puffed one and twirls it between his fingers. Then he holds it out to me. "What's a dandelion mean?"

I take it. The bloom's chardonnay notes are oakier when it matures to a puff. "Flirtation." The word slips out before I have a chance to catch it. A flash of heat sears my collar.

"And here I thought I was being subtle," he jokes, though I catch the unmistakable scent of smoked paprika, the mildest of the chilies and a telltale sign of embarrassment, creeping in from his direction. Or maybe it's coming from *my* direction.

Before my nose ties itself into knots, I add, "And hope. It also means hope." I lift the dandelion puff like a wineglass. "To your mother's happiness." I send the seeds sailing away in one breath, knowing it will take more than hope to set things right.

SIX

"THOUGH COWSLIPS LINE THY MAPLED CART,
THE WISE WILL CATCH A FALLING HEART."
—*Carmelita, Aromateur, 1728*

THE ROAD TO Parrot Hill is a winding two-lane highway no one uses except for the residents, who are few in number and mostly elderly. I've never seen any parrots myself, but they swarmed the sycamores when Mother was young, mini-F-18 bombers that dropped their loads wherever and whenever. After the parrots stopped coming, Mother bought chickens to enrich the soil, which are easier on the hair.

A burst of anxious energy helps me pedal up the incline, leaving a swampy bog in my wake. The wet-dog smell of forgotten cucumbers assails my nose, spiked by zingers of hoary tomatoes. Even though most of the homeowners no longer grow their own vegetables, the ghosts of produce past still linger.

At the break in the briar, I stop at the end of our long, stone driveway, breathing hard. If I'm not careful, Mother will smell my stress.

I step through bitter chicory plants with their jagged leaves, to reach a Merengue rosebush bursting with plump blossoms. Mother insists we plant them this way for the visitors. The bitter walnut scent of the chicory actually balances the sweetness of the roses, sort of like how coffee and sugar, working together, can create a more pleasing and complex taste. I inhale, letting its muscat-sweet fragrance cool my mood.

Calmer, but not by much, I pedal up to the covered walkway that leads into the round courtyard just outside our kitchen. Our cottage is a mishmash of stone blocks, as if the ancestor who built it simply employed whatever odds and ends were on hand. The whole lopsided structure has stayed intact through several earthquakes, but the wishing well is crumbling on one side where I crashed our old maple cart last month. Mother wouldn't speak to me for a week for taking out those two relics in one careless swoop, especially that cart. Aromateurs traditionally used handcarts made of maple, a hard wood whose scent won't react with the cargo, but true maple carts are hard to come by nowadays.

I lean my bike against the good side and peer through the window of the corner turret where Mother sometimes escapes, working her crossword puzzles. I don't see her, which I hope means she's in the workshop.

Cautiously, I enter the house, but not hearing or smelling Mother, I retreat into my room and perch on the edge of my bed. A handwritten journal our ancestors compiled in 1672, the

Rulebook sits on my nightstand. I flip through the tissue-thin pages to Rule Eighteen:

> *In the case of an error, the Wronged Party (WP) may be neutralized with a Potion to Undo Feelings (PUF) without consent until the time of the WP's first kiss with the client. Thereafter, the WP may only be PUF-ed with informed written consent.*

I don't know how I'll know when Alice and Mr. Frederics kiss, but the sooner I can make the PUF, the sooner I can avoid a meeting of their two lips. I skim through all the pages but can't find a single word about how to make the PUF. For something so important, seems *someone* should've written it down. We do keep index cards of all the elixirs we've made in my workshop desk. Maybe the card from the one time Mother made a PUF will be in there. It may not be helpful, since elixirs are client-specific. Still, it's a starting place.

Grimly, I trudge down the stairs and out the kitchen door. Mother's scent drifts from the direction of the workshop. Maybe I should wait until she leaves before searching for the card. But, I smell gardenias, which means she's making an enfleurage, a time-consuming oil extraction of the more delicate blooms. She could be in there all day and night.

I'll just have to keep my cool and hope she's too involved with her work to smell a few wayward stress fumes from me. Gardenias are heavy scenters, and might help mask my anxiety.

I travel down the path of stones. Everything is okay.

"Hi, honey." Mother looks up from the tray of oil on which she's carefully layering the flowers.

"Hi." My voice goes high. I try not to think as I head to my desk, but forget about the fist-size indentation in the hardwood floor. It's been there since before I was born but I never tripped on it until today.

"Mim!"

I catch myself before I fall. Bottles rattle at my jig. "I'm fine, I'm fine."

"We should've fixed that years ago."

Cool and easy. Conversational. "Why didn't you?"

"Your grandmother thought it would remind us not to play on chairs."

"Chairs?"

"It's a long story." Mother sighs and pulls off her reading glasses. "So . . ."

I freeze. She knows. Here it comes.

"I've decided not to interpret Rule One so strictly, given the circumstances." She points at me with the glasses, and for a moment, I'm vaguely aware that the eye of Medusa has somehow passed over me.

"But I meant what I said about you being overscheduled," she goes on. "You'll have to drop algebra if your work starts to slip."

Too late for that. "Thanks, Mother." I force myself to think happy thoughts of penguins frolicking in the snow.

"You notice any reactions in Ms. DiCarlo?"

"Not yet." Sunlight dapples the floor through the skylight. I haven't lied yet but my sweat glands are preparing to launch an attack. "The recipes are a mess. I'm going to move them onto the computer."

She beams at me. "Great. I've been wanting you to do that for years."

"I'll start right now."

Mother returns to her enfleurage. With tiny flicks of her wrist, she picks out the bruised flowers, something she could do blindfolded. Mother's nose is like two of mine. She once woke me up at four in the morning to help her cut out a root on her favorite oak that had caught disease. She smelled the rot in her sleep.

I park at my desk in the alcove and switch on the computer. Opening the drawer, I pull out the index cards containing the formulas to our elixirs and straighten them into piles, like a card dealer. Then I shuffle through the first pile, hunting down the card from the one time Mother made a PUF. The cards are a jumbled mess, some from the eighties when Mother and Aunt Bryony were teenagers themselves, and others from just last month. There's nothing indicating a PUF in the first deck. I move on to the second then third and fourth, flipping cards, scanning ingredients.

Mother clears her throat. I look up to see her twirling a

gardenia between her fingers. "Do you need to do that so loudly?"

My shoulders have risen to my ears, and I relax them. "Sorry."

I finish the fifth deck and still, no sign of a PUF.

Well, I *could* ask Mother. But lightly, tread lightly. "All done. They're all there, except . . . didn't you make a PUF once? I don't see that one in here."

Mother stands and stretches. The antique floorboards creak as she crosses to the far wall where the rare-plant terrariums gleam like cake stands. "Mark my words, this won't wait for December." She steps to one side. Long, smooth leaves drape from the center stalk of the orchid, Layla's Sacrifice, where a single white bud has begun to grow, its universally delicious jammy scent seeping through even the glass. The green sepals wrap the base of the bud as tight as a mother holding a swaddled baby. "I predict Thanksgiving."

"That early?" I lift my eyebrows and attempt to look interested. Why isn't she answering my question?

"Maybe we'll have time to replant the succulents like I wanted this Christmas."

When the once-a-year midnight bloomer opens, usually in December, the scent is so complex it can substitute for many elixirs, which saves us a ton of work. Though we never actually use the holidays to relax; love never takes a vacation. We do things like replanting cactus, which is as much fun as rolling around on tacks. I go with the flow. "Sure."

She poises one hand on the glass knob. "Ready for liftoff?"

65

"Yes." I hold my breath.

She lifts off the lid and sprays the plant. Even holding my breath, the jam scent assails me. Slowly, I let out my air. Only the initial release knocks me out. I broke a baby tooth learning that.

Now I'll have to bring it up *again*. When I'm breathing normally, I ask, "So about that PUF . . ."

"Why do you want to know about that?" She looks up sharply.

I quickly reign in my curiosity. Happy penguins. A note of defensiveness, like sour strawberries, wades from her direction. "No reason. Just didn't want to miss a card."

Spritz, spritz, goes her water sprayer. "Don't bother. I threw it out."

"What?" Stress fumes dribble out from me, but Mother doesn't notice. She seems to have drawn into herself, spraying Layla's Sacrifice at every angle even though she's gone over it twice already. "Why?"

"She refused to take it. No use keeping a record of something that was never used."

I begin to pick up threads of bitter chicory, the scent of regret, which resembles burning coffee fields. Why is she getting so emotional? "*Who* never took it?"

Mother makes an annoyed sound at the back of her throat. "Your aunt Bryony."

My eyes go round. She hardly ever talks about Aunt Bryony. So her sister was the one Mother tried to PUF? "Why didn't you just hit her from behind?"

"Mim! Of course I couldn't. She was already living in Hawaii by that time. She knew what I was up to as soon as I stepped off the jet."

I knew the basics of their fallout. The year that Grandmother Narcissa died, the governor of Hawaii commissioned the twins to make him an elixir, so they flew to Maui and hired a certain Captain Michael to help them collect marine flowers. Aunt Bryony married him within months.

Mother finally moves on to the next terrarium. "I knew I shouldn't have agreed to using that Captain Michael's boat. I could smell she was attracted to him." Her eyes grow large.

"How did it happen?"

She releases an especially vigorous round of her sprayer. "She fell into the ocean."

"But she couldn't swim, could she?" Aromateurs have a long-standing tradition of staying out of the ocean. Swimming pools are out, too, since the chlorine makes us nauseous.

"She was fine." Her nose wrinkles. "Michael gave her mouth-to-mouth resuscitation. After that, her ability to smell faded away like summer sweet peas."

She sits heavily at the large farm table that spans the length of the room.

"Poor Aunt Bryony," I mutter. If she had been born before our ancestor Larkspur jinxed us in 1698, she could've had love *and* her nose.

Mother gasps. "What do you mean poor Aunt Bryony? I had to make the governor's elixir by myself. And don't give me that smell. Larkspur's Last Word exists for a reason."

I make no attempt to suppress the lavandin notes of empathy lifting off me, which is the most camphorous form of lavender. "It's a Last Word, not a rule." We've tracked over this same patch of ground so many times the dirt's packed tight. Mother knows where I stand.

"Larkspur was a powerful aromateur and her grief over her sister's death was profound. Her Last Word might as well be a rule." With a sigh, Mother removes her reading glasses and rubs them against her shirt. The glasses leave tiny indents on the side of her petite nose.

Our spinster tradition began when Percy Adams, the Court Sawyer of his day, fell in love with a six-fingered aromateur named Hyacinth and she with him. The daughter of the mayor, who fancied Percy for herself, convinced her Puritan father that the only reason Percy could fall for someone so digitally challenged was that Hyacinth must be a witch. She was tied to a stone and cast into the sea.

Hyacinth's aggrieved sister, Larkspur, banned romantic relationships in her Last Word, reasoning, if aromateurs avoided romantic entanglement, there would be no more witch hunts.

"But why would she jinx us?" I ask in a huff, even though I already know what she's going to say. My mind flits back to Court, and I quickly shove those thoughts away.

Mother pops her glasses back on her face. "Larkspur was try-ing to *protect* us. She flicks her gaze to the skylight and shakes her head. A gunmetal streak on the right side of her hair lies in a flat line, like a disapproving mouth. "Romantic love, like all extreme emotions, distracts us from our life's work. *The wise will catch a falling heart.* We must keep our heart right here"—she taps her chest—"where it belongs. Your grandmother Narcissa only became great through her single-minded devotion to her craft. Bryony wanted it all."

She glances at my souring expression and adds more gently, "It's not as if you can't have love in your life—we do have each other, don't we?"

"Sure. You and me." I give her a reassuring smile. "So, how did you make her PUF?" Dirt. I sound way too eager. She's going to get suspicious. The cards make a clacking sound against my desktop as I straighten them.

"Sniff-matching, of course. It wasn't December, you know."

December? What does that matter? I wait for her to go on, but she doesn't. This is harder than extracting information from a baby. "Sniff-matching who?" I start whistling. Maybe I'll have a seizure projecting all this calm and I won't have to PUF anybody because I'll be dead.

"Bryony's, though of course, I knew her scentprint by heart."

Even though Mother and Bryony are identical, their scent-prints are not, just like their fingerprints.

"The PUF would've strengthened her innate scent notes,

overpowering any contamination by Michael's notes," Mother's voice twists when she says his name. She gets up from the farm table and rummages through a bucket of daffodil bulbs. "The effect is nearly always immediate, like neutralizing mist."

I let out a slow, even breath. So that's how it's done, sniff-matching the person contaminated, in this case, Alice, then fixing her with her own elixir.

Mother cuts her gaze to me, and I quickly ask, "What happened after Aunt Bryony refused to be PUF'd?"

She shrugs. "I went home. She sent me a letter, but I threw it away."

"Why?"

"If it was something important, she could have told me in person. She never came, of course." She holds up a misshapen bulb and her nose wrinkles.

The phone rings. Mother chucks the bulb into the recycle bin, then slaps the dirt off her hands before answering. "Sweetbriar Perfumes . . . Oh, hello, Mr. Frederics."

I don't move a muscle when I hear the name.

"Yes, everything went well, I think." She looks at me, and I smile and nod. I hope she's distracted by Mr. Frederics in her ear and doesn't smell the panicked zingers of habañero pepper flying off me.

"Oh, it could happen as early as tomorrow, but I always say give it a week. Everyone is different." Mother's fingers roll at the hem of her denim shirt as she listens. "You bet, anytime." She hangs up the phone and beams at me. "The man is just so thrilled. You see, now, this is why we make the sacrifices we make. People need us. We are the keepers of their hopes, their dreams."

She unties her apron and hangs it on a hook. Her nose twitches, and I go still. She's smelling me. "It's remarkable how similar you and Bryony are in the top notes, not just the zinnia." She pauses, knowing the zinnia comment stings me. It's a pleasing fragrance, peppery and flowery, but it tends to wander before settling squarely in the nose. She's not-so-subtly reminding me not to be a flake, like her sister. "There's the ginger, and the zinfandel with the stubborn liftoff, just like that bottle we sampled in Croatia last summer. Thankfully you're different enough in the heart notes, or I'd worry."

I can't help worrying about what *she's* worrying about—that I'd betray her, like Aunt Bryony. While the top notes make the first impression, heart notes are the soul of a fragrance, the thing that transforms random smells into scent. It's no accident that Mother's primary heart note is tuberose, a scent exceptional enough to be used for both weddings and funerals, and for which only a single blossom is enough to fill a temple with fragrance. A little of Mother goes a long way. But it's the interplay of the heart notes with the top and base notes that give the scent character. So even if I did have the same heart notes as Aunt Bryony, that doesn't mean we'd make the same choices.

"I'm going to soak the lentils. Don't forget to turn off the computer."

The blue door swings shut after her.

I should feel relieved that she's gone, but my limbs have gone cold and heavy. If Mother and I should ever have a falling out, would I receive the same treatment as my aunt? One moment, Mother and Aunt Bryony are as close as two daffodils on a double-headed stalk, and the next, each is a single-head species. If Mother ever cut me off, I would have to start anew, somewhere far away so we don't compete or, worse, eke out a living assisting the police in drug busts like a dog, or hunting expensive truffles like a pig.

Grimly, I replace the index cards in the drawer. Nothing against canines or ungulates, but that would be a humiliating way to live.

SEVEN

"THE GIFT OF FLOWERS OPENS MANY DOORS."
—*Hasenu-da, Aromateur, 1888*

KALI'S HEARTY VOICE wakes me out of a fitful sleep. Sitting up in bed, I peer through my window into the garden. Kali's leaning against the well edge, strapping aerating shoes over the red Vans she got at Twice Loved. The aerating shoes resemble sandals but with nail-like spikes on the bottom. A T-shirt, and a bright lavalava—a rectangle of fabric knotted to form a skirt—drapes her solid figure, topped by a plantation-style straw hat, her gardening uniform. Mother stands next to her, along with a third person whose identity I can't make out through the rock-rose bushes.

I lift the window and sniff. Mr. Frederics.

I jump out of bed. He just called yesterday. Something must have happened. Maybe he had tried to bust a move on Ms. DiCarlo and she slammed him to the mat. Or maybe Alice had begun making overtures. Mother will be onto me like Velcro.

I'm in trouble.

I wiggle into a sundress and shoes, then hurry outside. The three stand in a paved area shaded by palm trees, hung with containers of petunias and blue star jumpers.

Kali smoothly unfolds herself from the bench. *"Talofa."*

Mr. Frederics tugs a wrinkle out of his spinach-hued sweater vest. "Good morning, Mim." He doesn't smell mad, but maybe he's good at hiding his feelings.

"Good morning."

Mother claps the dirt off her garden gloves, which she stitched with the word *Saturday* across the back. She rotates her gloves because each day comes with different tasks, and the gloves match the activity. "Well, daughter."

Breathe. She doesn't smell mad either, but Mother can be good at controlling her emotions. "Mr. Frederics stopped by with good news."

I freeze. Good news?

The teacher's eyes crinkle and his mouth breaks into a smile, an expression that lifts years off him. "Ms. DiCarlo invited me to join the Puddle Jumpers' teachers' team with her."

"Great." Like an idiot, I give him a thumbs-up.

Mr. Frederics bats a hand in front of his face. "I know I'm overreacting, coming here like this, but I'm just so pleased." Now his hands don't know where to go and he stuffs them in his vest pockets.

Mother pats the sweat from her brow with the back of her glove. "You're not overreacting at all. Happiness is a gift that must be shared."

While Mother and Mr. Frederics converse, Kali starts punching holes into the ground with her feet to let in oxygen, walking back and forth in even rows. The chickens peck the ground around her. Normally, I would strap on a pair of aerating shoes and join her, but I have to sniff Alice, and the sooner the better. While I remember her overt notes, I didn't pay attention to the ones deeper down. I'll just ride my bike over to tell her I can't make the party, and am dropping off a "present" for her daughter, aka the fake elixir meant for Vicky. The fake elixir will buy us time. I'll take my whiff and go.

"We'd be happy to give you a tour, wouldn't we, Mim?" says Mother.

"Sure, but, actually, I have to go."

"Oh?" asks Mother, somehow managing to look down on me, despite my half-foot advantage.

Kali stops stomping and throws me a questioning glance.

"I have to drop off something for a classmate." No lies yet. "It's not far."

"Think I'll go with you." Kali pats her stomach. "Dahlia, my stomach's begging for one of Stan's donuts." Everyone calls my mother by her first name because, like all aromateurs, we gave up surnames when we gave up the institution of marriage.

Kali does smell a little hungry.

"You should have said something," says Mother. "We have oatmeal—"

"Thanks, but when your stomach wants donuts, it won't take oatmeal."

Mr. Frederics laughs. "Truer words have never been spoken."

"We'll be back soon, and then we'll take care of those leaves. Might even get to trimming that ivy." Kali knows how to stroke the belly of the crocodile. Mother hates it when the ivy gets leggy.

Mother pans her smiling face at Mr. Frederics, though fragments of her disapproval, like green tomatoes, loiter in the air. "Well then, I guess it's just you and me. Come, I'll show you what I mean about the pepita in your scentprint."

Together, they walk toward the workshop, chatting like old chums. I hope my mother and my math teacher don't become confidants. She doesn't need regular updates on Ms. DiCarlo's progress.

I bring my own confidant up to speed while we head back to the house. Tabitha the chicken dashes in front of Kali to catch a soil engineer skimming the dirt near Kali's foot. Kali picks it up. The chicken head jerks side to side, peering longingly at the morsel, which Kali dangles like a curly fry. "Today is your lucky day." She chucks the earthworm into the nearest compost bin.

Before we collect our bikes, we gather flowers to bring with us to the Sawyer house. The gift of flowers opens many doors. Kali kneels by an iris plant, shears poised.

"Not those!" I hiss.

"Why?"

"Irises say, 'your friendship means so much.' I couldn't give those to Melanie."

Kali rolls her eyes. "*Psshh.* Fine. Which ones then?"

I direct her to a rosebush with coral blooms, which simply represents girlhood. While she clips them, I pinch off orchid branches for Alice, symbolizing strength, which could fortify her broken heart. Working quickly, we bind our flowers with paper and twine.

My odd collection of hats line one side of the garage. I pluck off the cowboy hat and tuck my thick pollen-trapping hair inside. The last thing I take is a vial filled with nothing but water—fake elixir for Vicky to give Court. It'll buy us some time to figure out what to do about Kali's journal.

Soon, we're pedaling toward the eastern hills of Santa Guadalupe. I pray that Court has soccer practice on Saturday mornings. If I can just avoid him, I'll undo my mistake and he'll never be the wiser.

A fountain with a griffin guards the entrance of the tony neighborhood of Cypress Estates. Water cascades from the eagle's beak. Heavy clumps of "prosperity" bougainvillea drip from the rooftops of each mansion, which, despite variations in facade—hacienda, French villa, Tudor—still somehow manage to look the same. Wealth has a distinct odor that's the same throughout the world, the showy sweetness of bougainvillea mingled with weed killer and chlorine from all the swimming pools.

We steer our bikes past a lush expanse of golf course. Then the road veers sharply up. By the time we're halfway up the incline, I'm ready to collapse. I get off my bike and walk. Kali waits for me at the top, fresh as a plumeria lei.

The Sawyers' hacienda is the biggest house on the hill, a house whose extravagant parties always generate headlines like, "Sawyers' Fourth of July Bash Has Neighbors Seeing Red, White and Blue." The closest I've ever come to attending one was the night a westward wind blew the smell of roasted chicken and bourbon to our humble abode on Parrot Hill.

Clusters of palm trees draw the eye from one end of the house to the entryway and then across to the four carports. The sight of Court's Jeep with the surfboard poking out the back doubles my pulse.

In the driveway, men haul scaffolding from the back of a truck with the words "Black Tie Event Planners" painted on the side. Two women hang paper lanterns from ornamental brackets along the walls. Melanie's seventeenth birthday might beat out Christmas this year.

The lantern hangers greet Kali and me as we shuffle to the doorway, each of us holding a paper bag with a bouquet.

The door opens. It's Melanie, hair in rollers, and wearing a glare reserved for geeks with postnasal drip. Her new perfume screams fake fruit at me. I stop breathing through my nose so I don't pass out.

Synthetic perfume makes my skin crawl. Some lab rat concocted them in the late nineteenth century to cut the obscene costs of real perfume. It's understandable. A vial of rose oil the size of a double-A battery requires ten thousand pounds of petals. The irony is, nowadays, lab scents—petroleum byproducts mixed with assorted chemicals—often cost more than the botanical they're trying to imitate *and* smell nothing like the real thing.

Melanie gives us the once over. "Lemme guess, Lilo, from *Lilo and Stitch*, and Calamity Jane. Halloween's not 'til Monday, girls."

"I'll give you a stitch," mutters Kali.

Alice appears from behind her daughter, hair wrapped in a terry-cloth turban. I sniff. The smell of ammonia singes the air around her head, and trying to find her scentprint is like pushing through a mound of sand. The only note I make out is blueberries, which, of course, is a mood scent and not part of her inherent scentprint.

"Hi, girls," she says in a warm voice. A thread of honeysuckle weaves through the blueberry—she's delighted to see us. The woman must have just scrubbed her face, which looks as dewy and fresh as a teenager's. "What a lovely surprise."

We pull out our bouquets. I try to stop grimacing at Melanie. "We can't make it tonight, so we brought you both something from the garden." I hand Melanie my bouquet, glancing meaningfully into the blooms. When she sees the vial I tucked between two stems, she rolls her eyes and grabs my floral offering.

Alice frowns as her daughter scampers away. "I'm sorry."

Kali hands her the second bouquet, and Alice draws in her breath. "These are simply gorgeous. Thank you, and thank your mother for me, Mim. I love your style. A cowboy hat with a sundress and arm warmers is so fresh. Where do you do your shopping?"

"Kali found this dress at Twice Loved." I sniff but still can't get past the ammonia barrier.

Alice beams at Kali. "I love Twice Loved. Some great bargains there."

Kali glances at me, still trying to sniff on the sly, and nurses the conversation along, "So you finish your library books?"

"Sure did. I'm going back on Monday to get more, plus I'm bringing goodies for the homecoming fund-raiser."

I stop my useless sniffing, which just makes me look like I'm hyperventilating. "You can't go to school," I blurt out. I have to keep her and Mr. Frederics apart until I have a chance to remedy the situation. She's already primed to fall in love with him. If they bump into each other in the parking lot, and she looks into his soulful eyes . . .

"Why not?"

"Because they're trying to cut down on bake sale items."

Alice blinks, waiting for more of an explanation, but I am foiled by my ineptness at lying. Now what? I can't leave until I at least figure out her base notes. I take a last whiff in vain.

Kali smoothly cuts in. "Too many carbs aren't good for our developing bodies. They'd prefer you just send in a check."

Alice scratches at a pencil-thin eyebrow, and the doubt scent of trout floats toward us. "Well, I'll still need to pick up the books."

"Kali has books," I say. "What was the name of that series you couldn't put down? Goddesses of Guilt?"

Kali frowns. "I don't think Alice would be interested in Goddesses of Guilt." She says the title through her teeth. "It's not exactly her *genre*." She fixes me with a hard look.

Oh. I feed Kali an apologetic smile, wishing I had listened to her more carefully when she described the plot.

"It sounds intriguing," says Alice cheerfully. "Well, where are my manners? Won't you come in? I was just doing a rinse." Alice pats her head. "Just give me five minutes to wash out."

"We'd love to," I say too quickly. After she washes out the chemicals, I'll sniff and go. Hopefully, Court will be sleeping in like any normal teenager on a Saturday morning. Then again, he's an athlete. Maybe the type of athlete who rises with the sun and goes on jogs and makes protein shakes. My anxiety floods the air currents with dank, boggy smells.

Kali hooks one eyebrow at me as she follows Court's mom into the great room. White walls and high ceilings give the place an airy feel. Beneath the chemical smells—floor wax and the plasticky drip of polyester-blend slipcovered furniture—hums the comforting aromas of buttery croissants, orchids, and solid-oak ceiling beams.

Several vases line the rustic console in front of us. Most are crudely formed and unevenly painted, but one is a beauty with a pinkish-green patina and a well-proportioned body. Alice sticks her bouquet into this one, then sweeps her hand toward her prairie chic living room. "Please, make yourselves comfortable." She hurries down a hallway, slippers slapping the blond tiles.

Kali looks up at a chandelier dripping with crystals while I take a closer look at the odd-shaped vases. The initials "MNS" plus an age, 11, 12, etc., are carved at the base of each sculpture. Melanie Sawyer?

"Sorry about the books," I whisper to Kali when we can no longer hear Alice. "I'll pick up some paperbacks at Twice Loved."

"Forget it. My mom has a bunch we can borrow. So what's going on?"

"Can't get a read on her. It's all the hair stuff."

Kali whistles. "Maybe she's sprucing up for you-know-who."

Mr. Frederics? I don't say the name aloud but Kali nods at my horrified expression. I sink lower into my sandals. It certainly could've happened by now, though early show-ers are rare.

"Let's chill. Maybe it's nothing. Rich people like to keep up the package. Placenta facials, seaweed wraps." Kali hikes to the living room and plops down on one of the overstuffed couches. Feeling heavier than when I first entered, I join her, keeping my eyes, ears, and nose open for Court. Fluffy Sherpa carpets swallow my feet. At the far wall, the plantation shutters on the

French doors let in thin lines of white light between the slats.

Kali slides her foot out of her sneaker and runs her toes through the Sherpa. "This must be what it feels like to walk on clouds."

The muffled sound of men arguing in the backyard jars the serenity. Kali frowns at the French doors. I sit up when I recognize one of the voices as Court's. "You're the expert on that, aren't you?" he snaps.

"I deserve a say. You're still my son," says a huskier version of Court's voice.

"Biologically. You never cared about what I wanted. It's always about what you want, what will make you look good. But maybe I don't want to play for the Europeans—"

"—throw away millions—"

"—maybe I just want to be a bum on the beach. At least I wouldn't be a no-show, lying—"

"Uncomfortable," Kali whispers.

I nod, while trying to extract myself from the deep cushions. Worse than Court discovering me in his house would be finding me eavesdropping on an obviously private conversation. "Maybe I can scent her over there." There's a chance Alice's scent lingers on a favorite cushion, or the cashmere throw draped over the couch arm. The blanket tickles my nose. The rare plants in her scent are there, but I identify other scents that belong to Court and Melanie. Too contaminated.

Court's voice raises a notch. "—You never show up when

you're supposed to, and then when you do decide to drop in, you start bossing us around like—"

"I told you, I had a work emergency."

"Who has a work emergency on a Friday night? She waited a whole hour for you to take her to her *birthday* dinner last night, and you didn't even call to tell her you weren't coming. She had to find out from Darcy. And why is your intern answering your cell phone anyway? Oh, wait, don't tell me you *promoted* her."

Something crashes from outside followed by silence. Alice, hair wet and rinsed of most of the ammonia, hurries into the living room. "I'm so sorry." She hurries by me to get to the French doors.

Collecting my wits, I inhale.

As she peeks through the shutters, I edge along behind her, sniffing like a basset hound. Her scentprint plays to my nose like a complicated chord. Protea, of course, jasmine sambac, Malaysian coconut, hucklewood, and yarrow. Later, I'll analyze each note and sniff-match it to the most suitable plant fragrance.

Abruptly, Alice swings open her French doors.

The glare off the Caribbean-blue pool almost blinds me. Mr. Sawyer, in golfing gear, stands over a pile of pastel-colored shards and a tangle of daisies. A straight nose and Superman jawline are the only reminders of his once-handsome features, marred by too many martinis and not enough sunscreen.

Court kneels by the pile, grasping his head. The word *lifeguard* forms an arc of red letters over the back of his sweatshirt.

"You are such a jerk," Court seethes.

Alice gasps. "What happened?"

Both Court and his father turn around. Spotting me, Court stops glowering and his jaw slackens.

Mr. Sawyer combs his thick fingers into his hair. "Alice, I'm sorry." He waves his hand at the mess. "I shouldn't have smashed it. It was the first thing I grabbed. I just came to see if I could take Melanie out for pancakes. That's all I wanted to do."

"Just go," she says, her voice brittle. "Melanie's tired anyway. I'll give her your regrets."

Mr. Sawyer begins a loud protest, not caring that he has an audience. Kali casts me a meaningful look and clocks her head toward the front door.

"We'll visit another time," I say to Alice's back. For now, I have everything I need.

"Bye, Alice."

Alice is arguing with her ex-husband and doesn't hear us. Slowly, we back away from the melee, and fetch our bikes.

"You better PUF that woman soon. She doesn't deserve more grief," says Kali once we pass the neighborhood gate.

"I'm working on it." Pushing Court's astonished expression out of my mind, I mentally flip through the ingredients I will need for his mother. Alice's scent contains about a hundred different notes. Just my luck she comes from well-traveled stock. The more genetic variation, the more complex the scent. I already matched the strongest notes, but I will need to sniff around our garden for the others. Any missing components will require a trip to Meyer Botanical Garden, forty miles away in San Francisco, where we can usually find what we need.

One particular heart note I never smelled before. The note is soft and salty, reminiscent of miso soup. Of the eighty-one countries I've visited with Mother collecting botanicals, I don't remember encountering anything like it. While you can sometimes fudge the top notes, the heart notes are essential to an elixir—the secret in the sauce.

That miso note will be a problem.

EIGHT

"We do not pick our noses. Our noses pick us."
—*Calla, Aromateur, 1866*

KALI AND I spend the rest of the weekend raking, composting, and pruning. Whenever Mother's not watching, I sniff-match, pairing plant smells to the notes I recognized in Alice's scent-print. I roam our entire three acres for corresponding scents, from tropicals and subtropicals to conifer and deciduous. Since the warm air tends to accumulate in the center of our property, that's where we nurse the succulents, while evergreens with their sparkling notes crowd the cooler north side. I wouldn't have to log so many steps if we just kept track of all the notes that went with each plant, instead of doing everything the long way, one sniff at a time.

By the time the sun nestles into the folds of the mountains Sunday evening, I've sniffed every note in our garden, but am still short a third of Alice's ninety-eight notes. I won't cut anything here until I have the rest of what I need in hand. Plants must be cut close to the time they'll be used.

I untangle myself from the branches of a hemlock tree and brush cobweb moss off my hair. I'll definitely need a trip to Meyer Botanical Garden. It's closed on Mondays, which means I won't be able to get there until Tuesday.

Remembering one last plant, I take off toward the back of our lot where a natural spring runs down Parrot Hill and collects in a pond. Tabitha the chicken follows me, her salt-and-pepper feathers puffed out around her body. The sky is the color of irises, and a wet chill sits on my skin. I kneel at the edge of the pond and stretch as far as I can toward the water lilies growing in the middle, straining for even a whiff of Alice's miso note. I should've smelled them before they closed up for the night. Under full sunlight, water lily emits a heady, almost rotten perfume, but now I can barely find a thread.

My nose begins to bleed from the strain, both nostrils. It happens, usually, when I'm not getting enough sleep. I pinch its bump between my fingers and fall back onto my haunches. Tabitha scratches at the ground beside me. Mother works hard, but she's careful never to overwork her sniffer. To do otherwise leads to a headache and nose fatigue. But I'd gladly take those over what will happen if I don't undo my mistake.

After the bleeding stops, I try again, closing my eyes, and inhaling more gently this time. I filter out the iron scent of dried blood and zero in on the scent of the water lilies. Past the syrupy sweetness to the core, I find a medley of salty-sweet innards, but no miso.

With a deep sigh, I pick up Tabitha and head back to the workshop. I stroke the white plumage on top of her head, soft as a dandelion puff, and it washes away some of my anxiety. Tabitha clucks softly, head swiveling back and forth.

When I return to the workshop, Mother is looking up into our strangely prolific papaya tree, which fruits even in October. "Oh, there you are. Ready to get started?" Her head bobs to one side as she considers my blank expression. "Flower market? Last Monday of the month is tomorrow, remember?"

I stifle a groan. Tomorrow, a van will collect our excess flowers to sell at a flower market up in San Francisco, one of the ways we defray our living expenses. "No one buys in October. It's a dead month. Couldn't we just skip it this once?"

"Of course not. Why would we do that?"

"Because we've never taken a vacation. We're overdue."

"We travel every season. You've seen more of the world in your fifteen years than most people see in their lives. Not everyone gets a Cloud Air jet, you know." When Mother and Aunt Bryony were children, Grandmother Narcissa fixed the president of Cloud Airways with the love of his life, and in exchange, he gave Grandmother the use of a private jet. Technically, it's a gift, but Grandmother accepted it because the Aromateur Trust Fund wasn't written to include air travel.

"I don't mean traveling. I mean, not working. We could go surfing."

She snorts loudly, not bothering to remind me we don't swim.

"Or we could just chill somewhere."

She crosses her arms. "I'm chilling right now. Now put down the chicken and let's go."

Piles of flowers fight for space on the farm table that occupies the center of our workshop. The table, as well as most of our furniture, was made by a man named William, who lived here as groundskeeper when Mother and Aunt Bryony were growing up. I never knew the man, but I always imagined him to be a quiet, patient person. There's an exacting quality to his work, a marriage of artistry and craftsmanship.

I trim the flowers while Mother separates bushy stalks of snapdragons. Her cheerful humming grates on my nerves.

A rose thorn pricks me, and my irritation at Mother grows, though of course, it's my own fault my fingers ache and my nose is encrusted with blood. But if she'd just cut me a little slack, I wouldn't be in this mess.

She narrows her eyes, and I gather any stress scents to me like a full skirt. "I swear, Mim, ever since you started going to that high school, you're smelling more angsty every day. It's like it's rubbing off on you."

"Maybe it's just me being a teenager."

Her mouth twists to the side. Then she leans over our oak worktable and rubs my cheeks between her hands. "Not to mention, why do you look so wan?"

"Wan?" I draw out the word, hoping to divert her.

"Worn out." Sitting back in her chair, she lifts her chin and smiles.

"Weary." I throw back.

"Weak."

"Waifish."

Mother points her index finger. "Wilted."

I lean forward on my elbows and whisper, "Wasted."

She gives me a fake scowl then taps each of my shoulders with a snapdragon. "I dub you Sir Synonym, but there will be a rematch next week."

"I accept."

She starts humming again, and my anxiety subsides a notch. I lose myself in the rhythm of tying bundles up with twine. Wind, snip, and knot.

When I run out of twine, Mother gets up to fetch another spool from our cabinets. She yanks opens a drawer, and finding none, searches the shelves where we store the tinctures. "Mim." She plucks up a jar and shakes it by the lid, causing a single pod to rattle. "You didn't tell me we're low on cardamom."

I gulp. "Sorry." The itchy feeling that something bad is about to happen freezes me in place.

She stretches up on her toes and peers at the other jars. "And olibanum, too? These are key items, Mim!" She grabs a pad and pen and begins taking inventory. "Guess I'll be going to the

Middle East." Her voice is thick with annoyance. Mother selects each olibanum pod from vendors in Oman, where the most fragrant plants are grown. "If I had known I was going to travel, I wouldn't have taken so many clients. I just hope I can get the jet. The holidays are coming up, you know."

"I'm really sorry." I wilt further, imagining my small mother fighting the crowds in Oman without touching anyone.

"I knew something like this would happen." She runs a hand through her short hair. Here it comes. One little snag and the whole mitten unravels. She'll start checking my work, and somehow she'll find out about Alice.

"And school just started. What happens when things get rolling and you have exams? Term papers?" She faces me, arms crossed and mouth tight.

In desperation, I reach for something to say, something that's not a lie and won't invite further argument. Sweat beads form on the back of my neck. Maybe it's too late, and she already smells the sauerkraut of sour sap. She'll put the fearful scent together with the swampy stink of anxiety, and—

Mother's face relaxes, and her eyeballs shift to the side. She nods once, slowly, while I don't breathe. Whatever she's cooking up can't be good.

"Maybe you should come with me this time."

I gape. "To Oman?" The word comes out as "Oh, man."

"You just said we need a vacation. Oman's lovely in October." She lifts her eyes innocently to the skylight and says airily, "They have surfing there. We could chill."

"But, but—" I sputter. "What about the clients?"

Now she's not listening. "I need to call Alfie," she says, meaning our travel agent. "Finish up here, dear." Her clogs clap across the floorboards. Then, with a heavy thunk of the door, she's gone.

NINE

"THERE BE NO LADY QUITE SO FAIR,
AS SHE WITH ACACIA IN HER HAIR.
THERE BE NO LADY QUITE SO FINE,
WHO HAS A LOVER ON HER MIND."
—*Xanthe, Aromateur, 1789*

I CHECK THE calendar hanging on the back of the blue workshop door. We have several senior citizens coming up. Despite the complexity of their scentprints, Mother insists we fast track the aged wherever possible because they have less time left to enjoy the fruits of our labors. The next two clients are both in their eighties. It wouldn't be ethical for Mother and me to vacation right now. Plus, someone has to follow up on Ms. DiCarlo, and what if Layla's Sacrifice blooms? It'll go to waste.

If all these reasons still aren't enough to convince Mother I cannot go to Oman, I might have to break a leg. Of course, if I were serious, that'd make it trickier to get to Meyer Botanical. I imagine myself hobbling into the garden on crutches, sneaking around the bushes and taking furtive sniffs. If only it weren't closed tomorrow, I could take a train, and if all the plants were in alignment, "elix and fix" in the next twenty-four hours.

A hot shower does nothing to dissolve the knots in my stomach. I hop into bed without drying my hair, and pull Aunt Bryony's old quilt up to my chin. Grandmother Narcissa made the quilt along with the identical one on Mother's bed. Intertwining flowers run the length of the coverlet, representing each ancestor like a family tree. When I was born, Mother added mimosas, bristly balls like purple pom-poms.

I can smell the ginger and winter's bark in my aunt's scent-print, both of which contain a considerable amount of bite. She shares these notes with Mother and me, since heart notes run in families, but hers are a lot spicier. It's in the top notes, those volatile sprinters that reach the nose first, where Mother and Aunt Bryony vary wildly. Mother's top notes include cranberry and black currant—vigorous, eye-catching berries known for increasing memory—while my aunt favors linden, a lightweight but strong wood used by the Vikings to construct shields.

Life would be so much easier if I had an aunt. An aunt would understand how demanding Mother can be, and help with the workload so that her niece might attend algebra class. An aunt could convince Mother not to take me to Oman.

I pedal through the gray light of morning toward school, no closer to a solution for how to get out of the Oman crisis or how to teleport myself to Meyer. I just have to hang tight. Hope Mother sees reason and doesn't make me go. At least Kali dropped off her mom's stash of romance novels to Alice Sunday night. That should keep her away from school for a while.

I swerve around a dead opossum, trying not to breathe in its decaying stench as I pump through the last block to Santa Guadalupe High School. The banner above the entrance reads "Last Day! Halloween Candy Grams for the Boo of Your Dreams."

Swinging into school, I glide to my parking spot at the library bike racks, and wedge my trusty garage-sale bike next to Kali's Schwinn. Vicky leans against a post, cell phone to her ear. What is she doing here? Her eyes have lost focus and the angles of her jawline are softer. For the first time I notice a prettiness to her features. It's as if by dropping her guard, a quieter side peeks through, and I can see why Court found her attractive.

Her eyes snap to mine and vulnerable Vicky disappears. She clacks over to me in her dangerous-looking stilettos, which she could use as spikes to climb a wall in case she feels like going ninja. At the sight of my bucket hat, her eyeballs roll with the white of surrender, like she's giving me up as a lost cause.

She finishes her call and drops her phone into her Gucci purse, which is stuffed with so many beauty products, you'd think she was a klepto. The cloying scents of petroleum and polyurethane assault my nose. Vicky's designer purse is a knockoff.

"I dropped it in his drink Saturday night," she says in a low voice that boys might consider sexy. "Why is it taking so long? It's only supposed to take a couple of days."

How does she know that? "It can take up to a week. Plus, the chemistry has to be perfect."

"The chemistry *is* perfect," she hisses. A clot of mascara looks like a bug caught between her eyelashes.

"Well then, you have nothing to worry about." I fake a smile.

A woman and her toddler stroll by. The little boy reaches up for Vicky's skirt, and Vicky jerks away, with the urgency of someone who has just felt a spider graze her face. Her red lips compress disapprovingly, and the pickled cabbage of sour sap stings my nose.

The mother glares at Vicky, then tugs her child away.

Vicky shivers, as if casting off a bad dream. "The dance is in less than a week. If I don't get results by the homecoming game, I'm posting Kali's journal online." She sweeps away in a billow of fake Gucci, Poison Apple perfume, and burning rubber.

Four more days until the game, which kicks off a week of festivities leading up to the homecoming dance. I hurry to my locker. Vicky wasn't bluffing, I smelled vengeful sword fern on her breath, a plant that chokes out others through its sneaky underground tubers. Kali doesn't want me to fix Vicky with Drew Reaver, but my thought pot is empty of ideas.

Near the lockers, members of the student council hawk candy grams at a table.

"Mimosa, right?" Lauren Foster, student council president, points a neon-pink highlighter, which matches her fingernails, as well as the rubber bands in her braces.

"Yes," I say, hearing the surprise in my own voice. Lauren has a peaceful wild-olive-and-lemon scent that reminds me of sipping fruit-sweetened limoncello with Mother on a terrace on the Mediterranean—one of the rare times I'd ever seen her relaxing. I warm to Lauren instantly.

Pascha Hassan, her best friend, staples candy bars onto pieces of paper and stuffs them into a plastic pumpkin. Her delicate brown hands look like they should be modeling rings. She smells more floral than Lauren, with traces of superabsorbent polymers, the secret sauce in disposable diapers, which might mean she cares for a younger sibling.

"You want to buy a candy gram?" she asks.

"No, thanks. I don't eat candy."

Lauren and Pascha exchange a smile that I can't read.

"Well, it's not for you. You buy it for someone else. You write your message on this"—Lauren holds up an orange paper—"and we attach a candy to it and deliver it to your special someone. A buck each."

"Oh. No, thanks." A million times no, thanks. I begin to leave, but then I notice Pascha elbowing Lauren.

I split my gaze between them, not sure what I'm waiting for. Lauren hair sprayed glitter into her wavy blond hair and the sparkle makes me blink. She looks around, then leans closer to me and whispers, "Do you use potions for yourself?"

"Of course not." Is that what people think? "I'm not even allowed to date. Plus, that would be unethical."

Pascha stops stuffing. The folds of the scarf covering her head ripple in the breeze. "Then how do you do it?"

"Do what?"

The girls look at each other again.

"How do you get all those boys to like you?" Lauren asks.

I snort. Try living in a garden bursting with aphrodisiacs all your life. My particular brand of boy problems must be more obvious than I thought. I try to disinfect my followers as soon as I detect a problem, but I'll need to be more vigilant. Wouldn't want a jealous mob of teenage girls after me, like the ones who threw six-fingered Hyacinth into the sea. It hits me that maybe Larkspur's concerns weren't so far-fetched.

"I drywall better than I give love advice," I say. "Sorry."

Lauren deflates a little, and her sigh smells of diet soda and stomach acid. She could use more leafy greens. "I just want to know how I get a certain boy to ask me to the homecoming dance." She dabs her eyes with a tissue.

"Why don't you just ask him?"

"I couldn't do that!" she gasps. More dabbing.

"Why?"

"What if he said no? I'd need a sign that he'd say yes first. What are the signs that a guy likes you?" She clasps her hands together and implores me with her hazel eyes.

I tug at my sleeve. "When a person has a crush, their top notes become buttery and their middle notes brighten by a factor of sixteen. Plus, they smell like heartsease, which is a kind of wildflower."

A hundred yards out, the soccer team in their blue-and-white uniforms returns from their morning practice, slapping hands with members of the track team jogging past them. Number ten, Court, walks with his customary slouch. His shirt hugs his lean body like a wetsuit. Number nine, Whit Wu, runs to catch up with him.

Lauren's lips separate. "Um, what?"

Pascha's kohl-rimmed eyes narrow as she appraises me. Without lifting her gaze from me, she hands Lauren another tissue. "Listen to the witch. She knows what she's talking about."

I cough, putting into doubt *that* perception. My eyes drift toward the field again. Court looks up and our eyes connect. My heart does a backflip, and a dozen different scents burst from me, the sugar maple of happiness, the chicory of regret, and more rambling sunflower, a plant notable for its tendency to change directions several times during the day. I rarely smell like rambling sunflower. I usually have the Rulebook to circumscribe my path, and if not the rules, then Mother.

Court waves, then trots toward the locker rooms.

"But how am I supposed to know what, er, what she just said?" says Lauren to Pascha.

"Your body knows," says Pascha. "It's *hormones*. We just can't smell them like she can." Her dark eyes swing to me. "Am I right?"

Not exactly, but it's close enough.

Pascha doesn't wait for me to answer. She slaps her friend's arm. "Weren't you paying attention in sex ed? Hormones are like these candy grams that pass messages to people, only we get the messages mixed up because we're teens." She pulls a note out of the pumpkin. "'You're nice.' Ha! That one really means, 'You have nice buns.'"

"What does that have to do with whether he likes me?" asks Lauren.

"Just because you *think* you like him doesn't mean you do. Maybe *you* just like his buns." Pascha uses her spindly hands to help her talk.

"I do not." Lauren grabs a candy bar from the table and opens it. "You're so lucky you can just smell these things."

"Right," I say, not feeling lucky at all. "Well, I should go to class."

Pascha pushes a silver cuff up her arm. "Okay, well, try not to have too much fun today." Her brown lips fold into a smile.

Cautiously, I sniff but don't detect any disdainful dirty bathwater odors. "Okay." Shouldn't be hard. I've never had much fun, let alone too much.

I shift around on the plastic seat of my desk. Only ten minutes into algebra and my legs have already gone numb. Mr. Frederics's argyle cardigan bunches and pulls as he writes an equation on the board. The fluorescent lighting shines off his scalp.

As I copy the problem, Drew Reaver's pen scratches rapidly

behind me. I glance over my shoulder. Instead of the equation, he's flourishing the words "soul sucker" under a demon he etched into his notebook.

What would be so wrong about fixing Vicky with Drew? He likes drawing soul-sucking demons, and she *is* a soul-sucking demon. It's perfect.

As if sensing me lasering the back of her head with my eyes, Vicky turns languidly around and gives me the once-over. She taps the eraser tip of her pencil against her chin, then, just as unhurriedly, turns back around.

The door opens. A freshman enters, bearing a basket of candy grams.

Drew's pen stops. The freshman's sneakers squeak softly as she walks up and down the rows, doling out candy grams like communion wafers. Melanie shrieks in delight when she gets two.

The freshman stops at my desk, smiling oddly.

Dear God, no. I sense what she's going to do before she does it. It happens in slow motion. She puts a hand under her basket, then upends it onto my desk.

Candy grams overflow my desk and spill onto the floor. The cloying scent of chocolate and nougat makes my eyes tear. There's a shocked moment of silence, followed by exclamations and tittering. As I wilt in my chair, I realize why Lauren and Pascha singled me out for advice.

Vicky frowns while Melanie glares at me and stuffs her two

packs of candy into her purse.

As coolly as I can, I sweep the grams into my bag. It's just as I feared. I missed a few admirers, or ten or twenty. What if they're anonymous? How am I going to scent them all? No doubt they've been touched by several hands—the sender's, members of the student council, the messengers. I put one to my nose and sniff. Sure enough, the human smells are faint and hard to separate into individuals, plus they're overwhelmed by the chemical smells of felt-tip marker.

Drew helps me gather the grams that fell to the floor.

"Hey, thanks," I whisper.

"Bimbo's Chews." He holds up a candy bar. Each of his fingers is adorned with silver rings with skulls and crossbones. "These are the best."

"You can have all of them, but I'll keep the messages."

He grins, making his lip ring stand straight out. "Seriously? That's cool."

Mr. Frederics waves his hands. "Settle down, class, settle down. Let's return to the equations on the board. Do I have any volunteers for problem four?"

No one raises a hand.

"Mimosa, since you seem to be the lady of the hour, will you help us out?" He holds the dry-erase pen to me.

I fake some composure and walk to the board. As I start writing, I hear the door open once again, a sound that causes my spine to shrink. Oh no. No more candy grams, please.

Slowly, I turn around.

The dry-erase pen nearly falls out of my grip.

Alice strikes a pose, one hand on the doorframe, the other holding a pink pastry box that I can smell is full of chocolate cake with coconut buttercream frosting, no nuts. A plastic shopping bag dangles from her wrist. Gone is the velour tracksuit, and in its place, a dress in sapphire blue to match her eyes. Her hair is swept into a French chignon, and thanks to her rinse, contains not a hint of gray. She holds up the cake like a pizza and says in a huskier voice than I remember, "Hello, Franklin."

TEN

"An aromateur without ethics, nay,
she is a rhinoceros in a field of pansies."
—Myrtle, *Aromateur*, 1602

"MOM!" MELANIE CRIES out, gripping the sides of her chair like she's afraid it might eject her. Vicky bites the end of her pencil, eyes lit with amusement.

Still at the classroom door, Alice wiggles her fingers. Her nails are painted glossy red. "Hi, dear."

Mr. Frederics walks halfway to the door. "Mrs. Sawyer. What can we do for you?"

"Alice, call me Alice."

"All right, Alice."

She turns her bright smile to me. "I know you're all trying to watch your carbs, but what's life without a few treats now and then?"

Melanie's shocked expression doesn't change, but several people cheer. The box with the cake starts to slip but Alice catches it before it drops. "Oh!"

Mr. Frederics hurries the rest of the way to Court's mom. "Er, let me help you with that." He sets the cake and Alice's plastic bag, through which forks are sticking, on a bookshelf.

Alice, still standing in the doorway, beckons him back. Mr. Frederics waves his hand at me, carry on, then follows her into the hallway. We all watch them leave.

Standing at the white board, I break into a cold sweat. The elixir has kicked in. I'm too late.

Everyone's eyes shift to me. I turn back to the problem on the board, which suddenly looks like hieroglyphics. How do I do this again?

"Your mom's hot, Melanie," calls one of the smart mouths in the back of the room.

The guy next to him chortles. "Yeah, does she do home deliveries?"

"Shut up," says Melanie.

From the front row, Valerie, who prefers Val, probably because she fancies herself the future valedictorian, stabs her perfectly sharpened pencil toward the board. "Could you finish the problem?"

I start writing numbers while I run what-if scenarios in my head. If I don't PUF Alice soon, no amount of elixir will stop her crush from developing. Like a car with balding tires on black ice, she'll careen out of control.

"Um, wrong," says Val.

The string of numbers I wrote on the board are as random

as a lottery draw. Mr. Frederics is still out in the hallway chatting with Alice. What could they possibly be talking about for so long?

"Mr. Frederics?" I call loudly.

He reappears in the doorway. "Yes, Mimosa?"

"I'm just not sure what to do here." Probably it's the easiest problem on the planet. From behind Mr. Frederics, Alice stretches up on her tippy toes to see me.

Someone snickers, probably Vicky. I do my best to block her kumquat smell from my nose.

"Ah, well, I stumped you." Mr. Frederics chuckles.

"Yes, you sure did." My knees threaten to buckle under the weight of thirty pairs of eyeballs.

"Just sit down," Val mutters.

Mr. Frederics swivels his head back and forth between Alice and me.

"Oh, I don't mean to keep you," says Court and Melanie's mom. "Please, go back to your work. Enjoy the cake. Good-bye, Melanie."

Melanie's gone as white as the board. It's hard to say which of us is more horrified.

A trail of black scuff marks leads out the classroom door and into a marble hallway, ringing with the noise of the eight hundred kids who attend SGHS. I keep myself even more closed off than usual, eyes peeled for signs of pollen-induced crushes from everyone who passes too close. I've infected more people than I realize, more people than I have enough BBG for. My chest seems to squeeze my heart like a fist, and I can't help wondering if my being here is causing more harm than good.

Everything feels more acute when the body is stressed, and it's the same with my nose. All the smells barrel down on me, noisy as an orchestra of ten thousand instruments tuning up. As I walk, I identify them one at a time, an exercise that relaxes me.

Pictures of homecoming courts from years past line the walls, hairstyles broadcasting the decades. I stop in front of last year's photo, in which a taller and prettier version of Vicky smiles back at me. On her head is the tall, dazzling crown that marks the homecoming queen.

"That's Vicky's sister, Juliana." The student council president Lauren's voice causes me to jump. She shakes her hair, throwing off glitter, and pops the tab off her diet soda.

"Did you know her?"

"Yeah, she was a senior when we were sophomores. We all wanted to look like her. She was smart, too. Got into Oxford. And a nice person."

A trifecta of talents. Vicky has some pretty high heels to fill. Maybe that explains why homecoming is so important to her, because as far as I can tell, she is neither a nice person, nor valedictorian material.

Lauren's braces twinkle. "So you got your candy grams?"

"Yeah. Thanks."

"No, thank *you*. You boosted our sell-through rate by 10 percent."

"Oh wow." Nothing more original comes to mind.

"I got one and it said, 'You have nice buns.' Pascha thinks she's funny."

"I'd take one good friend over a hundred admirers any day."

She grins. "Me, too. Hey, Pascha and I are getting froyo after school. We used to do ice cream, but I need to lose some weight."

"You?" I eye her five-foot-two frame with its normal-size everything except for a larger-than-average chest.

"Yes, I'm totally gross. I can't fit into my favorite jeans anymore. Anyway, you want to come?"

I'm stuck between wondering why someone who seems to have her act together could think herself gross, and the realization that she's asking me to hang out. Like a normal person. "I'd love to, but I can't today." Someone finally seeks my friendship and I have to reverse an elixir. "Maybe next time?"

Her bracketed smile sags. "Sure. See you around."

My head throbs by the time I pass through a double door with the sunburst design that leads into the main courtyard. I trudge down interlocking cement tiles, looking for Kali. I haven't seen her all day since we don't have Cardio on Mondays. She's probably already scooping the goop. Kali works harder than any teenager I know, probably even me. She's saving up to be the first person in her family to attend college—a fancy creative writing program on the East Coast.

Through the library windows, I make out Ms. DiCarlo standing on a ladder, using a ruler to position the books into straight lines on the shelves. She glimpses me watching her and waves.

I halfheartedly wave back. If she only knew how my carelessness robbed her of a soul mate, she wouldn't be smiling like that. How can a nice librarian compete with an ex-model with money and a vivacious personality? If Mr. Frederics has any romantic interest in Alice, the elixir will send those feelings into orbit, eclipsing the ones he has for Ms. DiCarlo.

A fresh zing of anxiety courses through me, making my heart pound in time with my head. After the cake incident, it's imperative to keep Alice and Mr. Frederics apart until I can unfix her. If only there was a way to keep them busy, one or the other.

I pace in a circle and stop. Court could keep his mother busy, too busy to see Mr. Frederics. Maybe he could convince her to go on vacation, or sign her up for some classes. He'll want to keep his mom out of trouble as much as I do. Technically, aromateurs *"may not solicit nor accept the assistance of nonaromateurs in the creation of elixirs,"* but Kali helps us with the gardening. Surely, asking Court to run interference counts less than that.

Briskly, I walk toward the last lunch table, where the soccer players hang out, trying not to worry about how angry Court will be when he finds out what I've done, especially after confiding to me about his mom. The seeds of his admiration for me will wither and die, assuming there were seeds at all.

Whit Wu, Court's best friend, sprawls out in the space Court usually occupies, mowing down a slice of pizza. As everyone falls quiet and the mothball scent of suspicion spreads like poison gas, Whit finally notices me. His head jerks back and his black eyes go wide.

"Hi," I say. "I was just wondering if you knew where Court was?"

Whispering starts up, and I catch the words "candy grams."

Whit's throat bunches as food travels down the pipe. "Why do you want to know?" Casually, he flips back his black hair. It falls in waves around his broad shoulders. Despite his cool, I can smell his alarm at being accosted by the love witch. It smells like freezer burn.

"Maybe she wants to put a spell on him," someone cracks.

I ignore the jokers and address Whit. "I just need to talk to him. It's important."

"Why? Is there a love emergency?"

Everyone laughs. A slip of a girl scoots farther down her bench away from me, and a curtain of hair with purple highlights falls into her face. I recognize her as one of Vicky's friends and mentally kick myself for approaching this crowd. Half of Court's friends are Vicky's as well. If Vicky didn't already have enough reasons to dislike me, I think I just found her a new one. The girl casts me a suspicious eye, and moves her Tupperware farther from me, too.

Better to just make a quick and, hopefully, forgettable exit. Jaw clenched, I hurry away.

Court could be anywhere. Maybe he stayed after class. Or maybe . . .

I pull the brim of my bucket hat farther down to shade my eyes and hurry to the field. A lone figure sits with his back against the mulberry tree.

As I tread across the grass, a light breeze fills my nose with the chive-y smell of Jupiter grass. I will need to harvest some for Alice's elixir. At least that one won't require a field trip.

Number ten watches me slog toward him. I don't detect burning tires, or any of the other negative emotions. In fact, the happy smell of orange blossoms caresses my nostrils, carried by a southern breeze. He must not have heard about his mother's odd behavior yet. I'll just have to serve the truth, straight up, then move quickly to solutions.

The sleeves of his jersey are pushed up to his shoulders, showing the trace of a tan line on his bronzed biceps. "Was hoping to find you here. Guess you found me." The corners of his mouth budge upward.

"Guess so," I say, feigning cheer. Awkwardly, I settle beside him, still hugging my bag.

"Thanks for bringing those flowers to my rude sister on Saturday. My mom, too. It made her day." He flashes me that grin that stirs my pulse to a trot. "Power of the flower, even after my dad . . ."

A whiff of friar plums itches my nose, the bluesy note of sadness. Mood scents are often ephemeral, like sweaters we pull on and off. He chews on a hangnail, then drops his hand back into his lap.

"Is everything okay?" I ask, though I already know the answer.

He stares at his Converse All Stars, face darkening. "Melanie used to like making pottery, though she wasn't very good at it. When she was ten, she made this vase. It looked more like a . . . shoe." A smile flits across his face. "But Mom said she loved it, and so Melanie made her another one every year.

"Last weekend when Dad came to the house, Mom had moved that vase to the backyard for Melanie's birthday party." A dent appears in his smooth forehead and he lets out a held breath.

"The one he broke?"

Court nods. "Mom forgave him. Why? Beats the heck out of me. He's always breaking things. I just want him to leave us alone. Stop promising stuff he can't deliver. Mel got all dressed up when he said he was going to take her out for her birthday. I told her he wouldn't show up. I *knew* he would disappoint her." Scowling, he plucks up a handful of grass, then scatters it.

"Hope and disappointment are brothers," I hear myself saying.

Court's smooth forehead crinkles, and I explain, "Hope smells like pink hydrangea, but if you add a bit of acid to the soil—coffee grounds or eggshells work well—the petals turn blue, and the smell changes to something wetter and foggier, which is how disappointment smells."

"Disappointment smells like . . . fog?"

"It smells like blue hydrangea, which sort of smells like fog."

The confusion doesn't budge from his expression.

"What I'm saying is, without hope, there could not be disappointment."

The plum scent spikes noticeably, and he gathers his knees to him. "So I should stop hoping."

"No, it's human to hope. But you could stop adding acid to the soil. You can stop letting him hurt you." I can't help thinking about my own mom, who will be giving off a lot of blue hydrangea if she ever learns what *I* did. "As my mother says, forgiveness is a gift you give to yourself. At least that's what she tells me every time I'm mad at her."

"Yeah. I'm still working on that one." He gives me a rueful grin.

"It's nice that you're close to your sister."

"We used to be closer. Ever since Dad left, Mel thinks she's an actress. She used to be a tomboy. Used to surf with us on the weekends. Now she hardly talks to me." He squints as if trying to make out something on the field, but there's no one practicing there. "So that's my messed-up family."

I crease the cotton of my skirt with my fingernail. Now how am I supposed to tell him about his mom? Maybe I *shouldn't* tell him. But without his help, I might not PUF his mom in time.

"Hey, thanks for listening," he says, breaking the silence. "I didn't mean to dump. I'm not usually so mopey."

"It's okay, I like listening. Feel free to dump—I mean share—anytime."

"Thanks, and the same goes for you."

Oh great, way to sharpen the shears even more. Now we're confidantes. Better get it over with as soon as possible.

I straighten up and look him in the eye. "Actually, I do have something to tell you. I screwed up."

He goes very still, and the only noise is the breeze rustling the mulberry leaves above us. In as few words as possible, I tell him what I did. As he listens, his face is inscrutable, a placid palate of fair skin.

"Holy crap."

"I'm sorry." I dig my fingernails into my palms.

"I mean, I don't even—" His hand makes circles in the air then stops. "Are you messing with me?"

"No." I cringe that he could think that. My hat overheats my head. "I wouldn't do that."

The angry scent of burning tires soaks the air around us. "You know the crap she's been through this year?" His muscles tense, and he scoots onto his knees, like he's about to leave.

"I have a guess, and I am sorry. I have no excuse, except that I was . . ."

"You were what?" He wraps his hands around his head as if

preparing for a crash, then lets go, and his hands ball into fists.

I swallow hard. "I wasn't paying attention." A trickle of sweat inches down my neck. "I'll fix this. At least, I'll do everything I can to fix it."

He scowls. "How are you going to do that?"

I take a deep breath then explain about the PUF and why I need to go to Meyer. A large cloud of apple scab—one of the thirteen notes of horror—rushes at me, but I press on. "I just need you to keep her from coming to school, long enough for me to make the PUF. Maybe you could pick out her library books for her, or—"

"I don't believe this." His expression is too carefully neutral. "I mean, I thought it was cool you liked to garden, but this is seriously screwed up." He gets to his feet and hikes up his backpack.

He can't leave, and especially not smelling of rage. I jump to my feet. "I know, it's screwed up. But please don't go yet." Please see reason. "I'm only asking for a few days. Does she like movies? Maybe you can take her to a movie?" I sound desperate. He glances at my hands, stretched in the space between us, and I quickly clasp them together.

A gust of frustration blows from his lips. "What gives you the right to play with people's lives?"

"We don't play with their lives, we try to make them . . . happy." I wilt under his gaze, feeling the loose threads of our friendship untie. I had no right to expect his help anyway. "I'm sorry."

ELEVEN

"Love is revealed through sacrifice."
—*Shayla, Aromateur, 1633*

AT LEAST I learned one thing today in school. It's not possible to die of mortification. After the final bell rings, I numbly haul books out of my locker even though I won't have time to study.

"Hey, Nose!" Kali floats like a neon-hoodied lifesaver toward me. The sight of my best friend's smiling face, like aloe vera, instantly takes some of the burn out of my misery. Sometimes one friend is just enough.

"You're not going to believe what happened," I tell her.

"I believed it when you said you'd never eaten a Dorito."

As we tread toward the library, I fill her in.

A string of painted metal benches run along one side of the courtyard. Vicky and her posse perch atop one with their feet on the seat. They're engulfed in a cloud of perfumed beauty products.

The girls go quiet, and as we approach, Vicky smirks. Kali

slows and the sour sap scent of fear mingles with the burnt tires of her anger. I grab the crook of her arm and hurry her along.

"She's been giving me those snooty looks all day," Kali mutters.

"I can fix that."

Kali's eyes snap to mine. "You're not still thinking about fixing her with Drew?"

"Leave the guilt to me."

"Seems like you have more than you can handle right now." When I don't answer, she pokes me with her elbow. "I'm serious. Don't do it. Just worry about Alice. Want me to ask Mukmuk if he'll drive you to that garden?"

"Will he tell your parents?"

"Maybe. He's such a choir boy."

Even though Kali's brother is usually reliable, the Apulus are friendly with Mother. I can't risk a leak. "Thanks, but that's okay. I'll take the train." Assuming I'm not in Oman.

"You need me to come?"

It would be nice to have Kali's company, but I can't justify spending money on two train tickets, or breaking her perfect attendance record. The garden closes at five every night, and I can't wait until school lets out. "That's okay, I'll be fine." She can't smell it, but I wonder if she can hear my lie.

I set off for home. The autumn wind wrestles with my hat and the toggle bead strains against the hollow under my chin. When

I hit a pothole, my bag of candy grams nearly goes flying out of my basket. I'm tempted to dump them all into the next trash bin. In the time it will take me to scent them all and match them to their authors, I could probably spray every one of the five hundred boys that attend SGHS. Of course, then I would need to make several more bottles of the very expensive BBG.

Or maybe I'll just do nothing and wait for the mob to throw me into the ocean.

I ride around the block one more time to rid myself of the swampy stench of anxiety. When I pedal up the driveway, I catch a glimpse of Mother behind the turret window.

On the kitchen table sits a new crate of Creamsicle tulip bulbs, which smell of oranges and cream. A grower in Holland delivers these to us every year in October. Despite the pleasant fragrance, a scowl tugs at my face. The bulbs will be stressed from their flight and Mother will make me plant them today.

I trudge upstairs, mentally rehearsing the speech I prepared about why I should not go to Oman. In her room, an open suitcase lies on the bed. Mother is in her closet, sifting through her blue clothes.

We're leaving already? I open my mouth to speak, but my rehearsed words flee my head, and all that comes out is "The seniors need to be fixed."

"What?"

"I can't go to Oman. We have seniors coming up. And the papayas are ready to drop—you've seen them yourself. Who's going to look after things here?" I hold my breath.

"Relax. You don't have to go." Hangers squeak against wood.

"What? I mean, are you sure?" I lower myself next to her suitcase.

"We'll save that vacation for when it won't compromise love lives."

Like *that* will ever happen.

"Alfie got me the jet for tomorrow. Oh, I assume you saw the Creamsicles?" She bustles out of the closet carrying a navy sweater and navy slacks.

"Yes. I'll plant them tonight."

Briskly, she begins to roll up the sweater. "No. There's a problem with them. I'm sending them back."

"What kind of problem?"

She stops rolling the sweater and raises her chin. "You tell me."

A test. I begin to rise, intending to go to the kitchen, but she holds out a hand to stop me. "From here. I've babied you way too long."

I sink back into the bed. Why does she always make it so hard? The Creamsicles barely whisper here on the second floor, let alone reveal to me their defect.

"Close your eyes. It's easier to unlayer."

Mother moves about the room, noisily opening and closing drawers. I can't help wondering if she's putting as many obstacles as she can in my path. Even her own scent impedes my progress, especially the heart note of tuberose, that overbearing floral reminiscent of a throbbing headache on a hot summer day. My nose rummages for the bitter telltale signs of mold—one of the main reasons for rejection—but I don't find any more than normal levels coming from that direction.

Mother stops moving around. "Come on, Mim, don't try so hard. You look like you're going to pop a vein."

More smells tiptoe by: ink, a roll of postage stamps, cornflower water, old lace curtains.

A band of sweat forms around my forehead. Finally, the barest thread of something sour—formic acid—seems to chase on the heels of the Creamsicle scent. Before I catch it, it ducks back into hiding. "It's an insect."

"Yes, yes, go on."

I wait for it to resurface so I can get a clearer picture.

"Mites?" I open my eyes, and stars float around the room.

Mother, in the closet doorframe holding a denim dress, shakes her head. It stings me to smell the blue hydrangea of her disappointment. "Not mites. Aphids. You need to let go. If you try to force your way through the scents, they'll resist you."

I huff out my frustration. "What happens when there are no more aromateurs? Don't you think we should spend our time figuring out that problem instead of smelling aphids?" I don't think I could run the business all by myself, should something ever happen to Mother. Grandmother Narcissa was as vivacious as verbena, but still couldn't avoid getting hit by the taxi in Senegal.

"What do you mean, 'no more aromateurs'? One day, you'll have a daughter or two." She gives a tiny shrug and grins. "Or three."

I clamp my lip. I don't think I could ever inflict such a lonely life on anyone else.

Mother is hawking her eyes into mine, so I say, "Even if I did have kids, one family can't carry an entire species."

"Species," she says the words as if it tasted sour. "Aromateurs have existed for thousands of years. We're like the hostas; we'll never quite die out." She brushes past me with her dress and begins to roll it up. "I wore this when I was pregnant with you," she says brightly, indicating the discussion is over. "All it needs is a belt." After stuffing the roll into the suitcase, back into the closet she goes. Mother prides herself on her frugality. When the dress finally rots off her body, she'll use it as a rag, and after that she'll use it to line the chicken coop.

I trace my finger around the intertwining flowers that run the length of her quilt. Unlike their real-life counterparts, Mother's flower, a dahlia, twines tightly around my aunt's blue bryony.

She reemerges from the closet and tosses her belt into the suitcase, then starts rolling her underwear into neat bundles. "I'll be gone until next Monday. While I'm away, you'll need to finish Ms. Salzmann's elixir. It's done and all you'll need to do is agitate and clarify. Fix her Wednesday before you go to school. On Thursday, Dr. Lipinsky's coming in for a sniff analysis. Four p.m. Both senior specials."

Of course, I already knew about both appointments. "Okay, no problem."

Mother pauses in her underwear rolling to squint at me. Her nose wiggles, and I realize I've started to smell boggy again. I lower my eyes and meekly ask, "Is there anything else I can do?"

She sits beside me, and the mattress dips, rolling me toward her. "Just do the things you're supposed to do and we'll be fine."

"Right. Okay."

She pats my arm. "You could be a great aromateur, Mim. As great as your grandmother Narcissa."

Mother loves to tell me this, but today, it sounds like a warning.

"What makes you so sure?"

"When I was pregnant, your nose became combined with mine; I could smell things happening twenty miles away. Like that fire in Pheasant Hill."

"You never told me that."

"If you want to become great like her, you'll need to focus. Too many things going on in there right now." She taps my head. "Algebra, jumping jacks, blah, blah, blah. I know there's something else in there, too, something you're not telling me."

I freeze and force my mind to go blank.

Still focused on me, she begins coiling a leather belt while I impersonate a second suitcase. The belt buckle falls out of the middle and the whole thing unwinds, distracting her momentarily. She lets out a gasp of annoyance. "So what is it?"

"I, uh, really, uh—"

"You really what?"

I see an opportunity, like a single red bloom in a field of golden poppies. Keeping my thoughts carefully neutral, I say, "I smelled this scent on someone the other day and I didn't know what it was. It's been bothering me."

Her eyes narrow, reminding me of a cat that's unsure if it sees a mouse. "Go on."

"It had a dominant of miso soup, osha beats, a lick of buffalo weed, not too spicy, with a silvery finish. Do you know what it is?"

She goes back to rolling her belt. "There must be two hundred botanicals that fit that description."

"I know." I didn't really think she could tell me. Words can only take us so far in describing a scent. The English language is notoriously lacking in scent terminology. Of course, aromateurs have evolved their own terminology, but that can only narrow the field, not pinpoint. At least Mother's off the trail. I lead her further away. "What do you do if you can't match a scent?" From her open crossword book, I pick up her favorite bookmark and pretend to study the laminated pressed violets.

"Never happens anymore. It used to, when I was younger."

"So what *did* you do when it happened? When you were younger. It would be nice to know how to become . . . great."

"Don't worry, Dr. Lipinsky's easy. I met him once before. He's mostly fruits." She smiles. "It's wonderful to see you finally taking such an interest."

I let the matter drop now that I'm safe. "I better let you finish packing." I pass her the bookmark and haul myself up from the bed.

"Mim?"

I pause by the doorframe. Mother studies me with a curious expression. "Immerse yourself in the scent, then meditate on it. The notes will tell you where to go."

After dinner over a crossword puzzle with Mother, a challenging one I chose to keep both our minds occupied, I head to the workshop. I need to catalogue the scents to source on tomorrow's trip to Meyer. I bring textbooks, just in case Mother drops in and wonders what I'm doing in there. At least one good thing came of failing to inventory: when she leaves, I can work on Alice's elixir without fear of discovery.

I insert our old iron key with the heart-shaped grip. It sticks, the way it sometimes does. When I'm a hundred years old, I'll probably stick in a few places, too. I jiggle it a few times, until I hear the lock give way.

A tendril of Layla's Sacrifice pushes against the inside of its glass dome like it's trying to escape, in strange parallel to its namesake. A sixteenth-century aromateur, Layla, had a daughter, Shayla, who mistakenly fixed a Turkish prince with the wrong princess. For her crime, she was sentenced to three days in a locked tomb, a slow and horrible way to die. But so great was Layla's love for her daughter that she volunteered to stand in for the punishment. Layla stood with her back straight as a reed while they rolled a rock against the entrance of the tomb.

When they returned three days later, they found only an orchid.

"You have it easy in there. Three squirts of water a day, sunshine, peace of mind. It sure gets more complicated when you're on the outside."

I grab a notebook and pen. Before beginning my work, I run my hand along the narcissuses the groundskeeper William had carved into the farm table, an old ritual for resetting my mind. The simple act thins the anxious cloud hanging over me, but it doesn't evaporate altogether.

I write down plants I could use for the remaining notes in Alice's elixir. Her scentprint contains several exotics, which doesn't surprise me given her age and gender. The miso soup heart note still bothers me. It's the drum majorette in the woman's parade of scents, and totally necessary.

I turn on the computer and pull up our database of plants. Miso is made from soybean, and I run through all fifty-nine species, including four that I personally added to the list after a trip to Asia a few years ago.

None of them match Alice's miso scent. Then I pull up the Meyer website, which contains a list of all ten thousand species grown at the garden. As I read the names of each plant, I mentally call up their smells.

Again, no matches.

I drum a pencil against my temple. Meyer's database isn't regularly updated. They add new species all the time.

Then again, what are the chances they would add a plant with that particular note?

I fumble the pencil and it drops onto the desk, breaking the tip. If I can't find it at Meyer, I will have to look elsewhere, and elsewhere is somewhere between not here and everywhere.

TWELVE

"Harvest stinging nettle from the top, where it's least expecting you."
—*Tulipia, Aromateur, 1755*

THE ROOSTER'S CROWING jolts me awake. Mother's gone. I smell only the fraying threads of her winter's bark base notes. I wrestle on the nearest clothes—T-shirt, sundress, oversized sweater, and leggings—and then peer into my mirror. Dark circles bloomed overnight under my eyes, which look more snail brown than amber at the moment.

I employ a battalion of bobby pins to keep my hair out of my face, jamming them in wherever I see a stray lock. My chin-length bob is begging for a real trim after that last hack job I gave it.

I'm so jittery, I want to pedal to the train station right now, but Meyer doesn't open until one on Tuesdays. And I have to go to school anyway, because Mr. Frederics might wonder why I'm not at algebra.

Mother left a bowl of oatmeal sprinkled with raisins on the kitchen table with a note.

SEE YOU IN A WEEK. EMERGENCY CELL
ON FRIDGE.
LOVE, M.
P.S. CHECK ON MS. DiCARLO.

Did Mr. Frederics tell Mother about Alice's odd behavior? Did something happen or not happen between him and Ms. DiCarlo? We always follow up on the targets to make sure they don't adversely react to our potions. But Mother's never had to remind me to do it.

I choke down the oatmeal, grab a beret, and dash off to school.

I whiz through the parking lot, past Court's Jeep and Mr. Frederics's bamboo-green hybrid, feeling every glance thrown my way like a pie in the face. No one cares about my problems any more than they didn't yesterday, but I'm still self-conscious, as if everyone knows what I've done to Alice. I reassure myself that Court wouldn't say anything, for his mother's sake, if nothing else.

Today's Cardio Fitness leader, Vicky, stands in front of the class, fiddling with her phone. Kali stretches to one side, then the other. "Thought you were going to Meyer."

"I'm catching the 12:20 train."

The bluesy sounds of a guitar blare from the speakers, making the air ducts vibrate. We exchange a look when we recognize the song, "There's a Place for You and Me," a slow ballad that's not exactly cardio.

Ms. Bobrov waves her wristbanded hands at Vicky. "Wait, wait."

Vicky cuts the music and asks, "Something wrong?"

"This song ees not right." The teacher snaps her fingers.

"Oh, come on, Ms. B." Vicky slides her eyes to Kali, who's gone as still as an oak tree. "Some of us just move to a different beat."

Vicky jerks her head from side to side, cracking her neck, then pins me with her gaze. "It's just the warm-up song."

Melanie says, "Please, Ms. B!" in support of her BFF and then more voices join in. Ms. Bobrov throws up her hands. "Oh, very well. After zis, then we need something more zippy."

Vicky switches on the music again and the class starts following her lame moves. Kali follows, too, but at half her usual speed. I'm close enough to see that she's shaking.

The singer belts the chorus:

> *Just because we both wear heels, don't mean our love's not real.*
> *One day, the world will see, there's a place for you and me.*

Kali throws me a dark look then picks her way toward the exit, leaving a queasy trail of frogbit in her wake. She says something to

130

Ms. Bobrov, who nods curtly, then disappears out the door.

As Vicky executes the lamest jumping jack in the history of jack jumping, I'm resolved. I can't stand by while Vicky ruins Kali's life, one cruel prank at a time. Operation Fix Vicky officially begins.

On the way to algebra, I stop by the brick planters, though this time I'm not looking for aloe. Instead, I reach for a plant with straw-like flowers, otherwise known as sneezeweed, which likes to grow wherever it can find a layer of dirt to stand in. Nasal secretions can substitute for saliva in a pinch.

I pull off my beret and begin crumbling the flowers into my hair. Unlike the rest of the population, I'm immune to sneezeweed allergies.

Vicky is discussing the hotness of the pop star Tyson Badland with Melanie when I enter the classroom with my beret at a jaunty angle. Her gaze stretches toward an exposed pipe in the ceiling as if looking at that surely beats noticing what's coming through the door. Mr. Frederics is writing an equation in his neat block letters. He pauses midequation, stares up at the clock, and smiles. What's he thinking about? Or, more important, who?

I shake myself out of my thoughts and focus on the task at hand. Drew's doodling in his notebook again, this time with a calligraphy pen. He wrote, "'What doesn't kill you makes you stronger.'—Nietzsche."

He notices my interest.

"Nice calligraphy," I say, slipping into my chair. "Carolingian, right?"

His smile pulls his chin into a point. "Yeah, Carolingian. I'm branching out from Gothic. You know calligraphy?"

"Yes. You ever try parchment? It'll give you cleaner lines."

His head bobs up and down, and his red-rimmed glasses slip down his nose. "Cool."

I turn back around, and guilt nags me. Drew's a good egg. Would I be ruining his life forever by doing this?

No. He likes Vicky. This would be a dream come true for him. This would send his popularity soaring.

But what if he doesn't want that?

Before I change my mind, I pull off my beret, and shake out my hair. I count two seconds before Drew sneezes right into the back of my dress.

"Sorry," he mumbles.

"It's okay. It's allergy season."

After algebra, I use my hand clippers to snip a piece of contaminated fabric off my dress. I tuck the piece into one of the many canvas sacks I brought for the trip to Meyer. Next, I file an excuse with the school secretary. Upperclassmen don't need notes to come and go for appointments and the like. If I hurry, I can make the 12:20 train. As I push through the heavy door of the office, I pick up a scent that makes my heart jump.

Court is perched against a cement planter surrounding a

loquat tree, a few paces away. I consider retreating into the office, but Court already sees me.

He hurries toward me, backpack slung over one shoulder. "Saw you go in. I've been looking for you all morning." He squints and blinks, like his contacts bother him, and there are circles under his eyes. "Mom didn't play her uke in B minor last night. She played a happy song, 'Zip-a-Dee-Doo-Dah.'" He pushes the sleeve of his gray cashmere pullover up to his elbow, showing his golden arms. There's a pen stain on his finger. There's also a tear in the knee of his jeans that looks earned, not like the preripped jeans that cost a fortune.

I hug my bag to me. "She's in love."

He cusses and sweeps aside a fallen loquat with his foot. "Melanie's freaking out."

"Does she know?" I try not to panic.

"I had to tell her, or she'd call Mom's shrink."

Wonderful. Another leak in the boat.

"She thinks you did it on purpose, setting up Mom with a"—he frowns and looks away—"a teacher. Anyway, sometimes Mel doesn't know what she's saying."

From across the courtyard, Coach Juarez calls out, "Hey, Sawyer! Extra practice at four. Don't be late."

Court acknowledges his coach by holding up his thumbs.

"Will she tell your mom?"

"We decided not to. Mom's been through enough."

"What about Melanie's friends?" Like Vicky.

He shakes his head. "Don't worry, Mel won't talk. You said Mom would forget about her feelings for Mr. Frederics after you—" He makes loops with his finger, trying to conjure the right word.

"PUF her, yes."

"So it erases memories?"

"No. She'll remember what happened, but she won't have any romantic feelings attached to those memories. I have to go, but thanks for the update." I start toward the bike racks with a renewed sense of urgency. Despite his reassurance, I can't help worrying that Melanie will tell Vicky, who will then use the information to blackmail something out of *me*, and, by association, Mother.

He walks alongside me. "That's crazy. I mean, this whole thing is"—he rubs his chin—"unreal." He looks at me out of the corner of his eye. "I called my aunt. She's flying in for a visit. She'll take Mom out, which should give us some time."

I choke back my surprise. "Us?"

"I don't want to see my mom hurt again." He frowns.

I dump my stuff in my bike basket. "Thank you. I really appreciate it." It'll give me a needed safety cushion of time in case I don't find all the plants at Meyer today. Every bit helps.

Students drift in and out of the library, some of them staring at us. Court doesn't seem to notice. Through the library windows, I make out the time on the library clock: 12:07. If I don't leave, I'll never make my train.

I take up the handlebars. "Um, thanks again."

"You going somewhere?"

"Meyer."

"Right now?"

"Yes."

"You're *biking*?"

"Just to the train station. I'm not crazy."

He pushes up his other sleeve so now both sides are even. "I'll take you."

"That's okay. It's just a ten-minute ride."

"I meant, I'll drive you to Meyer."

"You'll have to miss practice—"

"It's my mom." He works an arm into his backpack strap, glancing across the courtyard where his coach was standing. The man has disappeared. "I'll need to sign out first and do a few things. Do you know which car is mine?"

"Yes." The word tumbles out too quickly as I remember the black Jeep with the surfboard sticking out the back. At least I could've pretended to think about it.

He fishes his keys from his pocket and hands them to me. They're still warm with his body heat. "I'll meet you there in ten."

He doesn't wait for answer, but strides back to the office. I'm so stunned, my nose stops working for a split second, and all I can think about is that the sun feels unbearably hot on my neck, even though it's a foggy day.

* * *

Court parks his Jeep in the row farthest from the school, where the alpha males park.

Females flock to this area of the parking lot to peruse the selection of mostly red, black or silver cars, some lowered, some raised, some with vestigial thingamabobs protruding off the sides with no real purpose, the way some cactus have leaves.

A waist-high brick wall separates the concrete path on which I'm walking from the lek, i.e., mating ground. I cautiously approach the area, head down, arms crossed tightly across my chest. Hopefully no one will notice me. I should have told Court I'd meet him outside the school. Someone's bound to see me get into his car. Tongues will wag and Vicky will hear of it. She might even publish Kali's journal to spite me.

Two teens with lettermen jackets challenge each other to a pushup contest on the other side of the wall. Court parked his Jeep in the opposite row.

I stop in my tracks when I pick up Vicky's scent somewhere nearby, celery and black elder. She's leaning her miniskirted bottom against the back of a Mustang just two cars down from Court's. A half dozen of her admirers, both female and male, vie for her attention.

If I keep walking, Vicky will see me for sure. Time to backtrack. I'll find Court—

Something bounces hard off my shoulder. "Oof!"

The object that hit me, a soccer ball, rebounds off the half wall, then rolls around by my feet. I pick it up.

"Hola," Vicky calls.

Everyone's looking at me. Instead of following my instincts to flee, I stand my ground, returning her saccharine grin with one of my own. Heart pounding, I square my shoulders and pass through the closest break in the wall, still clutching the ball. No one reaches for it.

Vicky's gravel-colored eyes glitter as we give each other the once-over. Her eyes fall to a stain on my dress I thought no one would notice. If she likes that, she'll love the hole I just cut in the back. I stick out like a hobo at a wine tasting.

"What are you doing here, Mimosa?" The way she says my name with the fake Spanish accent grates my nerves.

I shrug. "Just taking a walk." This is a mistake, but my other option, pretending I've lost my hearing, isn't much better. The strap of my messenger bag pulls my sundress in an indecent direction, and I shift and twist to get it back in alignment.

Vicky clicks her nails together. "Why would you be taking a walk in the smelly old parking lot? There aren't any flowers here." She doesn't lose her smile, and neither do I. Maybe we can smile each other to death. She puts her finger on her chin. "Are you meeting someone?"

I squeeze the ball so hard it nearly pops.

"Wh-who would I be meeting?" I lift my nose and try to act superior.

"I don't know. A boy?"

"I don't have a boyfriend."

"Of course you don't. Love witches can't *have* boyfriends. It wouldn't exactly be fair, would it? I mean, you could use your potions. No one's boyfriend would be safe."

The girl with the purple-highlighted black hair from Whit's table yesterday leans into the safety of her boyfriend's shoulder and gives me the stink eye. Those candy grams. Even if I could fumigate the whole world, Vicky could still run me out of town with a single rumor.

Vicky tilts her blunt chin. "Or girlfriend."

If I had any reservation over fixing Vicky with Drew's elixir, it disappears like a snowflake on a radiator. I smile thinly. "Believe me, if I could use potions like that, I would get Tyson Badland to take me to the homecoming dance."

A few people chuckle and Vicky's smirk weakens. Her knees lock, and she twists a gold cuff around her wrist. She's so focused on her prey, me, she doesn't notice when Court and his best buddy, Whit Wu, appear from behind her. Whit grins when he sees me with the ball.

"So how can you be a love witch if you've never experienced *el amor?*" She purrs out the Spanish word so that it sounds dirty.

Everyone watches me squirm. The bummer about blackmail is that it always gets worse. The blackmailer keeps testing limits, never stopping until the thing valued no longer seems worth it. But she hasn't cornered me yet.

Court and Whit close the distance, and Vicky's spidery lashes flick toward them. Whit holds his hands up for the ball, but I don't throw it to him.

Court frowns. "Vick, stop—"

I toss back my head, thankful my beret doesn't go flying off. "The same way I don't have to be a sanitation engineer to recognize garbage." This time, a few people laugh. Time to go. I hurry by Vicky and deposit the ball into Court's hands, at the same time slipping him his keys. "The sun did not shine, it was too wet to play," I murmur.

He lowers his eyelids and cocks an ear toward me. But that's the only line from *The Cat in the Hat* that I remember, and I hope it's enough to lead him to Dr. Seuss's hat, the windsock on the other side of the building. I beat a hasty retreat back toward the school. The scent of Vicky's anger stays in my nose long after I've left the parking lot, foul as burning rubber.

THIRTEEN

"WE ARE EACH A RAINBOW. EVERY RANK ONE OF US."
—*Gladys, Aromateur, 1855*

ON THE FAR side of the stadium field, a break in the shrubs leads to the main street. The red-and-white windsock fronting the school points east. It's been there so long, no one notices it anymore, much less uses it, even though the wind can tell a lot about the weather. It strikes me that windsocks are like most people's noses, outdated sources of information, more seen than used.

Near the windsock, Court waits in his Jeep. I slide into the leather seat. There's a sports magazine on the floor along with a box of number-two pencils. A soccer ball medallion swings from the mirror. How many girls would pay to be in my shoes? How many girls *have* been in my shoes?

I sniff. The synthetic scents almost always overpower the natural ones and can stick around for months. I count seven different perfumes billowing around me, trapped and ripened in the closed car. One of them is Vicky's Poison Apple. Though the scent's months old, my stomach tightens. I also detect potato chips, a whiff of marijuana, and sand mingling with Court's own scent.

We swing onto northbound 101. Court merges, waving in his mirror to the guy who let us in.

The tan leather of the backseat has been worn shiny. I sniff out of habit, and the human smells from that part of the car bring a blush to my cheeks. I have to stop snooping with my nose. Just because it's second nature doesn't mean it's right, like unlocking every door you encounter just because you own a skeleton key.

Court glances at me sitting stiffly in my seat, my cheeks baking. "Is everything okay?"

"Sure."

"I'm sorry about that back there." His face is somber, and so is his smell—yarrow with undertones of barn dust, like opening an old photo album.

"You don't need to apologize for Vicky." I weigh whether to tell him of the blackmail. No. He would confront her, and she'd know we ratted on her.

I could swear him to secrecy before I told him, but if he thought I was keeping things from him, the fragile threads of our temporary alliance could break. Besides, secrets have a way of untying on their own, though I cringe to think of my own secrets.

Court presses his fingers into the bones at the base of his

neck, glancing at me uncertainly. "I'm also sorry about yesterday. I was kind of a jerk."

"That's okay. I would be angry, too."

"Well, I'm not mad anymore. I'm more—I don't know how I feel."

I sniff, though his mood scents are as loud to my nose as the trio of Harley-Davidson motorcycles rumbling by. "You smell sad—"

He blinks, but when he notices me watching him, he shrugs. "Go on."

Awkwardly, I nose on. "I also smell guilt, which smells like cough syrup, mixed with loneliness—baby's tears."

"Baby's tears?"

"It's a kind of moss. There's also rabbit litter. Er, that means insecurity."

"I smell like rabbit litter." His face has acquired a pinched look. Clearly I've gone too far. He glances at me biting my lip. "Please continue. I'm enjoying this."

I clear my throat. "On the bright side, there's a healthy dose of excitement"—I falter, hoping that didn't come out wrong—"which smells like the strawberry tree, and, well—nervousness."

He swallows, then produces a queasy grin. "And what does that smell like?"

"Soap bubbles."

"Ah. You'd be a hard person to hide from."

"Yes—" I cough to prevent more words from slipping out.

An awkward silence follows. The accelerator nudges to seventy-five miles per hour, but then noticing it, Court eases up on the gas. I study the toe prints on the window in front of me. I could've admitted that I also smell like soap bubbles.

Or I could just change the subject. "Was your coach okay with you missing practice?"

He seems happy for the switch, and one hand releases the steering wheel. "I promised him a Kill Drill tomorrow at lunch."

"Kill Drill?"

"We scrimmage for forty-five minutes, no breaks."

"Oh, I'm sorry."

"We could use the practice." He flashes me a smile. "So the plants you need, will they just let you take them?"

"Ordinarily. The master gardener lets us clip what we want in exchange for cuttings from our garden. But I didn't arrange a visit because I don't want Mother to find out."

"How will we do it?"

I pull out my garden pruners, freshly oiled and sharpened. "Garden variety theft."

He whistles.

"You have any better ideas?"

"Would they sell them to us? I went to the ATM this morning."

"The common ones, maybe. But definitely not the rares. And we need several of those."

"Bribery?"

Is he serious? He's not smiling. Bribery would never have occurred to me, mostly because it's never been an option. But I'd feel weird using his money, even though it is for his mother. Plus, if the bribery didn't work, they'd toss us out for sure, maybe even call the cops. "Thanks, but no. My way is less risky. The squirrels do it all the time."

Conversation stalls the rest of the way to the garden, and it's hard to know exactly what he's thinking. Thoughts, unlike feelings, cannot be smelled. On the other hand, the soap bubble notes don't dissipate as Court concentrates on the driving and I concentrate on what's going on outside the car, instead of who's in it. I don't do a very good job.

FOURTEEN

"Every smell is a key, unlocking memories hidden in
the chambers of the soul."
—*Irisa, Aromateur, 1801*

RUTH MEYER WAS the only daughter of a toothpick manu-
facturer, who believed that the souls of all the trees her father
felled were conspiring to kill her. As penance, she built the larg-
est botanical garden this side of the Mississippi. At the time of
her death, she owned a hundred acres of prime real estate in the
heart of San Francisco, not to mention the cleanest gums in the
state.

As the town oddball with the big garden, sometimes I worry
that I'm destined for a lonely existence similar to Ruth's. She
probably talked to her plants, too.

We park, and I empty out my messenger bag so I have room
for the contraband. Then we make our way to the stone entrance
of the Meyer Botanical Garden, past yellow school buses parked
side by side like bakery loaves.

I notice a thin black case clipped onto Court's belt. Must be his EpiPen. "I guess gardens aren't your thing. You don't have to come in. I do tend to attract bees."

"As long as you don't mind sticking me, I don't mind being stuck by them," he jokes.

We pass the ticket office and go right to the gated entrance where I show my lifetime pass, which allows entry for me and a guest. The man studies it long enough to make me worry that he senses my evil designs. I sniff, but the winds are blowing his scents into the garden.

Finally, he hands back my pass. "You should get a new picture."

I laugh nervously. "Right, I'll do that." The picture on the pass was taken when I was eleven. "Have a nice day."

Once inside, I take in the millions of scents around me. I filter out all the animal odors and focus on the plants, which resonate at higher frequencies in my nose.

Court opens a brochure with a garden map, spreading it out before him like a tourist. The garden is divided into seven pie-shaped sections, one for each continent, with specialty gardens sprinkled throughout. The Children's Garden sits in the middle of the pizza, boasting a grassy field for running around, trees for climbing, and edible plants. I point at a small patch at the top of the Children's Garden labeled Ancient Plants. "This one. Follow me."

We travel down a gravelly path shaded by flowering dogwood that has a powdery fragrance, like a baby's nursery. Court, still looking at the brochure, whistles. "Mesozoic epoch? So my mom smells like dinosaurs?"

I chuckle. "Not quite. The plants here are like living fossils. They're resilient to pollutants, meaning they contain the truest core of scent. We all have a touch of the ancients in us."

I don't tell him that much of what we know about plants, especially the Ancients, is due to the effort of aromateurs, who believed that plants should be studied for themselves, not just for medicinal uses. It would sound like bragging. The textbooks say that Theophrastus, a student of Aristotle, founded what we call botany, but aromateurs had been categorizing plants for thousands of years before he was even born.

The amused animal cracker smell drifts from Court. "I had no idea plants could be so . . . cool."

A zing of nervous energy travels through me at the possibility that he could be talking about me, and not the plants. I laugh nervously and walk faster. The banksia gives way to bitter cherry trees. The leaves could substitute for two of Alice's notes. I stare up at the branches. Just out of arm's reach.

Court glances back at me. He stretches up for a branch. I jerk my thumb up. Higher. He lifts his heels and touches a slim branch, heavy with dark leaves. I nod.

He checks that nobody's watching then plucks off a handful. I stuff them into my bag.

"Why do I feel guilty about that?" he whispers.

"I heard it gets easier."

As we travel farther into the garden, we see more people, mostly senior citizens and kids on field trips. I let my nose guide us to Australia where I harvest kangaroo paw.

We cross a bridge lined on either side with planters of purple coneflowers. I stick my nose in the planters then quickly jerk away from its cloying grape scent.

Court notices my reaction, and carefully sniffs at the coneflowers. "Something wrong with them?"

"No, they just remind me of this time when I was five and ate through a whole quart of Mother's preserves. She was so mad, she cracked a spoon on the counter."

Emotional memories love to piggyback onto smells. Aromateurs have a saying, "Do not linger in the garden of memories, for there are many traps."

"I did that with my mom's lemon bars once. But that was only a month ago." He flashes me a grin, rousing one out of me. Then, with a mischievous quirk of his eyebrow, he tucks the flower behind his ear. "If I wear this all day, maybe you won't feel so bad next time you smell it."

His goofy gesture melts me like cocoa butter in the sun. Even my bones feel gooey and I pour myself, rather than walk, down the grassy pathway.

The sound of children laughing and yelling intensifies as we draw closer to the Ancients. A Frisbee whizzes one way, while a soccer ball flies in another direction. There must be at least fifty kids in the Children's Garden today, smelling like grubby hands and sock lint. Many of them are wandering from the grassy field into the Ancients. I pause by a statue of a half-naked woman and survey the under-five-foot crowd. Court shoots me a quizzical glance.

"Maybe they'll leave soon," I say, scratching my elbows.

He bends close to my ear. "How many more plants do you need?"

"Twenty-five."

"Are they all in the Ancients?"

"I hope so."

Below an engraved wooden sign that reads, "Ancient Plant Garden, Welcome to the Past," a group of eight- or nine-year-old boys cluster around a rare hellebore shrub, watching a kid in a Camp Snoopy T-shirt pluck off the delicate pink sepals. Children are often attracted to hellebores because of their primitive glands containing sugar that give off a taffy-like note.

I drift closer and sniff. "That one's a match for one of your mom's heart notes," I tell Court.

Out of nowhere, a soccer ball careens toward us like a meteorite. I gasp as something gray streaks past me.

Court traps the ball with his chest, letting it thump down against his thigh, then roll to his foot. Behind him, the hellebores remain unscathed, save for a few missing petals.

The kids who kicked the ball come running in from the grassy field, screaming with delight.

Court looks at me for a moment, the coneflower still

impossibly hanging on behind his ear. I freeze the image in my mind so I can remember it forever. Then he snaps his fingers toward the kids in the Ancients. "Hey, you guys want to play some ball?"

The kids bounce. A smile flickers over Court's lips as he takes a last look at me. "Girls against boys. Let's go!" He lets the ball drop, then kicks it long.

All the kids run after it, screaming loud enough to reach the soil engineers. Genius. With grim determination, I venture deeper into the now empty Ancient Garden. Most plants known from the fossil record—older than ten thousand years— are extinct, but the ones that survived evolved to form new species and adaptations. The scents envelope me with their low-frequency vibrations, which resonate in the nose far longer than other scents. They're like Gregorian chants to the ear; the older the species, the more complex their scents. It's the same way with people.

My heart still pounds, and my mind is a nest of randomly firing neurons. I hate working under pressure, but I have to get this done.

I run my nose through purple horsetail and ferns as ticklish as peacock feathers, hearing Mother's voice in my head. *Always inhale deeply in the presence of an Ancient; they've been around the longest and have many secrets to reveal.*

Using my hand spade and clippers, I quickly harvest what I need, being careful not to bruise anything or snip more than

I absolutely need. Sometimes I have to take parts of the roots, which pains me because a root is harder for the plant to regenerate than a leaf or a flower. As I tug at the base of an exotic fern, I swear to sign up for the volunteer program to make amends.

There. Only one left from this place, Alice's miso heart note, the problem one. I picked through every one of the Ancients and it's not here. Still crouching, I swab my forehead with the grass-stained hem of my dress.

"I saw you!" cries a kid. I nearly fall over, too deep in my own thoughts to smell him coming. The kid with the Camp Snoopy T-shirt, sweaty brown hair matted to his head, points a finger at me. "Touch with your eyes, not with your hands."

Well, isn't that the corpse flower telling the skunk cabbage it stinks?

I put my fingers over my lips and try to shush him but he's already sounding the alarm. "Ms. Jackson! There's a girl cutting plants!"

In a mild panic now, I consider standing my ground. If only I weren't clutching this heavy bag of damning evidence. With a groan, I step off the horseshoe path and let the ferns close up behind me. A branch knocks my beret off my head as I rush toward a wooded area, and I waste precious seconds stopping to snatch it back up.

"She went that way!" cries Camp Snoopy, his voice faint. Feeling ridiculous, I pick my way through the spiky ferns until I reach the edge of the forest, then sprint down a pathway lined with bark shavings. I could hide inside one of the redwoods with a rotted-out trunk, but I have a better idea. One less obvious.

I sniff around for the eastern red cedar with the hollow spot just large enough for a person to squeeze through, where Mother and I once found a Cinderella's slipper orchid growing on a high branch. The Cinderella traps bees into its "shoe," where they get dusted with pollen until they manage to escape.

The dense needles scratch at my arms but I manage to duck inside just before the kids rush by like a pack of bloodhounds.

A chaperone hurries after them, blowing her whistle. "Hey, kids, come back here!"

Not long after the chaperone passes my tree, I smell Court.

"Court!" I hiss.

He puts on the brakes, and quickly finds the entrance. The tree shudders as it swallows him up.

He's tied his sweater around his waist and the front of his polo shirt is soaked down the middle. Sweating magnifies a person's scent by tenfold. His scent, a heady blend of evergreens and roasting hickory nuts, is so strong I can almost wind my fingers through it. It muscles out the Cinderella still flourishing inside the tree, and makes my insides flutter. I lose mass with every *bump-bump* of my heart, and I'm thankful for the weight of my boots, anchoring me to the ground.

The kids' voices grow louder again, and I go still as a pine-cone. Our space is barely big enough to fit both of us, but we still manage not to touch. Court looks down at me, cheeks flushed from his game. A blanket of heat knits between us.

"Lost my flower," he whispers.

"We can find you a new one."

"I liked the old one."

I take a deep breath to beat back the giddy feeling in my stomach. That's when I catch it. Miso soup. I smell it. Alice's missing note. It's part of Court's scentprint, though a thousand times less intense. Heart notes run in families.

My startled eyes take in his, brown, flecked with striations of gold and even green. A tiny mole dots his jaw, just like his mother's. He's my answer, right in front of me.

What did Mother say? *Immerse yourself. Meditate on the scent. It will tell you where to go.*

The kids run back past us to their teacher, brushing so close, our cedar sways. Court's eyes, gazing at me, widen a fraction as our bristly capsule shakes. I grab onto a branch so I don't accidentally fall into him.

I'm vaguely aware of an adult on a megaphone calling the children back to the buses. But like those bees that are seduced into Cinderella's slippers, I am trapped, held captive while Court's pollen flies around me. Only unlike those bees, I don't want to escape.

The sound of children laughing diminishes completely.

Court peeks through the branches. "I think it's safe."

My palms begin to sweat. "I need to focus on something. Will you promise not t-to," I stammer, "not to move?"

"Okay. What are you going to do?"

"Smell you."

FIFTEEN

"Do they look like they're about to vomit?
They're in love."
—*Reseda, Aromateur, 1724*

"AREN'T YOU ALREADY smelling me?" Court asks around a smile. "I just played an hour of soccer with twenty-five third graders." He leans in as if telling me a secret, and my pulse spikes at the warmth of his breath caressing my forehead. "Girls won. And anyway, I thought you already knew how I smelled."

His throaty purr nearly liquefies me. Just like someone fixed by an elixir, my feelings for Court multiply like bacteria with each succeeding exposure to him.

I affect a business tone. "You have a bunch of smaller notes that aren't obvious. One of those you share with your mom. I haven't sourced it yet, but if I could get a better smell of it, I might be able to."

"Okay. Smell away." He spreads his arms, and if I were any other teenage girl, I would jump right into them.

I wrestle down my nervousness over what I'm about to do.

Analyze the scents, comes Mother's voice in my head, *don't give them the upper hand.* I am a professional. A love professional. "I have to warn you not to touch me."

His eyebrows lift in a question.

"I don't want to infect you." I already sprayed him once, after the bee sting, which should have been enough to last a lifetime. But why take chances? Especially when I've never hugged a boy before.

"Are you sick?"

"Not exactly." I lick my lips. "But you could get, er, sick if you touch me."

"What do you mean, sick?"

Wonderful. Now he's going to think I have some transmittable disease, which isn't far from the truth. "Lovesick."

The corners of his mouth tuck back even more in amusement. "Lovesick?" he asks.

"Yeah, crazy, I know." I try to keep a casual tone but I feel the flush.

My skin has gone clammy. What's wrong with me? I've never felt so nervous in my life. He's just a boy, human being like me, Homo sapiens. I lean in so that my nose is only an inch away from him and sniff.

Unlayering the mood notes, I find his scentprint. The nutmeg and cinnamon are especially strong and enticing.

I sniff again, and though his scentprint plays like a chord to my nose, I can still barely make out the miso.

I laugh nervously. "Don't mind me."

Hesitantly, I slip my arms around his slim waist and press my cheek against his chest. He takes in a short gasp of air and his chest clutches. The perfume of honeysuckle, heady and narcoleptic, escapes from him, the note of desire. Then again, we're so close, it could be coming from me. Court doesn't shrink away, but I feel him fidget as I hold him. His fists clench at his sides and his face is a tight mask. The two-step of his heartbeat chases after mine. I close my mind to the confusingly hard yet comfortable pillow under my cheek, and hone in on the miso note.

The scents are there, playing for you. Listen to them.

The miso note creeps, rather than sails into my nose, and I open my mind to its character, its essence. The saltiness doesn't have a lick of bitter, unlike table salt, and reminds me of seashells. It has to be a marine plant or a plant found near the ocean. I shut down thoughts of Court, shirtless and surfing, almost as soon as they crop up, and refocus. There's a buttery roundness to the scent, like it's used to sunshine. I inhale one more time.

Five years old, the beach. The fog sits on the ocean thick as cotton batting. Mother is wearing a floppy hat and sorting through a shiny black plant with floats that resemble lightbulbs. I close my fist around the clam and trudge over to a little girl about my age with daisies on her bathing suit.

I hold my clam out to the girl. "It smells like sea grass."

She scrunches her nose. "No, it smells like clams."

"Old oranges, too, and sunshine, and the lint trap. See?" I push the

clam farther toward her nose. She backs away, her face crumpling. "Stop it! You're gross!"

I sway as all the ugly scents swoop in through my nose and pour down my cheeks like hot fire.

That was the day Mother explained to me how our noses differed from everyone else's. The day she began to train me to objectify those emotions into scents, to protect myself the way a scientist can study diseases without getting infected. The day I began to wall myself into the brambles.

Tears prick my eyes, and as I look up into Court's confused gaze, his face softens.

I inhale his scent for the third time, and this time I don't let myself linger. My mind's eye zooms out from the beach to the cliff overlooking the beach. The water was peacock blue, frothing into a crescent of sand. Marine scents hung in the ocean's misty breath, which swirled all around me.

I remember where I was. "Playa del Rey." I slowly release Court. "I need to go there."

"Playa del Rey? In Las Ballenas?" He sounds short of breath, and his eyes look pinched, like he's in pain. I think I catch the fleeting note of wisteria, but wistful notes have always been quick to hide.

"Yes. That's where I'll find the missing plant."

"The missing plant. Right." He sags against a tangle of branches. "That's an hour from Santa Guadalupe in the other direction. Can you find it in the dark?"

It's already late afternoon. "Yes, but"—I chew on my lip—"Mother's supposed to call this evening. If she doesn't reach me, she might worry." She might even call the police. Plus, I need to get my plants home and properly stashed. "We can't go until tomorrow. Is that okay?"

"Yeah," he murmurs. I'm distracted by his chin, rounded like a guitar pick. I distract myself by focusing on a cluster of dark berries above his head.

His mouth opens, soft as the petals of a sweet pea. I can't stop staring, wondering how it would feel to kiss him. And the more I think about kissing him, the closer he comes to me. Or maybe I'm falling into him.

His physical proximity is screwing up my emotions, the way the Bermuda Triangle can make compasses malfunction. But I can't add kissing to my rap sheet. *Remember Aunt Bryony.* No falling in love.

His face hovers just inches from mine, drawing me in like a bee to a patch of sweet Williams. I try to fight it, distract myself with the berries, but now it strikes me that the sprigs look rather like mistletoe.

I tear my eyes away from his mouth just as he catches my wrist.

I gasp. No one besides Mother and Kali ever touches me. It's a strange sensation, the warmth of his hand on my skin. His fingertips slide to my grubby palm, then stop. Oh, sweet marjoram, I may never leave this tree again. As he holds my hand, we gaze at each other, so close now that I feel his breath graze my forehead and the happiness scent of sugar maple tickles my nose.

I break into a sweat as a chilling realization settles on me. I'm already in love. I don't know when it happened, but it happened. Invisible threads of attraction sewed him to me when I wasn't watching, trapping me tight. *That's* why I feel so sick every time he's near. I tug my hand away, and it's as painful as ripping out my own heart.

The future of love depends on me remaining true to our purpose. If not me, then who else? Mother and I are the world's last aromateurs.

My shoulders sag under the weight of my lineage. Perhaps this is why Mother let me go to school—because in the end, she knew I had no real choice. Like Ruth Meyer, the plants will haunt me if I leave them, and so in the garden I must stay.

I fumble around my bag for the BBG, nearly dropping the bottle in my agitation. I never had to respray before, but apparently, I didn't do it right the first time.

"Mim?" Court whispers almost shyly.

"We should go now." This is a business relationship, nothing more.

He winces, and the blue hydrangea of his disappointment is so strong, it almost makes me weep. I peer out at the now-empty garden, hoping he follows my gaze.

He does. I'm about to depress the pump of my bottle when

his eyes snap back to me. I snatch my hand behind my back. Real smooth.

"What . . . ?" One eyebrow quirks. "Was that a perfume bottle?"

Guiltily, I open my hand. "Oh, this?"

"Yeah, that." The gluey notes of confusion dribble out. "Did you spray something?"

I deflate. It's not a secret. We just spray in secret to avoid awkward explanations. "It's a special type of elixir." I gesture with my free hand. "You touched me, so I have to disinfect you."

"Or I'll get lovesick?" A grin tugs at his mouth, but when I don't change my expression, his own becomes serious. "Wait. You used it after the bee stung me. I remember now." He rubs a hand over his mouth and chin. "How long does it take for that thing to work?"

"It's almost always immediate."

"Well then, I guess I'm still waiting."

His words send a trill of happiness through me. For a nano-second, a vision of us strolling hand in hand through a golden meadow teases me. But then a thick and thorny vine entangles us, and all the flowers of ancestors past like the ones on Aunt Bryony's quilt look on, quietly censuring me with their gaze.

A branch pokes me in the thigh, jarring me back to the present. It's possible the BBG hasn't taken effect yet. Or a breeze might have blown it away, though that's never happened before.

"I definitely should remist you."

"What if the guy doesn't want those feelings taken away? Doesn't he get a say?"

My tongue stalls. This is where it gets messy. Mother warned me that men are just as emotional as women when they feel rejected.

"Yes, you get a say. But, love witches can't like people *that* way." The trouty odor of my doubt makes me wince. "So it's in your best interest for you to, er, not be interested." That is probably the oddest thing anyone has ever said to him. Seeing the good-natured face he puts on drives a cactus spine into my tender spots. I focus on a smudge of dirt on his cheek as my train of thought veers offtrack.

"So you're saying I can never take you out to smell dinner."

I sink my heels deeper into the bark-covered ground, wishing it would compost me. If you only knew I would trade an arm for a date with you.

But not my nose.

"I'm sorry." His eyes, probing mine, flicker, but don't lose their intensity. My knees begin to buckle, though I don't know if it's from standing so long inside these tree branches or standing so long next to Court.

His chest deflates and he gives the tiniest shrug. "Well then. Spray away."

Before he changes his mind, before I change *mine*, I spritz near his breathing space. I try to pump twice, just to be extra sure, but the lever catches at the end, meaning now I'm all out.

Mist shimmers between us like a rainbow veil. "Breathe in, please." I can't even meet his eyes. "Just to be sure."

He lets out a cough of tart disbelief. But after a last look at me, he closes his eyes and deeply inhales, a simple reflex that somehow devastates me.

His eyes flutter open, and an unseen ocean of blue notes fill the space between us. The bump on his throat hitches as he swallows. "Let's get out of here."

As we leave the garden, Court stuffs two crisp Benjamins into the donation box. "Hope that covers it."

SIXTEEN

"IF WE ARE THE MAGICIANS, LOVE IS THE MAGIC,
WITHOUT WHICH WE COULD PULL NO RABBITS,
WE COULD CONJURE NO COIN."
—*Poppy, Aromateur, 1819*

ON THE RIDE home, we stick to neutral subjects like math and soccer.

Court fiddles with the radio. "Whit's a better player than me. He should've been the one on Sports Illustrated cover. Cassandra says they chose me because I look more all-American."

Cassandra, the school songstress with the corkscrew hair. My toes clench.

"She told me not to get any tattoos or it'd ruin my image."

"Is she your"—I stop myself in time—"publicist?" It's none of my business if Cassandra is his girlfriend.

He chuckles. "She thinks she is. She set up a website for me, too." With his gaze still fixed on the UPS truck ahead of us, he adds, "Cass is just a friend, you know. I mean"—he releases the steering wheel with one hand and gestures with it—"obviously."

What's obvious? I don't ask in case it leads to tricky topics, like feelings. I have to keep things professional for his benefit and mine. Or at least neutral. "I like this music."

"Los Solitarios." He turns up the radio. The rich, rhythmic sounds of the Spanish guitar fill the void between us.

Before we drive back to Parrot Hill, we fetch my bike from school. The parking lot is mostly vacant. Court wedges my rusty steed into the back of his Jeep next to a pile of surfing gear.

Once we get home, he sets my bike down on the driveway. The familiar scents of our plants rush at me like children, wanting my attention. Not today, kids. I have an elixir to make, the most important elixir of my career so far.

"You *live* here? It's like something out of Disneyland." Court's gaze wanders up the stone blocks, skips around the hand-blown windows and stops at the corner turret with the pointed top.

"Is it? I've never been there."

"You've never went to Disneyland?"

"We don't do vacations." A chicken squawks. I slap my forehead. "I forgot to feed the chickens. They'll revolt soon. I should—"

Lingering thyme, the note of reluctance, tickles my nose. Saying good-bye has never been more complicated. I sigh. "Be right back."

I hurry down the path to our solid wooden gate and stand on my toes to unlatch it from the inside. The chickens peck the ground near our wishing well. "Sorry, guys."

I retrieve Mother's nut-and-seed mix from the kitchen.

When I return, Court is towing my bike into our courtyard.

"Um, thanks. Set it anywhere." I sprinkle the mix on the ground. The chickens dive for the goodies. "They get cranky when they don't get their treats."

Court lifts his eyes from the chickens to the bright clumps of rhododendron that spread across the ground like melting scoops of ice cream. Our plot of land could be the centerfold of *Extreme Home and Garden*, not that Mother would ever allow photographers in. "It's"—he searches for the word, and the awed scent of glory-of-the-snow, a plant that bursts with plum-scented flowers even in the highest alpines, thrums all around him—"unreal."

He walks to the first stone of our path and stares out at the grand procession of ancient oaks, crepe myrtles, and ash trees that lead to our workshop. Papery white poppies with yellow centers bloom along the path, nature's egg served sunny-side up. I consider giving him a tour, but I'm afraid of where that will lead. Our garden of aphrodisiacs could be a blooming love trap, especially if he's resistant to BBG.

Then again, I sprayed him good and through, twice. There's no real danger, despite the fact that he's lingering.

Court shakes himself out of his daze and walks back to where I'm leaning on the edge of the well. "A wishing well," he says in awe. "It looks old."

"Yes. People used to come here to draw their water in the nineteenth century."

He takes in the pile of rubble under the broken lip. "You

should repair that before it leaks."

"Haven't found the right contractor." An affordable one, that is. For him, the repair would simply mean a trip to the ATM. For us, well maintenance doesn't qualify for the Aromateur Trust Fund withdrawal since it's not a business necessity. During the medieval age when the trust was started, aromateurs were highly revered as healers, and society provided for their living much like they did for the clergy. Nowadays, any well repair money would have to come from our meager living allowance.

Court leans beside me on the well's outcropping and studies the wisteria dripping like bunches of grapes from the overhead trellis. An expression of wonder causes his dimples to flatten out. I bask in all the campfire smells of his scentprint, floating around relaxed and unguarded. When I realize I'm staring at him, I drop my gaze to his shirt. Even his alligator logo has perfect teeth.

I really should tell him to go, but my mouth won't form the words. Our rooster struts by, bobbing its head at Court. It decides Court's no match for it, and starts pecking at the ground.

"So where's your mom?" he asks.

"Oman."

"That's not an easy place to get to. We had a goodwill meet in Israel, once."

"It is when you have a private Cloud Air jet." I'm not supposed to tell people this, but surely there's an exception for when you're sitting next to the richest kid you know, and your dress has a stain and a hole, the well's crumbling, and your last haircut involved hedge clippers. My image could use bolstering.

He whistles. "Nice. Vicky said you charge a grand for your elixirs."

I snort. More like a grand zero. The thought of Vicky spreading rumors about me sticks a thorn under my seat, but I don't deny the rumor. Aromateurs are rule-bound to keep our no-charge policy a secret.

Court studies me squirming beside him. I try to dislodge the grimace from my face.

"Vicky's not a happy person, that's why she acts that way. Drives her stepmom crazy. They're always arguing. Her step-mom's a vinyasa yoga instructor, too, very chill."

An itchy feeling scuttles up my back. When I was eight, a Hollywood producer came to us seeking an elixir for a vinyasa yoga instructor. His wife had died the year before. He smelled of black elder. "Her father, is he a Hollywood producer?"

"Yep. That's why Mel hangs out with her. She hopes he'll make her a star."

That explains Vicky's disdain for me. She blames Mother, and therefore me, for giving her a stepmom. But Mother wouldn't have made a bad match. We always consider families when deal-ing with second marriages. My feet and hands go clammy. "Why don't Vicky and her stepmom get along?"

"Vicky says her stepmom spent all her dad's money, but the truth is, her dad was washed up a long time ago. And Mrs. Valdez doesn't let her get away with crap, but it's only because she cares."

Then maybe it wasn't a mismatch. Why do I care? Vicky's problems are not high on my list of wrongs to right.

Court twists and drags his fingers in the well water, which Mother filled with gardenia blossoms before she left this morning. The flowers' delicate scent plays around our noses, teasing us with its creamy, almost incense-like fragrance. Against my better judgment, I fish out one of the blossoms and hand it to him. He twirls it against his nose, a nose that would be perfect for leaning my own against, and his eyelids dip closed. I'm caught by the simple beauty of his appreciating a flower.

"Well, thanks for everything today." My voice sounds too loud and chipper. I could offer him a snack, but that would only prolong my torture. "I should be getting back to work."

He puts his elbows on his knees. "You know, aside from a few weird stares, people never treated me differently after that thing with Dad and the call girls hit the news. But I still felt ashamed. I didn't think I could ever hold my head up again.

"Then I saw you. First day of school, you sat at our lunch table. Tina screamed at you."

He saw that? My face flushes with the memory. I felt five years old all over again. The girl and all her friends left the table, like I was the grim reaper. I ate by myself, the first of many days of solo dining.

"You didn't leave, or even react. Even finished your lunch."

"I was hungry."

"Even with all the rumors, you still come to school, day after

169

day. I never see you whine or cry. You act like nothing bothers you. I figured if you could handle . . ."

"Public ridicule," I fill in for him.

He chuckles. "Right, then I should stop moping and get on with life."

"At least one good thing came of it."

His gaze softens. "I'd say a lot of good things came of it."

My skin tingles. I focus on Tabitha, who just caught herself a juicy soil engineer. The other chickens crowd her for a bite, but then something spooks the clutch and they all flutter away.

Twilight is my favorite time of day. All shimmery in the ceiling, violet on the carpet. The night bloomers are rolling up their sleeves to do their magic. I want to remember this moment, for after the BBG kicks in, it'll never come again: Court, staring at me as if I'm the only thing worth looking at in this garden of beauties. And me, sitting in a honeysuckle cloud of my own desire, wanting to kiss him, and cursing my nose for getting in the way.

"Why can't you like anyone?" he asks suddenly.

The intensity of his gaze makes me stammer. "I—I—" I want to slap myself. I can't tell him about Larkspur jinxing us from romantic relationships. If word got out aromateurs could jinx people, Mother and I would be driven out with the proverbial stakes. So I tell him the other reasons. "Ethics. The plants we use draw others to us like bees to pollen. People might think we were taking advantage. Our reputation would suffer." I sound like Mother.

"What if someone likes you for you, and not because of the flowers?"

"It would be impossible to tell."

"My mother always says, don't throw away a bucket of ice if you think there might be a diamond inside."

"We're not supposed to want diamonds."

"But do you?"

"No," I lie.

His eyelashes flicker, a movement so quick it could've been a trick of the light. But when the smell of blueberries mingles with my own, I realize his placid expression is just a front. A lie, like mine, though a hundred times less cruel.

SEVENTEEN

"Elixirs whisper to the mind what
the heart already knows."
—*Begonie, Aromateur, 1768*

AFTER COURT LEAVES, I head to the workshop, feeling hollow inside. Scents can be sneaky, making themselves so at home in your nose that when they are pulled away, it feels like something is missing.

To outsiders, our garden's the picture of serenity, an impressionistic painting of sight and smell. But if Mother saw it, she'd freak. It hasn't felt a rake or pruning shears for days. I can smell seven types of weeds, all gearing up to spawn weed babies. But I have bigger shoots to pull at the moment.

The workshop lock sticks again, but I jiggle the key patiently until it surrenders. Once inside, I cover all the plants I harvested today with muslin and set them under drying lamps. Alice's elixir must be as fresh as possible, so I won't start mixing them until I get the miso plant. Unlike Alice's complicated scentprint, Drew's only contains forty-two notes, basic ones that are all found in our garden. Most people don't grow into their full range until their twenties.

Back in the garden, I carefully dig out a woody stalk of horse-radish, one of Drew's main notes. Used to treat impotence, the horseradish looks like a horse-size phallus. Proof that nature has a sense of humor.

The nutmeg tree diffuses an eggnog scent from several paces away, and thoughts of Court wiggle their way in. Maybe I shouldn't go to Playa del Rey with him tomorrow. Who knows what will happen on a deserted strand of beach, sunlight glowing off his very ripped body . . .

But Court's my only option. Buses and trains don't go to Playa del Rey, and it's too far to bike. I could take a taxi, but then what? Is the taxi supposed to wait around while I find the plant? Mother would know if a few hundred dollars went missing from the account. I just need to pull it together. Act professional.

I trot back to the house for a shower. I need to clear my mind before I begin on Drew's elixir.

My neglected pile of books and papers nag at me from the dresser. So does the stack of candy grams on my nightstand, which I still haven't had time to scent, let alone read. But that's okay, because I also haven't had time to make another batch of BBG.

The pile of laundry collecting in the garage is rank enough for Mother to smell in Oman. As I strip off my clothes, the phone rings. It's Mother, finally calling. Thank God they haven't invented smell-e-phone yet, or she could smell the heartsease flooding from my pores.

"Hello, dear."

"Hello."

"Why are you yawning?"

"It's eleven."

"It is? Oh, I am sorry. I got my times mixed up. Then why aren't you sleeping?"

"Just . . . tidying up. Didn't want to miss your call. How's everything there?"

"The coconut palms are outstanding. I wish I could bring one home. What did you eat for dinner?"

"Um, leftovers. The thing in the fridge."

"Oh, the spinach quiche. Was the basil still fresh?"

"Top note retention of 70 percent at least, very zingy on the liftoff."

"Perfect. I worried about that." She wants to know if the weed situation is under control and if the camellia bushes smell like they'll bloom on time. I answer in between bouts of yawning.

"Tomorrow you have to fix Ms. Salzmann, remember?"

Oh, shallot. How could I forget? "Of course I remember."

"Lemon curry is her dominant."

"Right." It's going to be a late night.

"One more thing. Did you follow up with Ms. DiCarlo?"

"Yes." I let out giant yawn, this one purposeful, hoping to head off further questions and thereby avoid falsehoods. If

Mother senses trouble, she might return early.

"All right, good. I won't be able to call you until Sunday. I'm flying to Egypt to look at the cassia."

"Okay. Sunday. Got it."

"Mim? Have I told you how proud I am of you?"

No, but now is not the time to start. "Yes, Mother. Good night."

Ms. Salzmann's stucco bungalow with its peculiar dome shape sits at the end of a cul-de-sac. A bouquet of red and pink roses lies cradled in the basket of my bicycle. I managed to stick myself only once when I arranged them this morning.

After I park my bike, I pull my beret more securely over my head. The rest of me is dressed in leggings, an oversize men's shirt and a cardigan from Twice Loved with a reindeer on the back. A skirt would not be practical for climbing coastal rocks, which I may need to do to find the miso plant.

As I uncap the vial of Ms. Salzmann's elixir, the fleeting scent of lime blossoms gives way to a singular heart note of tamanu, which is nutty and green like walnuts picked from the tree. I sniff again. Mother never takes shortcuts, and it shows. There's a silkiness to her elixirs, achieved only through unflinching attention to detail, and patience, an ethereal quality that only another aromateur could appreciate. Given the shortage of aromateurs, at least in this galaxy, it's a wonder why she still bothers. I sprinkle the contents onto the silk handle of the bouquet. Then I hold the bouquet by the tissue paper and approach the target.

It's a little early to be ringing doorbells—just past seven in the morning, but I won't have time to deliver them after school. I press the button.

A senior wearing a terry turban and a kimono squints at me, pulling her wrinkles in new directions. She slips on the pair of reading glasses that dangle around her neck. Her nails are caked with something that smells like clay. "What's this?"

"Delivery for Ms. Salzmann. Is that you?"

"Yes, that's me."

I sniff to make sure. I can't afford another mistake. Lemon curry. Check. I hand her the bouquet, which she takes without incident. Fixed. I sigh. One down.

"How lovely." Her nostrils flex as she inhales. "Who could have sent them?" She pulls out the tiny card embedded in the bouquet on which I'd written "From Your Secret Admirer."

"My secret admirer? Good heavens. Don't you think I'm a little young to settle down?"

I laugh.

She peers more closely at me. "You look just like those twins who used to bring flowers for the still lifes, back when I was teaching."

"My mother and her sister are twins—Dahlia and Bryony." Mother never mentioned it, but it wouldn't surprise me. Aromateurs often donate flowers to worthy causes.

"Yes, those were their names. They'd always beg to stay and

watch the artists work. Of course I'd say yes, even if we were doing nudes." She winks.

Mother definitely never told me *that*.

"You have a second to give me an opinion on something? It'll only take a second. Come on in." Ms. Salzmann disappears into the house.

Before entering, I sniff. Acrylic paint. Bran muffins. No drugs, or smoke, or anything that would set off warning bells. I step inside.

A skylight washes the main room of the strange house with bright morning light. For a second, I think the room is filled with people, then realize they are life-size statues fashioned of recycled junk like beer bottles and cereal boxes. Ms. Salzmann sets the flowers in the arms of one of the statues, then crosses the room to a shelf stuffed with books. Nearby, a wingback chair is arranged next to a pottery wheel and a table. On the table, sits a bust of a man.

Ms. Salzmann glances at me rubbernecking her crowded room. She taps the table in front of the bust. "Tell me, who does this person look like to you?"

I study the face. The strong nose, wide-set eyes and Caesar-like bangs remind me of the face on all the current teen rags right now.

"Tyson Badland?"

She clasps her hands together and leans in. "He'll be so pleased."

I gape. "Is it for him?"

Her lips flatten into a sly smile. "All the stars must have a bust nowadays." She cups her hand beside her mouth. "He's shorter than you think."

"I better go. I'm late for school."

She escorts me to the front door. "You good with your hands?"

"I guess."

"I'm looking for an apprentice, you interested? My last girl moved to Singapore."

"Sounds interesting, but I have a lot of projects going on right now."

"Well, here's my card in case you change your mind." She hands me a business card from a shelf on the wall. "Thanks for the flowers."

Court can't leave until lunchtime, after his Kill Drill. That works out fine, since I have an arrow to shoot.

Kali fails to show for Cardio Fitness, a fact noted by Vicky's cohorts, who snicker as they look back at me. I ignore them. In a matter of hours, Operation Fix Vicky will be complete. Vicky always splits from Melanie after algebra when Melanie goes to dramatic arts.

An hour later, I take my usual spot in algebra with Vicky two desks away. Mr. Frederics's outfits have grown snazzier by the day, or maybe my bleary eyes are just more sensitive to color.

He's wearing a herringbone blazer and patent leather shoes, and the sugary notes of his happiness overpower even the tang of teenage angst. Is he sprucing up for the woman he expects to fall in love with him, or the one who's actually falling for him?

Mr. Frederics calculates the sum of an arithmetic series, and I hide behind my textbook, biding my time. Vicky knots her hair on her head, exposing a brown expanse of neck above her white tank top.

The moments tick by.

Only a week ago, I looked forward to coming to this classroom. Now, coming here only reminds me of my mistake—the first term in an arithmetic series that set off a whole chain of consequences. Finding the upper limit will be a monumental task.

Finally, Mr. Frederics frees us.

I quickly pack my things and begin to follow Vicky.

Mr. Frederics calls my name. "Do you have a moment?"

"Er, sure." Vicky sweeps out of the classroom and out of range. I step up to the teacher's desk, hoping this won't take long.

Mr. Frederics knits his fingers together, then bends them back, cracking the joints. "I asked Ms. DiCarlo to the homecoming game a few weeks ago but she never gave me a straight answer. Do you think I should renew my invitation, or is that too much, too soon, given the circumstances?" He leans closer, giving me a strong whiff of worry. "I don't want to mess up the, er, medicine."

"Um," I stall. There's a good chance she'd say yes even without the elixir, but if they get together before I've had a chance to undo my mistake, Alice will suffer. "I think . . . when Ms. DiCarlo is ready, she'll bring it up herself."

His eyebrow stretches up and his mouth pulls down in a thoughtful expression. "Okay. Good thinking. If she's still on the fence by the Puddle Jumpers event, I'll have to bring out my secret weapon."

"Er, what would that be?" I force a smile.

"If I told you, it wouldn't be a secret."

"Right. Well then, see you tomorrow." Then I hurry out the door, wondering what new surprise awaits me in this high school house of horrors. May his "secret weapon" not cause irreversible mortification, for him or Ms. DiCarlo. And may it not get me further in the hole with Mother for that matter.

I move briskly down the hallway, hoping Vicky's walking at her usual regal pace. Ahead, Lauren and Pascha are tacking up a poster. They spot me and smile. I return the smile but hurry by, not wanting to encourage conversation. They probably think I'm stuck up.

Thirty feet ahead, I spot Vicky's dark tresses. Like a stalker, I slip through the stream of students pouring from the class-rooms, edging closer to her.

Maybe it was a bad idea, me coming to school. I wasn't unhappy being homeschooled. I collected more than eighty stamps in my passport. Not many fifteen-year-olds can say they've smelled the orange blossoms in Granada, or stuck their nose in a peach-scented Osmanthus tree in Guilin, China. And

Mother wasn't all work and no play, either. We rode camels into a Luxor sunset. Hiked waterfalls in the Amazonian jungle. I even held a baby marmoset in the cup of my hand, its striped tail coiled around my finger.

I wanted it all, but maybe I already had it all. One thing's for sure: if I'd never come, neither Alice nor Kali would be in this mess.

Well, the elixir's ready to go and I have to do this. Vicky deserves what's coming. She stops at the vending machine. I tuck myself behind a partially open classroom door and wait.

"Mim?"

I nearly jump out of my ankle boots. Whipping around, I get a mouthful of hair—chestnut brown and curly. Cassandra Linney sweeps back her tresses and secures them into a rough braid.

"Hi," I say cautiously.

"I'm looking for her again. She didn't come to school and she's not answering texts." Her feathery brows stretch high above her wide-open eyes. She smells more concerned than uneasy today.

"I haven't spoken to her since yesterday." Having never texted Kali before, or anyone for that matter, I can't say whether it's unusual for her not to respond, but she never misses class. I should've called her last night.

Cassandra rocks forward on her toes. "Well, I hope she's not sick. We have homecoming rehearsal right now. I can't pull off the show without her."

I sniff for the insincerity scents of dirty bathwater and pond salt, but find only the freezer-burn smell of alarm and a little bit of pitcher plant. But Cassandra *was* the half-time show for the past three years before Kali came along. She's a born performer. At the beginning of the year, she'd climb up on the lunch tables to sing the daily specials until Principal Swizinger made her stop over liability concerns.

Cassandra fans her face with her hands and takes a few deep breaths as if she's preparing to either cry or break into song. I quickly say, "I'm sure she's fine." If Kali is sick, I hope it's not Vicky-induced nausea. And if it is, I'll take care of that right now. "I'll let her know you're concerned if I see her."

The ambivalent note of rambling sunflower crisscrosses my nose, but disappears when the girl stops hyperventilating. She smiles, an expression that tucks her mouth down at the corners in an oddly charming way. "Thanks. See you around."

Cassandra traipses back down the hall, passing Vicky who is still puzzling over her options at the vending machine. I uncap my vial and move in closer, hoping to get her while she's still distracted. A couple kissing in the hallway separates me from my target.

Vicky punches in a number and a canned soda falls to the bottom of the machine with a thud. She bends to collect it. As I pass her, I check that there are no eyewitnesses, then raise the vial. A twinge of guilt stops my hand in midair.

I wouldn't be here if she hadn't thrown the first punch. She did this to herself—

A kid bumps me from behind. I stumble forward, and a few droplets in my vial spray the back of Vicky's neck. In a hot panic, I retreat, tucking myself into the classroom across the hall. My heart pounds like a jackhammer, but I don't dare breathe.

Vicky pops the tab off her diet soda. Thank the lilies, she didn't see me.

I slump back against the wall, which feels cold and rough through my worn cardigan sweater. Well, that's that. Vicky will fall in love with Drew, forget about Court, and Kali will be off the hook. Everyone will be happy, even, perhaps Vicky.

Vicky's on the move again. She continues down the checker-tiled hall, then stops by an emergency exit. The door makes a metal crunching sound as she presses her back to it and slips out.

She's probably going outside to smoke. The door leads to a small grassy quad and an equipment shed.

Kids hurry to their classrooms. Chem lab will be starting soon.

Suddenly, Principal Swizinger hurries up the hall, her eyes and mouth all pulled into severe lines. She stops at the emergency door, then follows Vicky out.

I know a bust when I smell one. I'm not the only one who can smell the tobacco breath that Vicky covers with mint gum.

I emerge from my hiding place. I should get to class, but I suddenly have the urge to peek out the door. As I reach the emergency exit, the door swings open, and a sour-faced Vicky followed by the principal sweep by me.

"But I only wanted some fresh air," says Vicky. "You have no proof."

Her face screws up when she sees me. The principal gives me a curt nod. I pretend like I was about to get a drink from the water fountain and dip my head.

Principal Swizinger taps her toe. "I don't need proof. This isn't a courtroom. I've smelled it on you several times before. I'll need to call your stepmom."

"No, you can't do that. You don't understand. She'll ground me from *homecoming*."

"Maybe she should."

"But it's so unfair." She hiccups like she's about to cry.

The principal makes uncomfortable throat-clearing noises. I stop drinking and head back down the corridor.

"Mim?" The principal's voice resonates off the tiles.

I freeze, then slowly turn back around. Behind the principal, Vicky puts her hands on her hips and mutters something coarse.

"You're in charge of volunteers at Puddle Jumpers this year, aren't you?"

"Yes."

"How many volunteers do we have so far?"

"Thirty-two students, two faculty." I cringe, as a vision of Mr. Frederics breaking into the Latin Hustle in front of Ms. DiCarlo's startled eyes crosses my mind.

Her eyes become sly. "Make it thirty-three. Miss Valdez, you are lucky I have a soft spot for the Puddle Jumpers. Volunteer, and I will consider clemency."

Vicky's arms drop to her sides and her mouth falls open. Snapping it shut, she narrows her eyes at me. Either she's going to thank me or spit at me, and my nose tells me they're equally venomous.

EIGHTEEN

"Travel widely. When your feet
expand, so shall your nose."
—Marjoram, *Aromateur*, 1784

WHEN THE LUNCH bell rings, I head toward the library to
collect my bike. Through the library windows, I see Ms. DiCarlo
typing at her computer. The bleach smells emanating off her desk
are especially strong, which means she's been cleaning again. Still
stressed. I bet if I went in there, I'd come out a blonde.

I should unchain my bike and leave. Court will be meeting
me at the windsock soon.

But I can't.

Ms. DiCarlo looks up as I push through the familiar doors.
"Hi, Ms. DiCarlo."

"Oh, hello." Her features look especially pale today under
the harsh fluorescent lighting. "What can I help you with?" she
says a shade too brightly.

I fumble around for an answer, not knowing myself why I'm
here. Guilt, probably.

Her manuscript, *Avoiding the Torture Chamber of Medieval Library Collections*, lays open on her desk. "That looks interesting."

She touches her face. "Thank you. I'm hoping to get something published. It's hard to make a name for yourself as a medieval collections specialist, especially if you're a woman."

"Oh. I hadn't thought about that." Because I did not know medieval collections specialists existed until today.

"Yes, well, it's a huge problem. Most librarians are women, but the ones at the top are inevitably men." She squirts her desk with cleaner and rubs it with a paper towel, rubbing so hard, she may set the desk on fire. "I hate to say it, but women get the short end of the stick almost everywhere, especially middle-aged women." She chucks her paper towel in the garbage, then teases out a tissue and wipes her nose, which has started to run.

"That's . . . sad," I say lamely. If not for my mistake, Ms. DiCarlo would be sharing her lunch with a certain math teacher, instead of spending it contemplating gender treatment. "But I think that as long as there's hydrangea, there's hope."

Smile lines appear on her cheeks, but instead of making her look old, they give her face a sweet kind of vulnerability.

"Thanks. I'll keep that in mind."

Kali rolls up on her bike and parks it in the racks. I exit the library.

"*Talofa*," Kali says, jerking her chin up. "I'm late for lunch duty." She starts making tracks. Her nylon windbreaker swishes with each pump of her arms. I jog to keep up, and together we join the noisy mass of students on their way to the cafeteria. The nauseating smell of enchiladas and pizza intensifies with each step.

"You get your plants?"

"All but one. Court's taking me to Playa del Rey right now to find it."

Her head retracts. "Court?"

"Yeah. He had a change of heart. So where were you this morning?"

"Home. Thinking about earthworms."

"Why?"

"Those earthworms have to eat dirt all their life. Talk about a sucky existence. Not only that, they have to worry about being stepped on, chicken gangs, the sun baking them. They don't make SPF sleeves in their size, you know."

I let out a teensy smile.

"But do those things stop them? They keep eating dirt, and crapping it back out. And look how nice they make the grass." She holds her hand out to the smashed strip of crabgrass that runs along the building next to us.

"I know you're making a point."

"Never let fear stop you. I'm not going to let a squirrel push me around."

"That's good, but the squirrel still has your journal."

"Humph." Her face grows dark and her pace quickens.

"But you don't have to worry anymore. I took care of her."

Her eyes narrow to black slashes. "What do you mean?"

"I mean, it won't be long before she develops a little Reaver fever."

Kali stops so quickly I overtake her and have to retread my steps.

Frowning, she puts a hand on her hip. "I asked you not to fix her with Drew."

"After that stunt she pulled in Cardio, she had it coming."

A cloud of blue hydrangea has begun to form in the air around Kali. I stiffen at her disappointment, and the blood rushes to my cheeks.

"She might have had it coming, but you just can't . . . do that."

"I was trying to help, I—"

She angles her body so she's facing me square on. Her deep, all-seeing poet's eyes study me. "There are lines we can't cross, Mim, especially you." She points to me, then taps her finger against her chin.

"Why me?"

"Because, Nosey, you can do things the rest of us can't. Clark Kent was always getting stepped on, or chewed out, but did he ever use his superpowers against that kind of shit? No."

She's comparing me to *Superman*? "He was trying to keep his identity secret. And anyway, if Clark Kent's friends were being stepped on, he'd whip out the cape."

All six feet of her seems to bristle. "Do I look like someone who can be stepped on?"

"No, but—"

"Just leave it alone. I can take care of myself." Her flip-flops slap the pavement away from me, and the smell of burnt tires singes my nostrils, strong as a freeway underpass.

She's mad at me? I was just trying to protect her. What good is a superpower if you can't help your friends when they need it? I'm suddenly aware of all the faces casting me curious glances.

Closing my mouth, I steer myself back to the library. After I fetch my bike, I walk it toward the windsock, my heart full of injury, and my ears ringing. A tangle of clover weed pokes through a crack in the pavement, and I lengthen my stride just so I can crush it under my ankle boot. It doesn't make me feel any better. In fact, I feel like, well, a heel. So I fed Vicky a little giddy juice. It's not like I carjacked Ghandi. I dig a nail into my palm to stop thinking about her.

I exit the school grounds and roll toward where Court is already parked at the curb. He gets out of the Jeep, wearing aviator sunglasses, Levi's faded at the knees, and a navy T-shirt that hugs his lean frame without being tight. He jams my bike into the back.

Moments later, we're pulling into traffic. The Jeep has been vacuumed of sand, and smells of car shampoo and window cleaner. I can still smell the perfumes of girls past—those can stick around for years—but now there's a manufactured pine scent overlaying everything.

"I hope it smells better today," he says with a sideways glance at me.

Blushing bromeliad rises from my collar. I will have to learn

not to be so transparent. "It smells fine. You didn't have t-to—"
I stammer, "but thanks. Er, do you know the way to Playa del
Rey?"

His wet hair falls in waves and he smells like Ivory soap.
"Yeah. It's just north of where we surf."

We take the road west, toward the Pacific. The sun burns a
hole in the patchwork of gray and white clouds covering it. Highway traffic is sparse, and we ride the fast lane at just above the
speed limit, causing the red and white oleanders along the shoulder to blur into pink. The burnt rubber scent of the highway
breezes through the vents, and I begin thinking about Kali again.
She didn't even let me finish my sentence. She just stormed off.

I shoulder those thoughts away. "How did the Kill Drill go?"

"Not great. Coach decided to change strategy so we have a
meeting tonight. How's the potion making?"

"Fine." I feel shy because of how we left each other last night.
Unresolved. Like a crossword puzzle that gets too complicated to
finish. "Any updates on your mom?"

"My aunt took her shopping today. They hit up the yard
sales, collecting stuff to put in Christmas wreaths for the foster homes." He tenses his grip on the steering wheel and shakes
his head. "Last night, Mom took out all her cookbooks and
spread them out around her. Said she was looking for Savannah
Sweetpie."

I wince. Mr. Frederics is from Georgia. A jolt of panic hits
me again as the what-ifs crowd my mind. What if I can't find that

miso plant? What if I don't fix Alice before the first kiss?

Either Mother will have to make the PUF, and what a party that will be, or Alice's heart gets broken for a second time. The hum of the air conditioner and the outside traffic compete with the noise in my head.

"It's weird to think about Mom being in love with Mr. Frederics." Court interrupts my internal boxing match. "I mean, Mr. Frederics? Last week, he was just another of Mel's teachers."

"Mother says you never really see a person until you smell them."

He flashes me a smile, reminding me of my intimate and thorough sniff down of him yesterday in the tree. My cheeks warm. I scrap around for a new topic. The soccer ball medallion hanging from the rearview mirror catches my eye. "What would you do if you didn't play soccer?"

"That's easy. I'd study whales. Humpbacks swim half the globe to care for their young. Blows my mind."

"The power of a mother's love. Though it can make you crazy," I grumble.

He laughs. "But that's part of the job description. In fact, I'd been thinking about getting a degree in oceanography, though Dad's not happy about it."

"Why not?"

"He thinks it's a waste. He always wanted to play soccer, but didn't have the legs. If you draw the winning lottery ticket, you shouldn't burn it. What would your mother say if you didn't want to be a—?" His finger wiggles as he searches for the word.

"An aromateur. She'd probably lock me in a room with blackberry bramble until I changed my mind."

"Blackberry bramble?"

"The nonberry part of the plant smells like remorse. It's angular—it jabs at your nose until you want to mend your ways."

"You're kidding, right?"

"No. They used to plant it on graves to prevent the dead from climbing out."

"I meant about your mother locking you in a room."

"Oh yes." Mostly. "Thankfully, I enjoy using my nose to help people out." I also like being able to detect soap bubbles of his nervousness, and the blush of paprika. "I was born for it. It's not so much a talent as a calling. Though, it has its limitations." Like, the one sitting next to me.

"What would you do if you *couldn't* smell the way you do?"

"The list is long."

"Top three, then."

I answer without thinking. "Three. I would float in the Dead Sea. I heard it's just like flying, only wetter. Two. I'd load up on sugary, salty movie snacks. Buttered popcorn. M&M's. Peanut butter cups. Are they as good as I think they are?"

"The popcorn is, but I can't speak for the candy. I'm allergic to nuts." He glances down at the black case clipped to his belt that contains his EpiPen.

"Is it as bad as bees?"

"Worse. What's the first thing?"

"Um, I haven't decided," I stammer as I realize the first thing involves him.

We come off an incline and suddenly the Pacific Ocean opens on the horizon, nearly blinding us with her radiance. Court pulls down the sunshades.

The charcoal cliffs that mark Las Ballenas Reserve run like a black ribbon against a peacock-blue skirt. I inhale the air coming in through the ventilation. The briny scent of the ocean hits me first, mellowed by spicy sagebrush, bay laurel, and a hundred other back notes. I can't detect the miso-soup scent yet, but I suspect the air currents are chasing it away.

"There." I point to a sign partially hidden by shrubs that reads Playa del Rey.

We park in a clearing under a cypress tree with craggy branches that resemble a waving hand. There's no one around. Most people don't stop until three miles down where the paved parking lot and a wooden staircase make the ocean more accessible.

Court shrugs on his letterman jacket and I button my sweater. It's always ten degrees colder on the coast.

"When's the last time you came here?" he asks.

"When I was five. Mother wanted me to practice unlayering. The plants here are so dense, you have to concentrate to pick everything apart. Plus, the smell of the ocean blocks a lot of the subtler notes. It's like—" I search for the right analogy.

"Cheese sauce."

"Cheese sauce?"

"Mom used to put cheese sauce on our vegetables so we'd eat them. Blocks out the taste. Especially cauliflower."

"Right, cheese sauce."

A winding pathway cuts through a crazy quilt of coastal scrub with dense patches of somber golden yarrow and California lilac—a common heart note that attracts humans and bees alike. The bees go crazy for the pollen-rich clusters of the lilac's heady purple flowers, which are fruitier than the common variety grown on the East Coast. We follow the path to the edge of the cliff, where a sign reads Photography Allowed.

The skies are so blue, they erase the line of the horizon and melt into the Pacific Ocean. Despite its name, Playa del Rey, or King's Beach, is the smallest beach in the reserve. It gets its name from the glittering sand that surrounds the cove like a crown. A narrow pathway snakes two hundred feet down the side of the cliff to the beach.

Court whistles. "Makes me wish I could fly."

"Makes me wish I could swim."

"You don't know how?"

"There's not much time to learn with so many plants to tend." Cool wind burns my cheeks and I warm them with my sleeves. I survey the surroundings for somewhere to sit, and decide on a boulder at the top of the descent. "This might take awhile."

"All right. I'll just enjoy the view."

I try not to read into that and settle on the boulder, while Court takes himself to a spot a hundred feet away. Breathing deeply, I shut out the scent of Court, somewhere behind me, and focus on the air. I peel back the heavier scents layer by layer to reveal the more delicate ones hidden inside. The task requires all my concentration. The thicker scents keep folding back into my consciousness like the pages of a newly bound book. But remembering my failure with the Creamsicle tulips, I stop trying so hard. Instead, I take a deep breath, relax my jaw, and let the mystery scent reveal itself to me.

And soon it does. That subtle, salty smell, like miso soup, appears. I follow the wisp of its scent, as elusive as spider silk, and find it leads west. Toward the ocean. Into the ocean.

When I open my eyes, Court is gone. I don't remember him leaving. The sun won't drop for another few hours, but the sky has turned a desolate shade of gray. I stand and the breeze whips my clothes all around me. I hug myself. I can't go into the ocean. That would be suicide for a nonswimmer like me.

The crash of the waves echoes off the high sandstone walls, sounding like the angry roar of a lion, warning me to stay back. Court's scent reaches my nose as he comes up behind me. "Find your plant?"

I nod grimly.

"What's wrong?"

"I'm going to need to swim."

NINETEEN

"Just because we're born with it,
doesn't mean it's easy."
—*Torenia, Aromateur, 1922*

COURT COUGHS. "IT'S seaweed?"

"I think so."

"There's a ton on the beach."

"That isn't the kind I need." I cast around for a solution—a boat, or even an abandoned fishing pole—but see nothing. "Er, could I borrow your surfboard?"

"Didn't you just tell me you don't know how to swim?"

"It's not far." I gaze down into the cove where a curve of white foam upon the sand grins at me. "It's on the surface."

"It's cold in there. Plus, that tide will fight you."

I shake my head, not seeing any other way. The miso-soup scent is one of Alice's heart notes, and therefore, essential.

He snorts. "You're not going in there."

"If I don't, I can't fix things."

"If you do, you might drown." He starts walking back to the Jeep.

I trot after him. "Where are you going?"

"To get my wetsuit."

"You can't do it for me. You won't know which plant to pick."

He stops. His shoulders slump as he lets out a great sigh. "Well then, I guess you'll be borrowing Mel's steamer. But we'll do this together."

Mel's steamer turns out to be a winter wetsuit with long arms and legs. It's not something you just throw on. A pink stripe runs down the middle of the black rubbery fabric. I thought we were the same size, save my longer legs, but rethink that as I sit in the passenger seat of the Jeep, struggling to pull my calf through. The suit is like a thing alive, resisting me every time I try to get a good grip. By the time I bring it to heel, my hair is damp with sweat.

I lay back against the headrest, panting. Court opens my door, though I'm not sure how he knew I was finished. Well, almost. My back zipper's still undone.

He hands me a pair of black booties. "Water shoes."

Those are easier to put on than the suit. Finally, I'm ready.

"Come out and I'll zip you." His black suit shows every chiseled cut and projection on his body.

As he fiddles with my zipper, goose bumps prick the skin of my back. I can't help blushing. It's just my back, but please let him not be staring at the birthmark lower down that looks like a pair of lips. When he brushes the hair off my neck, I nearly faint at the whispery heat of his hand.

He zips me up as carefully as if he's trying to draw the straightest line he can. In the time it takes to finish the job—a few seconds at most—I feel as if I've circled the earth in the Cloud Air jet and landed, disoriented and giddy.

Finally, he pulls his board out of the trunk. It's white and roughed up around the edges with a No Fear sticker on the tip.

"This will keep us topside."

I clear my throat. "How, exactly, will this work?"

"I'll lie across the deck and paddle us frontside."

"Where will I be?"

He flashes me a lopsided grin. "On top of me."

My stomach flip-flops, and my flush travels all the way down to my toes. The thrilled scent of flame lily, also called Gloriosa, peels off me in a thick layer. I blush even more furiously, though of course he can't smell the honey scent.

"We'll have two layers of neoprene between us. No skin contact, I promise." He holds up his hands in surrender. I mumble something agreeable, as if the idea of me riding him like a human surfboard doesn't affect me in the least.

After clipping a pair of gloves to my waist tag, he hands me a canvas bag with towels, and bottled water. "Let's go before the sun goes down."

I sling the canvas bag around my body. After I grab my mesh

collection bag, I follow him down the cliff.

The cove is shaped like a scallop shell. A rock twenty feet across juts out of the water like a black pearl. Two sea lions sun themselves on the rock, two bumps on an otherwise craggy outcropping.

We pick our way down the zigzagging cliffside pathway. Somehow he manages to get himself and the surfboard down without falling, while I find myself scrabbling down the steeper parts like a crab.

We rest on a ledge halfway down the cliff.

After I catch my breath, I ask, "When did you learn how to surf?"

"When I was ten. Dad used to take Melanie and me down to Santa Cruz when we were kids. Mel could kick my ass back then. Afterward, we'd get Snowshoe Cones." A shadow crosses his face and I catch the scent of friar plums again, mingled with the damp earth of longing.

"You miss him."

One of his cheek muscles tightens. "I miss thinking I have the coolest father in the world. Now I'm the son of the town lecher. I mean, my *dad*."

I try to imagine how it would feel to be in Court's shoes. I can smell the bleeding heart that pervades his mood, and I know how angry I would be if anyone ever hurt Mother. But having never had a father, the precise dimensions of his emotions are hard to conjure. Perhaps I've been spared a degree of pain by *not* having one.

Was my father spared a degree of pain by not having me? I nearly snort aloud. It's different for him. As a sperm donor, he probably thinks he's made some infertile couple very happy. But I will always wonder if there's a part of me that failed to thrive in his absence, like an unrotated watermelon that stays yellow on one side.

Then again, I can't imagine anyone brave enough to take on Mother. She's a one-woman show, and though I may have my hang-ups over the running of said show, her moral virtue has never been one of them. In fact, I often wish I had her convictions. Somehow, I think it would make life easier.

Court stares into the ocean, his mouth a tight line.

"Certain people are supposed to be reliable, like rhubarb," I tell him. "Once you plant the crowns in the ground, you don't have to worry about them. They take care of themselves. Parents should be like that."

"Yeah. Well, he was no rhubarb. More like . . ." He looks at me for help.

"Eggplant? They're sensitive to flea beetles."

"Right, eggplant." He smiles. "You ready?"

A line of black cormorants swoop down to land on the beach. When we finally touch down on sand, they fly off again.

The noise of the ocean echoes off the cliff walls. Waves rush up to kiss our feet. I hiss in my breath at the arctic temperature, which freezes me all the way to my teeth. Suddenly, swimming doesn't seem as easy as it did from above.

A crop of bull kelp pokes out of the water like Paul Bunyan–size jalapeño peppers, growing and shrinking with the flow of the tides. Massive fronds of giant kelp spread their arms over the surface, making me wonder if they're hiding something. Water blocks my sense of smell so if something's down there, I won't know unless it surfaces.

Court sets down his board and the tiny No Fear sticker seems to thumb its nose at me. Well, I said I wanted to try surfing, and now it's come back to bite me. At least I didn't say crocodile wrestling.

He pulls on his gloves. "You okay?"

"Fine." I try to keep my teeth from chattering.

As I work on Melanie's gloves, Court stands the board in front of me. "After I get on, you'll have to crawl on top of me. Think you can do that?"

If I didn't, I definitely wouldn't tell him. "Sure."

The musty scent of elbow bush for awkwardness creeps from his direction. It eases my own awkwardness to smell some on him, too. He slings my collection bag across his own body, then secures the leash dangling from the bottom of the board to my ankle. "Always find the board if you fall off, okay? And try to relax."

"Got it." I take his neoprene-covered arm with my gloved hand, and into the ocean we go. The water shocks me again, but I grit my teeth and keep moving forward.

When the water comes to my waist, he drops the board. "At least it's calm."

"This is calm?"

He lifts his chin toward the open ocean beyond our cove. "Sure. Compared to out there, this is a swimming pool."

I stare at the board, suddenly worrying that the dings in the side came from sharks. Big-teeth sharks whose sense of smell rivals my own.

But I don't have time to obsess on it further because Court's already rolled onto the board and now it's my turn. I put one hand on the edge and the other on top of his waist, then hoist myself up. My top half lands in a crisscross over his midsection and I quickly try to scoot the rest of me on top. The board bobs, but he uses his arms to keep it in one place as I maneuver myself in fits and spurts.

I yelp as a wave splashes me from the side. But soon enough, I'm all the way on top of him. We float for a moment like a hastily made sandwich, and I worry that I'm crushing him, but then he paddles us off.

"Anchors aweigh," he says.

More freezing water hits me in the face and stings my eyes, so I rest my cheek between his shoulder blades.

I never imagined I'd be this close to SGHS's star soccer player, but if I had, it would not have been in this particular configuration. Or in this particular outfit. The warmth of his body makes even my hair tingle. I wonder if my inexperience with human touch makes me that much more sensitive to it, or perhaps it's simply Court who, despite the two layers of neoprene, is setting off every alarm bell in my body. If I can feel every single bump, ridge, and dip on his body, then he can feel every one on mine. I stiffen. Just focus on finding the plant and getting the heck out of the water.

"Which way?" he asks. At least one of us is still using his brain.

I sniff. The miso-soup smell comes from somewhere farther right, near the rock with the sea lions. I lift my hand off the board to point. "Over there."

Paddling with strong, even strokes, Court bears us toward the rock. It lies about twenty yards away, with the open sea another ten yards beyond. The movement of the water coming into the cove causes turbulence around the rock, forming mini-whirlpools.

Water sprays into my mouth, burning my tongue with its saltiness. I cry out.

"What's wrong?" He looks over his shoulder at me.

I spit to rid myself of the taste and wipe my mouth on the shoulder of my suit, though that only makes my lips sting. "It tastes terrible," I say, panting.

The water splashes my face again but this time I clamp my mouth shut.

The going is slow since the ocean wants to push us back to

the shore. If our motor had not been a varsity soccer player, we might be at a standstill altogether.

Ten yards out.

A large swell shoves us at an angle, but Court counterbalances it with his weight. Suddenly we're moving toward the greater ocean. The water's fickle, and it's hard to know if we're coming or going. My stomach roils at the topsy-turvy movement as we flatten out again.

"You do this for fun?" I gasp.

"You'd like it better if you had your own board." He glances back at me again. The water collecting on his eyelashes drips onto his cheek as he winks. "But I wouldn't."

Oddly, his flirting eases the queasiness in my gut, but I don't let on.

He starts paddling again and after a few more yards, I spot it, a small tangle of black kelp with hollow bulbs that grow in intervals like Christmas lights. It's some subspecies of bladder wrack, a kelp commonly found in the Baltic Sea. The tangle floats in a four-yard-wide channel between the sea lion rock and the high volcanic walls that surround the cove. Water churns like a giant washing machine around the rock and through the channel. We couldn't go through that. The water would toss us around like a pair of socks.

"See that blackish stuff tangled in the giant kelp?"

He stops paddling and lifts himself up to see.

"I should've brought a fishing pole," I mutter.

"I'll swim it. But that means you'll be on your own for a minute."

"Are you sure? It looks kind of rough."

"Piece of cake. I'm a certified lifeguard."

I remember the lifeguard sweatshirt he was wearing the day of the bee sting. Still, even seals drown.

"I'm going to slide out from the right."

"Okay," I say dubiously.

Shifting one limb at a time, I uncage him. He barrel rolls into the water in one smooth motion, then quickly resurfaces. As he holds the board steady, I spread myself on top of it.

"Relax, okay? The easiest way to float is to relax."

"Relax. Got it." Laying my cheek on the board, I command my muscles to melt. Just another comatose sea lion here. Nothing's going to happen.

He treads water beside me for a moment, then smoothly glides away.

When Court reaches the channel, the water pulls him behind the rock and out of sight. I push myself up to try to see better, causing the board to slide around under me. Don't panic. Relax. "Court?"

One of the sea lions barks, then flips onto its other side.

What if the water current's too strong? What if it drags him out to sea? The seconds plod by. This was a bad idea, a very bad idea. So I'm locked in the tower, it's not worth Court's life. Why didn't I think this through a little more? "Court!"

No response.

The board starts to turn to the left so I no longer face the channel. Water chases itself around the black rock, throwing up white mist and seafoam. Cupping my hands the way Court did, I dig in and try to turn the ship around. The water numbs my arms but I keep going, until finally I'm facing the channel again.

Court's head pops out of the surface. He drags himself by long strokes toward me.

I whimper in relief.

"You didn't miss me, did you?" His voice carries across the water.

"A little." Now the board's turning away again. I hoist up my arms and let it. He's halfway back to me when I hear him cry out. I jerk my head around. Court, not ten feet away, puts a hand to the side of his head. His face pinches like he's in pain.

"Mim," he gasps. "A bee."

TWENTY

"The aromateur's power lies not in her ability to smell, but her power to give."
—*Ferne, Aromateur, 1832*

I DIG IN both arms and paddle furiously. "I'm coming!"

My floating platform threatens to derail at my frenzied splashing. I can't help Court if I don't calm down. Relax. One arm after the other like he did.

The water is thick as cement, and each stroke leaves me breathless. Bees don't like the ocean. One of the bees buzzing around the California lilac must've fallen asleep in my hair and then awoken when I got splashed.

Court struggles to keep his face above water. Where is his EpiPen? Left back on the shore when he changed. There's not exactly anywhere to put it on a wetsuit. Who knows if an EpiPen is even waterproof?

The ocean swells and when it drains back out of the cove, it pushes us toward the channel, toward the whirlpool. My stomach drops at the movement, and I break into a cold sweat. "Hang on, I'm almost there."

Gritting my teeth, I redouble my efforts to paddle toward Court but a wave hits me from the side, and the board flips over.

I remember to close my mouth just as I plunge into the icy depths. In a panic, I clutch at the board, but I can't get a grip. It's too slippery. My head dips underwater. Madly bicycling my legs, I try to pull myself up, but the water pushes me back. Shoving aside thoughts of imminent death, I try again.

If I die, so will Court.

With a last burst of effort, I reach up and grasp the edge of the board with my fingertips. Hoisting myself back out of the water, I fling my arm over the board, filling my lungs again with air.

Court's submerged to his nose.

"Court!" I use my free arm to pull myself closer to him. My limbs feel numb and sluggish. Move faster! Just a few feet more.

I reach out to Court, but miss and the board flips again. Back under the water, I sink. Court's body dangles in front of me, the collection bag with the bladder wrack floating next to him. His leg kicks out once, pushing his head above water.

I wiggle and thrash my way back to the surface as well, desperately flinging my arm over my fickle raft once again. Got it. Keep going.

Finally, I catch him under the shoulder. With more strength

than I thought I owned, I lift him up a few inches and lug him toward me. Gasping, he heaves his arm over the board, somehow managing to tuck it under him again.

I yank off my glove with my teeth and comb my frozen hand through Court's hair in search of the stinger. It's right behind his ear. I dig it out, though I know it won't do much. The poison has already spread.

My eyes fill with tears as Court struggles to breathe, his grip on the board weakening. To help keep him afloat, I jam my arm under his and pedal my legs back and forth so I don't sink, racking my brains for a solution. No plantain weed, no EpiPen, only salt water, seaweed, and myself.

Myself.

Human saliva is a powerful thing, and the secret ingredient for our elixirs. How powerful, then, is a love witch's saliva? Mother says our bodies contain the memories of the plants we handle. It's why we never get sick and heal so quickly. But kissing him? It's anyone's guess where Larkspur drew the line, but clearly kissing lies on the other side of it. I could end up like Aunt Bryony.

I almost laugh out loud. Who cares at this point? The ocean has closed a fist around us anyway. We will die here and no know will know except the sea lions.

Court blinks as if trying to straighten his vision. His mouth hangs slack, lips blue with cold or shock, probably both. I wait until he draws in a breath, then without wasting another second, I press my lips into his.

Since this will likely be the only kiss I ever get, I give it all I've got, despite the tangle of hair covering my face, the salt burning my eyes. Ours noses bump together and his lips, half-parted already, yield under mine. He tastes sweet as apples, his mouth deliciously warm despite the frigid temperature. My stomach drops as if I'm in free fall, and for a moment, I think I have joined the cormorants diving somewhere near. But then his gasp catches in my throat and vibrates down to the deepest chambers of my heart.

The sea swells again, lifting us higher, but the movement doesn't break our connection. Finally, though I want to stay there longer, I pull my head back. Court's skin loses its bluish cast, and his eyes regard me like I startled him out of a dream.

I cry out as another wave yanks the board from my one-armed grip. Then the water swells over my head, cutting off sound and holding me in place. I kick my body upward, but the sea squats on me like a twenty-ton giant. I stop moving to preserve breath.

They say in the moments before death, significant events rise to the mind, the last bubble of memory. I see my seven-year-old self running through a South African warehouse full of spider plants, great blooming things that sucked up Mother's scent with their powerful odor collectors. Their spiky fronds grabbed at me as I shouldered past them, sniffing desperately though my nose was so swollen from crying that I could barely breathe. At last, I picked up a filament of Mother's black currant top note. When

I finally found her, she was looking at her watch. "Impressive, dear. That only took you seven minutes. I thought it would take at least ten."

Incredibly, the ocean shifts, and my head pops up again. Though I strain to keep it above water this time, another wave crashes above me, and I can't draw a breath before going under. The currents pull me this way and that, and I'm not even sure which way is up anymore. I'm a single berry trapped in a shaking mold of Jell-O.

I'm sorry, Mother, I blew it. May the news fall gently.

TWENTY-ONE

"The difference between infatuation and love can be
measured by the distance between two pairs of lips."
—*Justicia, Aromateur,* 1836

A HAND CATCHES mine, and then his strong arms snatch me
from the grave and gather me to him. I suck in air, sweet air. Just
as I seize a lungful, I start to sink back under. But Court's arm
tightens around me.

"Mim, grab the board! Listen to me, grab the board. You
can do this." His voice sounds different than I remember, tighter,
and I can hear him panting.

Despite the hundred-pound barbell attached to my arm, I
throw it over the surfboard.

"Catch your breath," he murmurs from behind me, arm circled around my waist. "You're doing great. Think you can get
your legs over?"

"Sure," I pant. "Right after I"—gasp—"finish running this
marathon."

His grip tightens, as if he thought I might be serious. Perhaps it's against lifeguard protocol to joke while you're on a rescue mission. I accidentally kick him and he lets out a soft gasp.

"Sorry."

"Relax for a second. I'll just hold you."

I muse at my stomach's ability to do somersaults, even after its owner has been starched and hung to dry.

I rest in Court's warm embrace until I can catch my breath again.

"You ready?"

No. "Yes." I push myself up over the surfboard, aided by Court who pops up on the other side to hold it steady. Then I'm once again lying on top of the wobbly mattress. Court grabs the flat end, and with more power than I thought he had left in his engine, kicks us back to shore.

We slide onto the sand, my mouth so parched and salty that my tongue feels like a piece of jerky. I'm vaguely aware of Court handing me a bottle, and then I'm glugging water down greedily. A searing sunset lights the ocean on fire.

We pull ourselves back up the cliff, though the going is slow, even with Court helping me. My head reels, and the giddiness in my stomach has spun into something more like nausea. Melanie's steamer feels tight and clammy, like it's eating me alive. My every movement causes the sand trapped inside to rub my already-raw skin. When Court finally unlocks the passenger door, I collapse in the seat with my legs hanging out, feeling dangerously close to throwing up. Court helps tug the suit off me. I don't care that the towel covering me slips, exposing my white legs. I just want the steamer off.

Then Court's back in the driver seat, somehow clothed again.

"You okay to drive home?" I murmur, too tired to move more than my head.

"Good as new." He feeds me a sweet grin.

My saliva must be pretty potent. He should be in the hospital. I sniff for confirmation that he's alert, but don't catch much beyond salt, and more salt. My nose must be worn out, too. I search his neck for signs of the bee sting, but don't see a single mark. "How?"

"I don't know."

His hands seem steady on the wheel, and his gaze, alert. I rub my eyes but the sand scratches my lids, so I shut them. Just a moment to recharge.

The next thing I know, we're in my driveway and Court is opening the door to the Jeep. He offers his hand, but I shake my head.

"I'm sorry I fell asleep," I croak, thirsty all over again.

"You needed it."

He collects my bike and bag. Soon, I am stumbling into the house. "Kitchen's over there if you want something to drink or eat. Mind if I go put something on?"

"Sure."

I ascend the staircase, taking a long whiff as I go. Dust motes. Pillow feathers. Dried violet blossoms. Thank the lilies, I still have my nose. Larkspur's Last Word didn't bite me.

Once in my bedroom, I step into clean underwear, then hastily wrap myself in my chenille bathrobe. It makes me look like a whorl of cotton candy, but after the suffocating grip of Melanie's steamer, it feels like heaven against my skin. I stick my head out the window and shake the sand out of my hair.

The creaking stair warns me that Court's on his way up.

"In here," I call out.

He appears holding two full glasses of water.

"Thank you. You saved my life."

He shrugs. "You saved mine, twice. So I still owe you." As we gulp down our glasses, his eyes take in each of my possessions: the stuffed alpaca, the chipped mirror that never lies to me, and my bamboo alarm clock that currently reads 7:06. The wainscot surrounding the room suddenly strikes me as babyish, like the rails of a crib.

"I can't believe I conked out. What happened?"

"Besides nearly drowning, you might have had vertigo. We learned about it in lifeguard school. The movement of the ocean can make you pass out." He sets his glass down on my dresser next to my empty vial of BBG. "I don't know how you did it, but you saved us. My throat was closing. I couldn't see straight and everything was cramping inside. But when you kissed me, all of it stopped. I felt strong again, like I could do a triathlon."

"I can't explain it. Mother says we're walking medicine cabinets."

"So as long as I have you around, I'll never fear a bee again."

"As long as I'm around, there will be bees. I'm like honey to them."

"You trying to scare me away?" He steps closer to me. "Because, if I had you around to kiss me, I might even want to get stung."

His gaze brushes my mouth, and I start babbling. "What happened to your board?" I don't remember him retrieving it after he helped me up the cliff.

"My board?" He takes my hand and tugs me even closer. His touch sends a shock down to my toes. "I sacrificed it to Poseidon. But your seaweed's safe. I left it in the garden."

My seaweed? Oh good gerbera, I nearly forgot. Most of the day is gone. I need to start sorting and processing the botanicals before everything loses its potency.

"You swam pretty good for someone who doesn't know how to swim." He puts his arms around me, goading my heart to a trot. "But when you let go, well, I've never been so scared in all my life."

Now he's studying my face like he did the room. His eyes rest on my forehead. Then they creep down to my nose with the bump. Finally, they land on my mouth, and there they stay for at least a count of ten. I'm sure he can hear my heart pounding, the *whoosh* of the blood racing through my veins, and maybe even the creaking of my knees as they buckle.

"I—I can't—" Larkspur's Last Word. I can't fall into the

trap. Think about Aunt Bryony. Mother.

"Can't what?" he asks softly.

"This." I stumble backward into the dress rack I forgot was behind me. I grab it before it falls.

"I don't think your spray works on me. You said it should work immediately. But even after you sprayed me the first time, it didn't change how I felt. I still spent a night writing cheesy Halloween poems for your candy grams."

The candy grams were from him?

"Then you sprayed me again at Meyer, and nothing changed for me. If anything, I have it worse now."

It doesn't make sense. Maybe the BBG went bad, though that's never happened before. Or maybe Court is immune. We've never come across a BBG-immunity before either, but it doesn't mean one can't exist. Of course, it would be my luck that the one person I've fallen for is the one person who is resistant. What am I talking about? I can't fall for anyone, especially right now, when I've already made such a muddle of things. It would muck up both of our lives, destroy everything I've worked for.

I attempt to organize my thoughts, but it's hard when he's standing just a few feet away. The Rulebook sits primly on my nightstand. A layer of dust dulls the gold lettering on its leather cover. I can smell the particles . . . actually, I can't smell the particles. Maybe it's not as dusty as I thought.

He closes the distance between us in one step, gazing at me with an intensity that makes every nerve in my body tingle.

My head feels floaty, like its full of helium, and it's not his smell that is causing it, but a hyperawareness of what could happen, of what could be. In fact, I can hardly smell the campfire scents. He encircles my waist with his hands, tugging me closer, tilting his head . . .

The phone rings. I jerk back at the sound. Mother. It's as if she knew.

I put my finger to my lips in the universal hush sign, then answer.

"Mim? I've been trying to call you for the last few hours."

"I was in the garden. I thought you weren't going to call until Sunday."

"Why do you sound out of breath?"

"Just running to get the phone."

"So what happened?"

"What h-happened? With what?"

"Ms. Salzmann."

"Ms. Salzmann." It takes me a few moments to remember. "Fine, she's fine. Everything went fine." I cringe. If I have to repeat fine three times, obviously things are not fine. "I delivered the flowers—the Prescott roses. She—"

"Oh, Mim." I can hear the disapproval even through the static.

She knows. Somehow, she can see through the phone to Court brushing sand off my cheek. I give him an apologetic smile and turn toward the window. "Yes?"

"Prescott says 'let's be friends,'" comes her breathy scolding. "I've told you that. Next time, try the Bourbon."

"Right." I nearly laugh with relief. "So, how are you doing?"

"You got my email, didn't you? You never replied."

"I haven't checked yet."

Court's cell phone rings. He hurries to silence it.

"What was that?"

"Just the computer." Dummy. The computer's in the workshop. Oh, but maybe *I'm* in the workshop. Come on, Mim, pull it together. Pretend he's not so close he could reach down and place a kiss on your neck. Everything is fine.

"So look at the pictures and tell me what you think."

"Pictures?"

Her sigh sounds like paper rattling. "In your *email*. You said the computer's on, right?"

"Right. Well ... hmm ... something seems to be wrong with the connection." I draw it out, like I'm actually waiting for my inbox to open. Court lifts his head from his cell phone.

"Oh, I'll just tell you. I saw these beaded bags at the market. One had a tiger, the other had a dolphin or whale or something. Which would you prefer?"

"Whale or something."

Court smiles.

"All right," says Mother. "Are you eating well?"

"Yes."

"Don't forget about tomorrow."

Tomorrow? Tomorrow. "Oh yes, Dr. Lipizzaner."

"Lipizzaner is a horse. *Lipinsky.*"

"Right."

"He's hard of hearing, so remember to speak loudly. Now, get some sleep tonight. Oh, but first, make sure the orchids are getting enough water. I'll call you Sunday."

"Okay."

Even after we hang up, I swear Mother's still in the room somewhere.

"Everything okay?" Court murmurs into my hair.

I spook away. "Yes. You?"

He sighs. "Coach is going to kill me for missing tonight's strategy meeting."

"Will he bench you?"

"I don't know. I'll have to talk to him. But I don't want to leave you."

"No, you should go. The Panthers need their captain." That, and if he stays any longer, I might be tempted to do something that would cause the Rulebook to spontaneously combust. I lead the way out of the room before I can change my mind. "And I should start your mom's elixir."

At the front door, I nearly push him into the driveway in my haste to avoid further romantic entanglement. He turns and stands firm in the doorway.

"Mim, we nearly died today. Maybe we should both take it easy."

"I will." I give him a too-bright smile.

"Okay, well, I'll see you tomorrow, right?" A dab of sand by one of his ears challenges me to rub it off, but I resist.

"Of course. Thank you for driving me today, and for everything else," I say in a rush. Before he construes that as an invitation, I firmly close the door.

I watch from the window as he backs out his Jeep, then motors off. Then I collapse on a rocking chair, a little trembly in the knees. As the chair gently rocks me, Court's eyes appear in my mind, dark like ash bark with hints of gold. His dimples seem perfectly placed in their asymmetry. I linger over the expressive line of his mouth, a mouth that tells me so much without speaking a word. And, then, of course, there is his smell—

My eyes pop open as I remember his mother's scentprint. I cannot sit here and daydream. Certain ideas, once they take hold, like the ruthlessly creeping kudzu plant, require years to eradicate. I'll need to avoid any further amorous encounters with Court before I can remake the BBG. Next time, I'll make it twice as concentrated.

Before I know it, my eyes blur. I bury my face in the Welcome Home pillow Mother embroidered when she was expecting me. The truth is, I don't want to BBG Court with a stronger dose. I *like* that he likes me. In her last letter to her love, Percy, before she died, Hyacinth wrote, *Somewhere between right and wrong lies a garden surrounded by thorns, and I have met you there.*

TWENTY-TWO

"Uproot your weeds by the root, lest,
like the heads of the hydra, they multiply,
destroying all in their path."
—*Angelica, Aromateur, 1723*

MORNING LIGHT FILTERS through the window of the storage room at the back of the workshop. The ottoman on which I'm sprawled is too short for a bed, but that didn't stop me from falling asleep on it after an intimate night with bladder wrack. I carefully dried each frond, then processed it into a fine powder.

A million things to do today, starting with a change of clothes. I'll have to skip school again. I'll probably be suspended before Mother can pull me out. What a waste, made even worse because there is no one to blame but myself.

I eye the phone. I need to talk to Kali, sort things out with her so she can sort things out for me. Yet, why should I call her? I'm the one who nearly died yesterday. She should be calling *me*.

Pettiness aside, would it kill her to be concerned or at least curious about my state of emergency? Not to mention, I really need to tell her that I kissed Court, an event that, though admittedly ambrosial, will probably come back to bite me one day.

Sniffing, I wipe away hot, indulgent tears. Kali must care. Haven't we plowed through our share of dirt together? I knew her back when she ate rival gangsters for lunch. She stuck by my side during those awful first weeks of school when people ran from me.

I dial. The sound of her cell phone ringing jangles my ear, and after several rings, her phone goes to voicemail. I can't help wondering if she saw it was me calling, and switched her phone off. I don't leave a message.

Still thinking about Kali, I scamper to the house for a quick bite, shielding my eyes in the bright glare. In the kitchen, I remove one of Mother's homemade raspberry granola bars from a canister. Instead of Brazil nuts and pumpkin seeds, the bar tastes wooden, almost as if I've bitten a chunk off the wall. Even the raspberry bits barely register on my taste buds. Strange. Maybe they went bad.

Something slick and queasy loops through me. I grimly head back into the garden, anxious more than ever to start on Alice's elixir. Several papayas dropped off the tree and lie squashed, black seeds oozing out like guts. I forgot all about harvesting them. Once they fall, the seeds are useless for elixirs.

I brake so abruptly, I nearly knock my knee out of joint. Why did I have to *see* the papayas before I knew they were rotten? Why didn't I *smell* them first? I point my nose toward the tree and inhale. I definitely smell the rotting papayas, like stinky socks, but only because I'm searching for it. My hand flies to my nose. It feels stuffed up, like I caught a cold.

My skin breaks out in goose bumps. I race to the workshop.

Another bud has started growing out of the center stalk of Layla's Sacrifice. A sister bud means the plant should be twice as fragrant. I line the floors with thick towels in case I faint. The glass lid rattles as I close my trembling fingers around the knob. It occurs to me, the habañero scent of panic dribbling off me should be a lot stronger, given my current levels of stress, but I will know soon enough. I brace myself. If my nose is fine, I'll definitely pass out once I lift the lid. One, two . . .

I lift off the cover.

The juicy sour scents of marmalade waft up to my nostrils and cheerfully hum. But I'm still standing, at least, kneeling. I'm not even dizzy.

I replace the cover and crumple over my knees. My eyes fill with hot tears, and Mother's words ring in my head. *Her ability to smell faded away like summer sweet peas.*

Pushing open the workshop door, I run around the garden, smelling plant after plant. I step onto a stool and inhale the blue star juniper tentacling out of a hanging container. It's an unmistakable scent, like a baby Christmas tree, but today I can barely distinguish it from the skyrocket juniper growing beside it.

I jump off the stool and crouch by the common herbs rosemary, tarragon, oregano, sage—notes that are notorious for bossing other scents around. Tearing off handfuls of the plants more carelessly than I should, I crush them under my nose.

It's useless. They're a bunch of shrinking wallflowers, all of them. I collapse onto a patch of dwarf grass and put my head in my arms.

I tempted fate by going to school. I lied to Mother, defied the rules, and gave Larkspur the finger. No wonder my nose is becoming ordinary.

Mother would understand that I needed to save Court's life, but not why I lied to her. For that matter, did I have to *kiss* him? A little spit on his bee sting—that might've done the trick. Why didn't I think of that?

I didn't think of that because I wanted to kiss him. *That* was my undoing. My stomach roils at the thought that I may never smell again. I wouldn't be able to help Mother with the elixirs. I'd only be able to clear branches and weed like Kali, but unlike Kali, I don't have anything else to aspire to, no other talents to build on. Plus, I'd have to face Mother's disappointment in me, day after tedious day.

I drag myself back to the kitchen where Mother left the number to the cell phone she carries in case of emergency. I pick up the receiver of our old kitchen telephone with the curly wire and begin to punch in the numbers. Before the call connects, I hang up. I need some Kali therapy, first. She would know what to do. At the very least, she could recite a last poem of solace before I march to the gallows.

But before Kali's phone rings, I replace the receiver. She can see that I called not even an hour ago. She must not want to talk to me. A hot colony of misery blooms inside me.

I dial Mother's emergency number. As I wait for the line to be connected, I knead my knuckles into my temple. *Mother, you might want to sit down.* No. If I say that, she'll think someone died. That's what they always say when someone dies.

The phone rings. Once, twice.

Mother, I blew it. No, too much too soon. Ease into it. Make small talk first, ask how the palm trees are.

Three rings, four. Finally, an answer. I squeeze the phone to my ear. "We're sorry, all circuits are busy right now. Please hang up and try your call later."

Busy? This is an emergency! I hang up and dial again.

Same message. After trying for a third time and getting nowhere, I suddenly worry about her safety. I hurry to the workshop where we keep our only computer.

The old PC whirrs to life. Egypt's latest headline: record-breaking heat of 108 degrees. Nothing newsworthy is happening in the Middle East either besides the usual oil-price acrobatics.

I try calling again, but no luck. Even if I did reach her, the most she could do is scold me. It'll take her at least a day to return, maybe two, and that's assuming she gets the jet. By then, Alice could be baking Mr. Frederics a wedding cake.

I pace the length of the workshop, forcing myself not to panic. Maybe it's a cold. It's flu season, isn't it? My ears are ringing, too, and my head feels like someone stuffed it with Styrofoam peanuts. I am a human being after all, and I did nearly drown yesterday.

Ten. I was ten the only time I had a cold. I could hardly smell my breakfast, and the loss immobilized me as much as if I had suddenly gone blind. Mother wiped my tears and tucked me into bed with *The Complete Fairy Tales* by Hans Christian Andersen. By the time I finished the last one—*The Steadfast Tin Soldier*—I was good as new.

Only time will tell. Meanwhile, I'm wasting daylight wearing down the floorboards. I need to get on that elixir. If my nose is on the way out, I have to make it before it fades completely.

Staring through the fist-size indentation in the floorboard, I review the plants I will need for Alice's elixir. Moss oak, protea majora, Jupiter grass . . . I groan. I still need to collect that one from the school field. Jupiter grass needs to be harvested when the sun's shining and its oil's at full potency. Of course, it's just my luck that the day is overcast.

Grimly, I head back to the house. Guess I'll be going to school after all. At least I won't arrive until after Cardio, which might be the only good thing I can squeeze out of this day.

TWENTY-THREE

"Two hearts in synchronicity have little use for our magic."
—*Wisteria, Aromateur, 1935*

THE SUN STILL ducks behind a gloomy curtain of clouds by the time I roll into the parking lot of SGHS. The clouds usually burn off by noon, but what if they don't? Lady Luck and I haven't been on speaking terms lately.

Overnight, the homecoming fairies visited, leaving streamers and signs everywhere, like Go Panthers! and Eat Our Shorts, Bulldogs. I even spot one that reads Warrior Sawyer Kicks Ass, with a picture of a donkey, checkered white and black like a soccer ball.

An image of Court's easy smile slips into my head, but I try my best to banish it. If there's any chance of recovering my nose, then I will have to be on my best behavior. There is no PUF for aromateurs, no shortcut around heartbreak to make me forget that exquisite sparkle of joy at his touch, the warm safety in his arms—not that I want to. But if being in love is causing me to lose my nose, maybe falling out of love will make it return.

Kali's bike is missing, once again. She's becoming as delinquent as I am. Maybe she *is* sick. Or maybe she's avoiding Cardio, or worse, me. I swallow the sour taste in my mouth. I might be able to cross the tightrope of my error eventually, but it will be twice as hard without my six-foot safety net. Maybe this is the problem with having so few people in my life. The ones I have count more than they should.

Then again, maybe they shouldn't count at all.

Too late, I begin to understand why our ancestor Carmelita cautioned in her Last Word to catch a heart before it falls. Attachments, whether romantic or filial, just lead to disappointment and pain, emotions that distract us from our life's work.

Though I try not to look, my gaze travels through the library windows to Ms. DiCarlo, hunched over her desk. Towers of books form a wall in front of her, but I can see her in profile. She puts her head in her hands, as if it's too heavy to support. The wistful wisteria notes lay heavy and talc-like all around her. Oh, for peat moss' sake, I need to start parking my bike somewhere else. She spots me through the window and gives me a smile so tight, it might shatter.

With a sigh, I head into the library.

"Good morning, Ms. DiCarlo." I peek over the skyline of books. Her eyes are bloodshot and begin to water.

230

"Oh, hello," she says in a falsely bright voice. "Shouldn't you be in class?"

"I'm late today. Is everything okay?"

She sniffs loudly. "Yes, everything is fine." She takes a book off her pile and runs it through a bar code scanner. *Beep.* "Something must be in the air."

I scratch under my straw hat, trying to decide if the situation requires more conversation. Suddenly, she sneezes three times in a row, slinging her red curls around her shoulders. She tugs a tissue from a box.

"Well, if there's anything I can do, just let me know." I inch away.

She dabs her watery eyes, and says in a conspiratorial whisper. "I sent out twenty queries."

"Oh, that's nice," I say hesitantly.

"It's hard to know what anyone's looking for nowadays, but I'm hoping the right one comes along. If all twenty reject me, I might need a long vacation." She dabs at her eyes.

She must be using an online dating service. I can't help feeling guilty about that, even though online dating services are perfectly viable tools. Elixirs are just more organic.

She misreads my queasy expression. "Oh, you think twenty is too many? Maybe I should've started small."

"No," I quickly say. "I'm happy for you. Mother likes to say, the bees don't land on unopened flowers."

Ms. DiCarlo looks at me like I have aluminum foil antennae in my hair. Another sneeze comes between us and she holds her tissue to her nose. "Thank you, Mim." The tissue waves up and down, telling me to leave already.

I arrive several minutes late to algebra. The sight of another pink pastry box sitting cheerfully on Mr. Frederics's desk strikes fear in my heart the same as if it were a bomb. Alice struck again, despite the yard sales.

As quietly as I can, I slip into my desk. Mr. Frederics raises an eyebrow at my tardiness, but doesn't say anything. Vicky, at her desk in the center of the room, lets the shiny necklace she's chewing fall from her mouth when she sees me. The elixir must be working by now. But will she fall in love before she publishes Kali's journal? She shifts back around.

"Very good." Mr. Frederics beams as Val Valedictorian completes a problem on the board in her neat block letters. Though her answer requires the entire board to complete, I have to sniff hard to pick up the marker fumes.

Mr. Frederics taps the board. "This is exactly the kind of problem you might find on the final."

"What?" cries someone. "That's stupid hard."

He gives the kid a hard eyeball, then chuckles. "Math is like love, isn't it? Simple, yet, so complicated."

A few people laugh, but not Melanie, who grimaces. She

catches me watching her, and I shift my gaze to the window. Still overcast.

"Who will do problem number five from your homework?" Mr. Frederics's gaze sweeps over the classroom and lands on me, the tardy one. I freeze for a moment. Not only do I not know the answer, I don't know the question. I shuffle through my folder for the homework pages when Drew's chair squeaks behind me. Oh, sweet relief. It's not me.

As Drew completes the problem, everyone copies it down. Everyone but Vicky, who's watching Drew's derriere shake as he flourishes his numbers with flags and scrolls.

She rouses herself from her daze, and a flush creeps up her face.

Oh my, she's definitely coming down with something, either the common cold, or the love bug. Symptoms can be similar: hot and cold flashes, nausea, difficulty breathing. Maybe that will teach you to pick on someone your own size, and by size, I mean ego-wise.

At last, the bell sounds. "Great work today everybody," says Mr. Frederics over the noise of people scrambling to leave.

Drew stuffs his notebook into his frayed backpack. "Hey, Mim?"

"Yes?"

His pale skin makes his blue eyes pop. He glances at the paper on my desk. "Can I still sign up for Puddle Jumpers?"

"Sure. Algebra?"

He blinks. "Huh?"

"You want extra credit for algebra, right?"

"No, I just wanted to hang out with the kids."

My cheeks warm. "Oh, right."

"I like kids. My mom's a kindergarten teacher."

"That's cool. You must get killer bedtime stories."

"Yeah, we do 'Wheels on the Bus' every night, too." He smiles, lifting me momentarily from my mushroom cloud of anxiety. He's wearing clear braces. Once his teeth don't stick out so much, he might find that more girls than Vicky are attracted to him.

The itchy guilt makes me fidget. Maybe I don't have the ethical backbone to be an aromateur after all, fixing a minor with an innocent party like Drew, even if he did have a crush on her. If I ever get my nose back, perhaps I should consider a career in drug detection, or truffle hunting.

I shove those thoughts away. There'll be plenty of time later to wallow in guilt. Right now, I need to get the Jupiter grass. I hurry outside and scan the skies. Still, not a single break in the gray blanket overhead.

TWENTY-FOUR

"O HUMBLE GARDENIA! HIDDEN AMONG BASE-LYING BUSH.
YOUR HEAD MAY BE SMALL, AND PALE BE YOUR FACE, BUT
MY! HOW THE CREATURES ADORE YOU."
—Sorrelia, *Aromateur*, 1645

FINALLY, THE LUNCH bell rings, and right on schedule, the clouds burn off. Time to collect the Jupiter grass, then check out early.

I hurry to the field. The soccer players are drilling, which isn't surprising, given the upcoming game. As I draw closer to the field, I spy Court's familiar form, feet moving quicker than a sandpiper's. He taps the ball left, then pivots to catch it again, throwing his opponent off balance. It's mesmerizing. The cheerleaders scream his name, but he doesn't even look up.

Mother calls that kind of focus "the flow." Once you're in, you connect with your task so closely that doing it is almost an act of magic. It's the same way with elixirs. When we focus on the scents, they sing to us in all their complex glory. Mixing a potion is just a matter of choosing the right singers for the chorus.

Hopefully, Court's so involved in his game he won't notice me.

A patch of Jupiter grass grows where the cement ends. I drop down on still-wet lawn and comb through the hairy weed. A handful of students eye me suspiciously, but I ignore them.

I pluck off a tendril and sniff. Jupiter grass always announces itself like a soprano hitting high C. But today, it's just a background voice.

Swiping my forehead with my sleeve, I pluck another, and another. They're no stronger than the first. The sun is shining, strong enough to give me a tan, but everything is so weak, even weaker than the papaya this morning. Come on, nose, don't go yet.

Someone calls my name. In front of me, Whit Wu appears, giving me a grin and flipping his ponytail. I didn't even smell him coming.

"Hi there." He shakes out his lanky legs, the kind that require an aisle seat. There's a natural pout to his mouth, and his olive skin is blemish-free. I sniff by reflex, but only catch the synthetic fragrance of his deodorant.

"Hi." I silently implore him to leave so I can continue panicking in peace.

He reaches into the front pocket of his sweatpants, but whatever he's searching for isn't forthcoming, so he tries the ones in the back. Not there, either.

"Don't you need to practice?"

He cocks his head to one side, exposing a jawline straight enough to chart courses. "Nah. We got this. Coach is taking us to Spaghetti Station for carb upload tonight. So you coming?"

"Spaghetti Station?"

He chuckles. "No. The game."

"Oh, yes."

Now he's checking the inside pockets of his sweatpants. What's he looking for? What does he want from me? And how many pockets do you need to play soccer?

I know I couldn't have infected him. I only see him when he's on the field—except the last time when the soccer ball hit me in the parking lot. His soccer ball.

I grimace. I must have contaminated Whit's soccer ball with aromateur's pollen. Voilà, infection.

Whit finally finds what he wants. Chapstick. Cherry-flavored. He pops off the cap and draws it on his mouth in two quick circles. "You like miniature golf?"

I rein back my horror and reflexively reach for my BBG. Then I remember that it's sitting on my dresser at home, empty. "It's not really my thing. Er, do you?"

Court appears from behind Whit, and wipes his brow with his arm. "Hi."

I drum up a smile. "Hello."

Whit looks from me to Court.

I could just tell Whit I infected him. That usually undupes the duped, though it can get messy, and he could refuse the BBG once I remake it.

Whit turns his back on Court, and cracks his knuckles. "All

righty then, well, I was wondering if you wanted to, uh—"

Court clears his voice loudly. "Hey, Whit! Coach says tow in or he'll tow it for you."

Whit groans. "I'll be there in a sec."

Court doesn't budge. "He said, now."

"All right. Chill."

Court's eyes shift to a spot somewhere behind me.

I turn around to see Vicky picking her way toward us. The realization that I didn't smell her approaching, despite her severe risk rating on my personal security advisory system, nearly causes me to fall. Inhaling deeply, I catch only the fragments of her skulking black elder. The celery top note barely registers.

"Hey, guys," she says.

"Hey." Court's tone flattens.

Her eyes fall to me, squatting in her shadow, and become flinty. "What *ever* are you doing?"

A clump of Jupiter grass rolls off my knee. "Weeding."

She gasps-laughs in a way that says, "Loser." Then her attention locks on Court. "We're going to get froyo after school. Want to come?"

"Sorry, we've got practice."

Vicky squeezes her Gucci purse so hard, I think I hear it scream.

Court glances back at the coach, who has his hands on his hips and is glaring at all four of us. "Come on, Whit, we gotta go."

Whit curses. "Can't we have a little privacy?"

Vicky's chalky red lips thin into a smile. "Who? You and Mimosa?"

Whit's head bobs up and down and he looks at me like he wants to eat me. "Yeah."

Court glares at Whit. "No."

The coach blows his whistle and beckons his players back with his hands.

"See you later." Court grabs Whit and tows him back to the field.

Vicky's nose wrinkles, and she pierces me with her gaze. "See *who* later?"

"You."

She crosses her arms and her pupils don't budge from mine for a full five seconds.

At last, she relaxes her stance and flips back her hair. "Well, maybe it's working, finally." She turns on her heel and stomps away.

Desperately, I twist off handfuls of Jupiter grass and stuff them in a canvas bag, past caring about quality. Clustered with his teammates, Court watches me. My stomach twists into a knot as the memory of his sweet taste now fills me with dread.

TWENTY-FIVE

"Trade a flower for a smile.
Give a pumpkin and reap a grin."
—Cassis, *Aromateur, 1689*

I DON'T BOTHER filing an excuse with the secretary. I just pedal home as fast as I can, though a bullying headwind fights me all the way. The clouds coming in from the coast roll out over the sky. Rain wasn't in the forecast, but maybe the sky changed its mind when it saw me biking.

At least I got that Jupiter grass. First, I have to process it and the other ingredients that need to be steeped over night. Then, I'll have to pray I still have enough of my nose left tomorrow to blend them.

By the time I pull into our courtyard I'm so full of adrenaline, I could pedal all the way to the moon without stopping.

The left half of the Virginia creeper that frames the workshop door swapped its green coat for red overnight. If I had my nose, I would've known that happened before I even stepped out of the house. I should get used to figuring things out by sight or sound. Too bad those senses can't help me make elixirs.

As I unlock the door, some of the Virginia creeper's pinwheel-like leaves drop on my head.

I arrange all the plants on the familiar worktable, grouping them by the methods of oil extraction. In one pile, I put the specimens that I will wrap in muslin and steep in sweet almond oil. In a second pile, I gather the ones I will run through our copper distillers. Plants in the last pile, larger than the first and second combined, require pressing through a vise-like contraption called a cold press. Those, I will save for last.

I work faster than I ever have, sniffing like a hound dog every few seconds to gauge any change in my nose. Soon, I lose myself in the physical work of prepping the ingredients. I shred ash bark and pommel pomegranate seeds, break yucca strips into fine threads and cut the bad spots off alder leaves with tiny scissors. Then I warm a kukui nut in my palm that's the exact shade of Court's eyes. The memory of our one kiss halts all other thoughts, and I replay it in my mind for a guilty moment.

One of the distillers begins to boil over. I dash to the burner and adjust it lower. Wrong way! The flame shoots higher and I burn my hand. Quickly, I switch it off and run my hand in the sink, cursing myself for spacing out. Mistakes happen when you're not paying attention. I never seem to learn.

Groaning, I rub aloe vera onto my burned skin, then get back to work. With my left hand now, I mince pine needles. Sweat drips down my forehead, stinging my eyes.

My nose begins to bleed, forcing me to take another break. The duller my sense of smell becomes, the harder I have to sniff. If it vanishes by tomorrow, I won't be able to gauge the right proportions for the elixir. Might as well make a cake without measuring cups.

My breath comes in short gasps, and it feels as if someone is using my heart as a punching bag. More from desperation than logic, I cross the room to the computer.

"How to fall out of love," I type.

My search generates forty-six million results. I click on the first link.

> **Tip 1: Make a list of all the reasons why it wasn't meant to be.**

My list isn't long: loss of livelihood.

> **Tip 2: Remove all traces of him from your life.**

Also easy, since I won't be attending SGHS for much longer.

> **Tip 3: Practice thought stopping.**

Every time I think about him, I should say, out loud, *stop*. Are they kidding?

I try calling Mother again. The line is still busy.

I wipe my sweating palms on my apron and rummage through the cabinets to find the lavender to calm myself. Even if I can't smell it as well as I used to, it still works, in the same way loud music can damage your hearing even if you're not listening.

My twitchy hands fumble the bottle, and with a clunk, it shimmers across the floorboards.

I pick up the bottle, managing to save a few last drops. The spill quickly transforms into a wet spot on the floor. I don't notice I'm crying until I feel the sting of the salt water on my cheeks.

My knees scrape against the hard floor. I'm drowning in a sea of plant debris, staring at a stain that looks suspiciously like a surfboard. But unlike yesterday, there will be no rescue for me here. If only Mother and I weren't the only love witches on the planet.

Wait a minute. Aunt Bryony.

Though she can't use her nose anymore, my aunt was a love witch. Maybe she knows how to fall out of love. At the least, maybe she'll give me a place to stay when Mother disowns me.

I go to the People Finder website. How many Bryonys could there be in Hawaii? I hope she didn't move. How many Bryonys could there be in the United States? The world?

A man's voice calls out, and even though it's faint, I jump.

"Hello? Anyone home?"

I freeze as I remember. Dr. Lipinsky. I'm scheduled to do his intake, though I can hardly do that now with this bare excuse of a nose. For a moment, I'm tempted to hide out here in the workshop. But the poor man drove all the way from Santa Barbara.

"Coming!" I call back.

A stooped figure stands midway down the path of stones. I hurry to him.

Mother said Dr. Lipinsky was in his seventies. But this man before me couldn't be more than fifty. When he sees me, he straightens his slim posture. He's fit and neatly put together, with combed hair parted straight down the middle. His pressed pants break neatly over his shined shoes.

"I'm sorry, the gate was open." He gestures behind him. "I'm Dr. Lipinsky."

I paste on a smile. "That's okay, we were expecting you. I'm Mim." Welcome to my house of horrors.

"Nice to meet you." He reaches out his hand, but I don't shake it.

"I'm sorry, we're not supposed to shake people's hands. Contamination."

An eyebrow lifts.

"How was your drive?" I quickly ask. Maybe I can convince him to give up his shirt, and then Mother can scent it out later. Or even a sock. He'd probably prefer driving home with a bare foot over a bare chest.

"My drive? Er, fine."

He'll think I'm crazy. *Hello, nice to meet you, now could you take off your sock?* My knuckles crack as I crunch a fist.

He straightens his bow tie. "See, the thing is—"

"I'm sorry," I blurt out, on the verge of blubbering now. "I can't help you today."

His eyes grow a fraction, then he scratches his head. "Oh. Well, I think you have the wrong idea. Because I'm not the Dr. Lipinsky you're expecting."

"Oh? There are two of you?"

"My father passed away just days ago. It was out of the blue, a heart attack."

My troubles recede into the background. "I'm very sorry for your unexpected loss."

He nods, his mouth grim. "Well, it was quick and he was seventy-one. They sent a real bugler to play 'Taps.' He served in Vietnam."

"Oh wow. Was he in combat?"

"Sure. Got a Purple Heart." His nose pinkens, and he sniffs.

"May I get you something to drink?"

"I'm fine."

"I'm sorry you had to drive all this way."

"I live just ten minutes away. I called, but the line was busy, so I thought I'd just stop by on my way home." He sticks his hands in his pockets and stares at a cluster of rosebushes.

"Would you like some roses?" It's the least I could do. Somehow I dodged a bullet, but not in a way I would have wanted.

"I'm afraid we can't have flowers in the office because of our patients' allergies."

"If you don't mind me asking, what kind of doctor are you?"

"An otolaryngologist."

"Excuse me?"

He smiles. "Ear, nose, and throat."

Nose? Why not? I have nothing to lose. "Um, Doctor, could you tell if I have a cold?"

"Probably. Haven't you had a cold before?"

"When I was ten, but I don't remember much about it."

"What about allergies?"

"No."

"Well, what are your symptoms?"

"I can't smell. I mean, I can smell, but not *smell* smell." What the heck does that mean?

His forehead creases. "Any coughing? Malaise? Phlegm? Fever?"

I shake my head.

The doctor reaches out toward my face. "Mind if I?"

"Okay, but first I have to get something." I wave my hand at a bench. "Please make yourself comfortable."

I dash to the garage. Pulling my sleeve over my hand, I rummage through a cabinet for surgical gloves. We use them to handle plants that stain. At least doctors are accustomed to wearing gloves. I better make that BBG ASAP.

Bloody bladder wrack. I can't make BBG without my nose.

I return to the doctor and hand him the gloves. "Here you go."

He draws back in surprise, but takes the gloves. "Oh, well, thank you."

After snapping them on, he feels both sides of my throat below my jaw. "Mm hm." Then he pulls what looks like a pen from his pocket. It turns out to be a mini-flashlight. He shines it into my eyes, then peeks down my throat, my nose, and in both ears.

Switching off the light, he announces, "Good news. You don't have a cold or allergies."

My heart sinks. I knew it. Now it's been confirmed by a medical expert. "Are you sure?"

"Pretty sure. You look disappointed."

"Oh no. Sometimes I just look disappointed when I'm really not disappointed." I perk up my expression though I'm cringing inside. Still a horrible liar. Some things will never change.

He peels off his gloves and hands them back to me. "Well, if you start having any, er, symptoms, feel free to call me." Removing a business card from his wallet, he hands it to me. "I don't want to keep you. Do I owe you anything?"

"Owe? Of course not. I'm sorry about your father again. If I can't get you flowers, would you like to choose a pumpkin?" I look toward our pumpkin patch, twenty feet away, where gourds shaped like turbans and bottles form an odd junkyard of squash.

"That sounds wonderful. A pumpkin would sure cheer up my quiet apartment." He chooses a tangerine one shaped like a turban, and then I walk him back to the gate. He surveys the garden as we go, eyes brighter than when he came in. "My dad would've loved this garden. He was a big gardener. Ever since losing his sight."

"You mean, he was blind?"

"That's how he got the Purple Heart. Never let it stop him, though. He won state awards for his cloud forest orchids."

"Cloud forest orchids are notoriously fussy."

"Exactly."

"But he couldn't see them."

"Not the usual way."

I visualize an older version of Dr. Lipinsky with dark shades over his eyes, gently rummaging through the leaves of a lush orchid. He understood, like aromateurs, that a flower's beauty is more than visual, and not even blindness stopped him from pursuing that beauty.

Somehow, the thought gives me a poppy seed of hope.

He offers a smile and extends his hand for a final shake.

"Oh, I don't want to get you sick," I say.

His eyebrows lift. Maybe now he agrees I'm sick, but not with a cold. "Thanks for the squash."

TWENTY-SIX

"NEVER USE PENNYROYAL.
ITS NAME MEANS, 'YOU HAD BETTER GO.'"
—*Nasreen, Aromateur, 1840*

IF AUNT BRYONY took on a last name when she got married, Mother never mentioned it. People Finder brings up over three hundred Bryonys in the United States alone. Who knew it was such a popular name? I take a side trip to search *Mimosa* and find even more.

Next, I narrow my Bryony search by typing in *Hawaii*. Seven results. I pick up the phone and start dialing.

Of the seven, two are wrong numbers, two are definitely not Aunt Bryony judging by the accents, and three are answering machines. I leave messages on all three machines. Again, I try calling Mother's emergency number but get the same irritating message.

Finally, I attempt Kali's cell once again, clasping the receiver anxiously to my ear while her phone rings. This time, her nineteen-year-old brother, Mukmuk, answers the phone. "Hey, Mim. Kali's asleep."

It could be an excuse, but Kali has never deceived me before. "Is she okay?"

"Yeah, why?"

I better not say anything in case her brother doesn't know she's been skipping classes. "She's usually a night owl. Just tell her I called."

"'Kay. Hang loose."

She has to come to school tomorrow. We've been planning this event together for months and a hundred Puddle Jumpers are counting on us. This was my chance to show the school that they need not fear me, that I can be fun. Not to mention, I have to make sure that whatever Mr. Frederics is planning to surprise Ms. DiCarlo does not cause further catastrophe. If by some miracle, his "secret weapon" does entice Ms. DiCarlo into his arms, it would come at the expense of Alice. I simply need to maintain the status quo until I can fix her. *If* I can fix her.

After I finish steeping all the plants that need steeping, I slog through the leaves piling in the courtyard to get back to the house. It must be close to nine.

I draw a hot bath infused with rosemary and eucalyptus, hoping they might improve my olfaction, but . . . nothing. Sinking up to my neck, I consider the bleakness of my situation.

I won't be able to do anymore tonight. The distilled plants have been extracted, the steeped plants need time to steep, and the third pile of cold-pressed plants can't be mixed until tomorrow or they'll go bad. If my nose fails completely by the time everything's ready to mix, I'll have to make the PUF from my memory of the strengths of the ingredients. It will be a rough approximation, but I don't have much of a choice.

I heave myself out of the tub and towel off, rubbing my face extra hard as if I could erase the grimace there. The door chime rings.

I grab my robe and pad downstairs. If I still had my nose, I could tell who's on the other side without opening the door, assuming I know the person. But now, I have to find out the normal way. The peephole.

Court leans against the post holding up our entryway, his hands in the pockets of his Panthers hoodie.

My chest suddenly feels tight. Court doesn't know about my nose, about what our kiss cost me. And I can't tell him, because he would blame himself. Besides, telling him wouldn't change a thing. I'd still have to let him go. If there was a chance I could get my nose back, Mother would surely demand it.

I consider pretending I'm not home, but then he might worry. I'm not ready for this. Not now, not here. Tomorrow's the big game, anyway. I'll tell him after the half-time show, when there's less at stake for him.

I open the door. His eyes crinkle into half moons and he points the toe of his sneaker. "Hi."

"Hi." How is it possible for him to be so shyly awkward and

hot at the same time? His smile broadens and he glances toward the driveway, as if his own smile embarrasses him. What were those tips again? Tip 3: Practice thought stopping. But how am I supposed to not think about him when he's standing right in front of me?

My heart turns a cartwheel as his gaze skims down my pink chenille robe.

"I'm starting to develop a weird craving for cotton candy." He leans down and tries to kiss me, but I step back.

"I think I have a cold. And I would hate for you to catch it."

His eyebrows draw together. "We shouldn't stand out here then." He hangs an arm around my shoulders and ushers me back into the house. "Can I do anything? I'm pretty good at opening soup cans. I can even do those childproof Tylenol bottles." He looks down at me with a goofy grin.

I turn to face him so his arm drops off me. Clutching at the plushy weave of my robe, I shift from foot to foot. "No, thank you. I'll be fine. How's your mom?"

"I found a book on her nightstand."

"Another cookbook?"

"Worse. *How to Ask Out a Man and Keep Him.* I think she's going to make a move tomorrow night. Melanie said Mom bought herself four-hundred-dollar jeans for the game."

"I thought your aunt was keeping her occupied."

"She left this morning, but don't freak. The earliest they can kiss is at the game. She's busy all tomorrow with alumni stuff.

How's the potion making going?"

"Haven't finished it yet." My voice goes high and slightly hysterical, but I clamp my lips together. "I'm prepping the ingredients."

"Hey, it's okay." He reaches out to take my hand, but I shake my head.

"Germs."

"You know, maybe it's not such a bad thing, Mom tripping over Mr. Frederics. I admit, I never thought it would work. They're so different. I mean, he's—"

I fill in the blank. Poor? Bald? Obsessive about recycling his Ziploc Baggies?

He shakes his head. "He seems like he has his act together. Mom's a bit of a wreck. But who am I to judge? She seems happy for once. Maybe she's finally over Dad."

"But it's not supposed to be that way. Mr. Frederics likes Ms. DiCarlo. Your mother might get hurt."

"I know. But you can't score if you're always playing defense." His voice lowers. "We wouldn't be here if you didn't take a risk on me. And I feel so good, I could win tomorrow's game all by myself."

His words pull my emotions all out of shape. His smile is weak as a shoestring and even his eyes are full of wonder. If he keeps looking at me that way, I might jump into his arms and beg him to take me to the moon. Somewhere with no flowers to remind me of my failure, only space and starlight.

My shoulders slump. The ceiling feels like it's sagging down on top of me. Even my robe weighs me down. "I'm sorry, I'm a little beat."

"Okay, I'll let you rest. Do you want me to get you a burger? Dad always got us McDonald's when we were sick. Oh, right. You don't eat those. Maybe I should—"

"I'll be fine."

After another long look at me, he kisses me on the forehead, leaving a warm imprint there. "Good night, Mim. Feel better soon."

"Thanks."

After he leaves, I lean on the door to prevent myself from flinging it back open and running after him. I don't move until I hear his Jeep start up and power away.

The rooster's crowing. I bolt upright in my bed and sniff.

Still can't smell the dust motes. But, am I worse than yesterday?

I shower and wiggle into fresh clothes, then hurry back to the workshop.

Now the Virginia creeper has completely switched its spring coat for autumn attire. Traffic-light red. I sniff a leaf, but only get a vague impression of its ivy-like scent.

I'm tempted to return to my bed and throw another pity party under the covers. But pity is a luxury I have to save for later.

In the workshop, the two tendrils of Layla's Sacrifice spread out in opposite directions like the plant's opening its arms to me. I rip off the glass cover and inhale.

Now, instead of the jam-like humming of marmalade, all I get is its shadow, quickly fading to nothing.

My nose has become ordinary, or, as Mother would say, useless.

The room tilts and my locked knees suddenly sag. Though I'd been dreading this moment of truth, now that it's here, I feel weirdly calm, or maybe just numb. At least now I don't have to worry about losing my nose anymore. It's gone. Gone.

I drop into my place at the worktable.

Breathe. Clear your mind. Mother says that before we work, we need a tabula rasa, a blank mind, since so much of what we do requires sensing, not reflection.

But now, I can't sense, only think. The plants, once my only company, seem to turn their shoulders to me, cloaking their scents like strangers. I run my fingers over the narcissuses that William the handyman carved into the table, but the ritual brings me no comfort. On the edge of panic now, I grab a twig of partridge berries and set it between the steel plates of the vise. Keep moving.

I crank out oils by brute force, until the sun's rays light up the terrariums, meaning it's around eleven. All sense of self-respect has evaporated by now and I try Kali's cell not once, but three times. No answer. Maybe this is how a friendship dies. One blast of hot air is enough to kill a begonia, but I hoped our friendship could weather more than one argument.

Grimly, I set off for school. Puddle Jumpers starts at noon. I'll just take care of the event and be back by one thirty. If I don't finish the elixir in time for the big game, at least it will have been for a good cause.

TWENTY-SEVEN

PRINCIPAL SWIZINGER AND a bunch of adults wearing orange shirts stand in the field surrounded by folding tables. The tables bear washtubs of produce, from shiny eggplant to bloodred tomatoes. A banner proclaims, "Fruits and Vegetables Love Our Bodies."

There's no sign of Kali anywhere. Principal Swizinger points at me and a woman with a blond crew cut hurries over. "Mimosa, right? I'm Hope. Thank you so much for helping us."

"You're welcome."

Hope scratches the side of her head with her pencil. "Is Kali coming?"

"I'm not sure. She hasn't been feeling well."

"Oh, that's too bad. We sure appreciate all the work she put in. Kids should be here in fifteen. Do you mind checking people in?"

"Of course not."

"Great." The woman hands me a clipboard. "Here are the teams, and those are the shirts." She nods at a box under one of the tables. "Have people wait by their traffic cones."

"Got it."

The woman leaves.

Students drift out from the main buildings. Most hang back when they see me. I stifle my irritation. I promise not to touch you or breathe in your face. "Step right up. Todd Sze, Ann Abrams, you're both on Team Eight. Take a shirt and find your cone."

Those at the back of the line start pressuring those in the front to hurry up, and soon I have a crowd on my hands. I strain my eyes for signs of the math teacher and the librarian, and finally spot them approaching from the lunch tables. This is the first time I've seen them together. I can't read their chemistry anymore, but they aren't exactly brimming with conversation, which for the moment, is good. Ms. DiCarlo lifts her feet, but her heels keep sinking into the grass.

"Hi, Mr. Frederics and Ms. DiCarlo." I sniff, trying to read their chemistry, even though it's futile. Nothing but sunscreen and grass. "We decided to separate the adults this year to even out the competition. So, Mr. Frederics, you're on Team Two, and Ms. DiCarlo, you're on Team Eleven."

Ms. DiCarlo spreads the neck of her T-shirt wide as she maneuvers it around her hairdo. Mr. Frederics makes eye contact with me, pupils shifting meaningfully to Ms. DiCarlo, who's still tented in her shirt. I give him an apologetic shrug, and tick my head toward Principal Swizinger, as if she made me do it. His mouth rounds into an O and he nods. He tugs on his shirt. "You know, Ms. DiCarlo, eleven is very special. Do you know why?"

"It's the first number we can't count on our fingers?"

"Well, yes." His zinc-smeared nose bobs up and down as he nods. "But it's also the fifth smallest prime number." He slips on a baseball cap. "You know, my colleagues used to call me the human calculator." He winks at me. Is this the secret weapon? "Give me any problem and I'll do it in my head. Go on."

Ms. DiCarlo frowns, eyes bobbing around as she thinks. "572 times 1,008."

Without missing a beat, he answers, "576,576."

"Wow, that certainly is . . . impressive." She blinks.

"Cool, Mr. Frederics," I add. "But you should get to your cones. We'll be starting soon."

"After you," he says to Ms. DiCarlo, extending his hand toward the cones. "Give me a harder one," I hear him say as they stroll away. I watch him drop her off at Cone Eleven, then amble to his own Cone Two. Hopefully there'll be no more romancing for today.

People crowd around me, loud and impatient. Some start rummaging through the shirt box before I can check them in.

"One at a time, people!" barks a familiar voice. "What are you, piranha?"

"Kali!" I nearly weep at the sight of her solid self. She sweeps her arms at the crowd and they finally begin to line up. There's a healthy glow to her cheeks and a swagger to her stride. The plumeria on the print of her lavalava wrap are so vibrant they might burst off her dress.

"Thanks for picking up the slack."

She didn't say *talofa* or call me Nosey. It's not something I would ordinarily notice, but today, the lack of familiars stings. I sniff for her mood out of reflex, but of course, don't get anything but grass. "Where have you been?"

"Thinking about earthworms again."

"Earthworms?" People start crowding around us, halting further conversation. At least she doesn't seem to be actively mad at me anymore, despite her relative aloofness. I check off names while she hands out T-shirts and dispatches people to their cones.

Her hand shoots up. "Next!"

Cassandra bounces up, fidgety as a sunbeam on water. "Hi!"

"Oh, hey," says Kali, handing Cassandra her clipboard, instead of a T-shirt. "Oops, sorry." Kali's cheeks flush and she exchanges the clipboard back for the T-shirt.

"Are you feeling better?" Cassandra's voice goes squeaky. "I was worried about you."

I could swear Kali blushes. "Yeah, I'm cool. You ready?"

"I was born ready." The songbird trills out a high note to prove it. "Which poem are you doing?"

"Made up a new one." Kali hands Cassandra an extra small.

"Thanks! I can't wait to hear it." She skips away.

After dispensing with several more volunteers, we're down to one. Vicky arrives by herself, sporting dark sunglasses, maybe to shield her from the glare off her gold tracksuit. Crossing her arms in front of her, she shows us her profile. Without her peeps, and in the middle of this festooned field, she looks like a cat floating on a pool chair, nervous and slightly ridiculous.

Kali tosses a shirt at her. "Designer, for you."

Vicky tosses it back. "There's no way I'm putting that on."

"No shirt, no service." Kali chucks the shirt back at Vicky.

Principal Swizinger, standing only a few feet away, lasers Vicky with her eyes. This time, Vicky hangs on to the shirt, and her scowl morphs into a smile. "This is going to be so . . . gay."

Kali's wide nostrils flare and her mouth tightens, as if she's trying to keep her tongue from letting loose. I jerk my head toward one of the orange cones. "Team Four."

Vicky picks her way across the grass toward the cone.

"Psh." Kali lobs her gaze to the sky. "So did you fix Alice?"

"I ran into some complications."

"What complications?"

"I lost my nose," I say in a tight voice.

"Looks like it's still there to me."

I shake my head, forcing my tears back into their corners. "I'm toast."

"Hey, it's gonna be okay," Kali bumps my arm with hers, and I'm so grateful for her sympathy, I nearly lose it.

"Oh, great, Kali, you made it." Hope with the blond crew cut holds out a megaphone to her.

"*Talofa.* Sorry I'm late."

"Let me show you the buttons." Hope leads Kali to an adjacent table. The two consult while I regain my composure.

"Did I miss anything?" In front of me, Drew runs a hand through his blond hair.

"Oh, hello." A pang of guilt hits me again at his guileless face, with his blue eyes enlarged by his glasses and his clear skin. "You're with your friend Parker, Team Seventeen. Grab a shirt."

Drew gamely pulls the Day-Glo tee over his black ensemble. He shades his eyes as he scans the field for his friend. "Wait. Can I be with her?"

My eyes travel to where he's pointing. Fifty feet toward the school, Vicky clutches her purse like she's on a New York City subway. Before I can reply, Drew skips away. The chain linking his pants to his wallet slaps him on the back of his thigh with each stride. Kali notices, and frowns at me.

I smash my clipboard to my chest. If I had it to do over again, would I choose differently? Undecided. Vicky might be a shark out of water right now, but once we get off the field, Kali's chum number one. Kali deserves to live her life on her own terms.

A cloud passes over the sun, and the change in temperature chills my skin. In some way, I feel responsible for Kali's predicament. If I hadn't come to school, Vicky would not have seen an opportunity in me. I'm like a strange magnet whose very presence seems to screw with people's compasses, shifting them in new directions. I couldn't have foreseen the trouble I would cause here. But it doesn't erase any of my guilt.

A bus rumbles onto the field, then parks. The happy faces of dozens of kids stare out the windows.

Kali fiddles with the megaphone, then holds it to her mouth. "Sup, everyone." Her friendly voice booms across the field. "We're makin' Thanksgiving baskets with the kids. Teach 'em about veggies, like radishes and sh—"

The principal clears her throat loudly and gives Kali a severe look.

"Shit-ake mushrooms," Kali corrects. Everyone laughs. "Stay with your kids at all times, and don't squeeze the tomatoes."

The bus door opens with a metallic gasp. Moments later, the kids burst out and run to their cones. The energy and noise level shoots up by a factor of ten.

Kali turns off her megaphone and heads back to me. "So how'd it happen?"

"I fell in love with Court Sawyer."

She snorts. "I coulda told you that." Her ironic expression fades when she sees my face. "Look, you're still you without your nose, right?"

"I don't know." I sniff. "My smell started fading, and now it's gone completely."

"After all that work you put it through, maybe it's on vacation."

"Noses don't take vacations."

"Well, maybe they should."

"How am I going to mix if I can't smell?"

"What did you do when you didn't prepare for a choreography for Cardio class?"

"I don't know, blew it off?"

"Nope." She pokes my shoulder. "*You* sweated it. You didn't give any excuses, you just powered through the routine, grapevines and everything, and you got a B plus."

"Thanks. But there are no grades here. It's either pass or fail."

Vicky stands apart from her group, nervously picking at her sleeves. Drew pulls three onions from his basket and begins a juggling act. His kids bounce up and down. Kali watches, then turns her back to them, as if she can't bear to look any longer.

"So what if you're wrong? Alice ain't gonna sprout an extra head." Kali cocks an eyebrow. "Is she?"

"No."

"You going to tell Court?"

I shake my head. "What's the point? Mother would never let us date, even if he did save my life."

"Your *life?*"

"It's a long story."

"Okay." Her lips press together, then unstick with a smacking sound. "You go home and work on the elixir. I can handle things here."

"Thanks, but I still want to hear about your earthworms."

She shakes her head. "Not today."

I can't tell if she's brushing me off, or just looking out for my time. "Good luck tonight."

"Same to you." She blinks, but her face remains unreadable. Without another word, my only friend moves toward a group of kids throwing grapes at one another.

Things still aren't right between us, but at least she still cares. That refills some of the air in my leaking inner tube, makes me feel I can float a little while longer. If I still had my nose, I bet I would smell like cucumber, that cooling scent of relief.

I weave through people and baskets of fruit back to school, passing by Team Four. Drew, still juggling, throws Vicky his onions, and she catches them, well, one of them. Then he starts a new act with beets. Vicky tosses him back all the onions, one by one, which he neatly adds to his routine.

Now Drew's juggling six tubers. The guy's talented. Vicky smiles. Not a fake one, either—a real smile, like the one I saw on her sister, Juliana. Drew urges Vicky to throw one more. This time, she hefts a pineapple. She winks at one of the kids, then tosses it to Drew. His whole act falls apart.

But now all of the kids on Team Four are holding their sides, laughing.

The sight of Drew and Vicky's burgeoning chemistry should make me feel relieved, but instead, something rancid burns inside me. If not for that arm-twisting squirrel, Kali and I would still be okay. I might still have Kali's respect, and not just her pity.

I move beyond Team Four to where Ms. DiCarlo holds a coconut for her kids to pet. Mr. Frederics studies her from far away, his expression thoughtful.

Does the man still care for the timid librarian? Or did Alice's attentions cool his ardor, and kindle a new one? If so, where does that leave Mr. Frederics when I PUF Alice? He'll be damaged goods. We'll have to tell him to plant rosebushes, the best way to get over a broken heart.

Love is so chancy. If Alice hadn't gotten hooked on romance books, I might never have fixed her. Or if Ms. DiCarlo's rabbit hadn't died, Mr. Frederics and Ms. DiCarlo might be making some of their own sunshine, without our help.

I would still simply be Mimosa, the oddball with the hats, she who should not be touched.

TWENTY-EIGHT

"THE EASIEST WAY TO RUIN
A GOOD ELIXIR IS TO THINK ABOUT IT."
—*Xanthe, Aromateur, 1877*

AT LAST, ALL oils are ready for blending. The homecoming game starts at seven. Two hours to get this right. Ordinarily, it would take me an hour, and that's with a nose. I work at a Frankensteinian pace, transferring oils into test tubes, and occasionally banging my head on the table. Finally, ninety-eight glass tubes stand at attention in front of me like the pipes of an organ.

I try again to smell, and nearly pass out from the effort.

A mathematical formula would be really handy, something that told me exactly how much of each oil to use. If the aromateurs of yesteryear had allowed scientists to study their noses, perhaps they could've invented tools to quantify smells by now. I take a slow breath in, trying to steady my heart.

Going from memory, I begin to layer the oils onto a square of cotton using pipettes the size of straight pins. Certain notes, like kangaroo paw, are typically "shy" and like to hide, and so for these, I use more. Others, like blue tansy, a flower with an appley scent, are notorious for being the loudest one in the room, so I use only the smallest drop I can manage.

I should try calling Mother again. She'll be livid. I imagine her clutching her heart and sucking in her bottom lip the way she does when the soup's too hot.

The thought causes my hand to shake, knocking over the vial of blue tansy. The tansy quickly seeps into the entire cotton square. Holy dirt, that's the second spill in twenty-four hours! I grab the vial before I lose all the precious scent. Between the tansy and the lavender, Mother will smell the mistakes before she even gets to the driveway. I'll need to bring in the spider plants, with their pure oxygen smells, to erase the evidence.

Sinking into my chair, I clutch my head in my hands and curse myself. The square is useless now. Breathe and start over, one singer at a time.

It's dark by the time I finish. Why doesn't Mother get a clock in here? Quickly, I put the cotton square in a test tube and add carrier solution. I shake it fifty times, unlid, filter, and retube. Then I run back to the house. The homecoming game must have already started.

My heart sinks when I see it's 7:14. Games always start late, don't they? They have to do the anthem, the welcome home speech to the alums. I pull a sweater over my sundress, stuff my hair into a beret, and grab my gloves. Then I hop on my bike and

I'm riding as fast as my legs can pump toward the biggest game of the year.

Most people think homecoming means football, but not in Santa Guadalupe. Some of the greatest soccer players in the country come from our narrow strip of the world, which is why cars are parked along the shoulder at least two miles before the school. Opening car doors and strewn beer bottles force me to slow down as I draw closer.

I leave my bike near the library and race to the stadium. The trash cans are already overflowing with empty cans and hot dog trays. A group of kids blow their noisemakers right by my ear.

According to the scoreboard, visible from outside the stadium, no one's made a goal yet. The words Half Time inch across the screen as the announcer reads advertisements. I hope Kali hasn't performed yet, though I have to focus on finding Alice. My blend may be the worst elixir ever in the history of elixir making, but it's all I have right now.

I pull my beret over my ears and work on my cotton gloves. With no BBG, I must be extra careful to avoid skin contact with anybody who could possibly take more than a friendly interest in me. Keeping my elbows in, I make myself as small as possible as I hurry into the stadium, passing people wearing panther ears, and others sporting opposition T-shirts for the Bulldogs.

The half-time show has begun. Someone, I think Cassandra, begins to sing. Definitely Cassandra. She chose a ballad so syrupy, my teeth ache.

"Hey, Mim!" yells Lauren. She and Pascha, linking arms, rush up beside me. Lauren's fully decked out in panther wear, complete with black ears, whiskers drawn on her cheeks, even a tail pinned in the back. Pascha's wearing the same ears atop her headscarf.

"Hello."

Pascha pushes her friend with her arm, causing both of them to stumble sideways. "Lauren's going to ask him tonight."

It takes me a moment to figure out what she's talking about. Ah, the boy Lauren wanted to ask to the homecoming dance. "That's great."

"Assuming I can find him. There's a full house."

I look up, swaying a little. The stadium's crammed even at the highest levels, a dot matrix of color. The din of horns and people yelling feels like somone is pushing needles into my brain.

"Just look for the red glasses," says Pascha.

My eyes fall back to the girls. Drew has red glasses. "Is it Drew Reaver?"

Lauren squeezes Pascha's arm so hard, Pascha makes a face. "How do you know that?" Lauren asks me. "Can you smell that I like him? Or can you smell that he likes me?"

Pascha untangles her arm from her friend's, and her bracelets jangle. "He's the only junior with red glasses, dummy."

"Oh, right." Lauren has changed the rubber bands in her braces to silver, making her smile extra tinselly.

I look around me, as if I could be the butt of some colossal joke. Lauren likes Drew, but thanks to me, he already has one pant leg caught in the Vicky vacuum, and soon he'll be whirling around in the vortex of her affections. There will be no room for Lauren.

"Now we have to work on a date for Pascha."

"It's okay. I need to babysit my brother. Plus, my dad thinks people just go to dances to make out."

"He's sort of right. But you're on the *committee*. You'll be too busy working to make out."

A wave of vertigo passes through me again, and I grab a rail on one side of the pathway to steady myself. The lights hurt my eyes, and my head might explode soon with the combination of Cassandra's high notes and the noisemakers.

Breathe. I close my eyes and inhale a few more times.

When I open them again, Pascha and Lauren are staring at me.

"Are you okay?" asks Lauren.

"Yes, thanks. I'm fine." I still have a mission to accomplish and I can't get sidelined. "Have either of you seen Alice, er, Court's mom?"

"No," says Lauren.

Pascha shakes her head. "Why?"

"I have to give her something."

"There's an empty seat by us," says Pascha. "Front row because we're officers. She might have seats there, too."

"Thanks," I murmur gratefully.

I scan the bleachers as I follow the girls, trying not to bump anyone.

Cassandra holds her final note long enough for my clothes to come back into fashion. When she finally cuts it off, the crowd applauds and she spends the next few minutes bowing, her curly tresses flipping up and down like she's giving the crowd a car wash.

Pascha and Lauren finally park in front-row seats, right at the midline. I slide into the empty seat beside Pascha, then crane my neck in both directions. No Alice.

At last, the announcer hooks Cassandra away. "Now, get ready for the Panther's own poet laureate performing her poem, 'The Way We Are,' Kali Apulu!"

Kali's appearance distracts me for the moment. She lights up the stage in her neon ensemble and I yell like crazy, finding my second wind. The cheering is especially loud two sections up, where I spot her family, jumping up and down and waving.

Kali adjusts the microphone headset then gives a thumbs-up to the audio guys. A bass beat starts rocking the stadium, and a synthesizer adds a syncopated rhythm. She's going to rap.

> *I'm-a get square with you,*
> *Gonna share with you,*
> *Kick a chair, let down my hair, and spare the air with you.*

Living out loud is the way we groove it,
If they don't like our crowd, they can go move it.

Kali bends her knees and begins moving them from side to side like she's slaloming, and the crowd goes crazy.

They think we don't know jack,
They think we just throw smack
Racing cars, hiding, and getting cash,

Rolling down the lane is how we're strollin',
If they don't like the groove, they can get rollin'.

This time, everyone joins Kali in the dance move. Despite my sensory overload, and the noise of the bass pummeling my brain, I can't help smiling. That's my friend, smoking up the stadium.

I continue straining my eyes for Alice and finally locate her—right behind the goal, another prime viewing section. She's wearing a hot-pink sweater over her four-hundred-dollar jeans and waving pom-poms. Her head swivels side to side, then looks behind her, below her. She must be looking for Mr. Frederics, who I don't see anywhere. That's good. Maybe he decided not to come to the game.

On one side of Alice are three empty chairs, and on the other, Melanie and Vicky. Unlike the rest of the crowd, the girls are sitting, both staring at their cell phones.

Time to move. If I can reach Alice while Kali still has the crowd pumped up and on their feet, maybe I can dose her without anyone noticing.

"I'll be back," I tell Pascha, then slip away.

The path to Alice is slow and treacherous. I skirt bodies flinging their arms around, some still holding their drinks. I dodge hoards of barking Bulldog fans. The journey's as slow as wading through mounds of sand.

> *I'm an extra large*
> *And I charge by the pound,*
> *So get your nuts and chews before I come around.*

> *Living loud and queer is how I travel*
> *If they don't like my gear, they can hit the gravel.*

What did she say? Living loud and *queer*? I stop in my tracks. Kali just outted herself.

Vicky's hands fly to her mouth. She turns her astonished eyes toward Melanie, and the two of them have a staring contest. Kali keeps up her flow, knees now bowing inward and outward and arms pumping up and down. Her audience copies her, yelling out the chorus and nearly drowning her out. Besides Vicky and Melanie, no one even notices Kali's confession.

So that's what Kali was talking about when she said no

squirrel was going to push her around. And her speech about earthworms and not letting fear stop her.

> With a winning state of mind,
> We're gonna catch you from behind,
> We iPhone, homegrown, won't go home until we own.
>
> In your face, keep the pace, pass, and unlock it,
> Shooting from the line, Panthers go rock it!

Kali didn't need me to break any rules for her. She could hold her own.

I sag into the metal railing and it digs into the bumps of my spine. Kali didn't even confide in me about what she planned to do, more proof that she doesn't need me, not like I need her. My eyes grows misty, and I cage my chest with my arms, feeling like the emotions that swarm inside might suddenly fly away and leave me empty. I have to keep moving.

By the time I finally arrive at Alice's section, Kali has finished and everyone's back in their seats. I want to bang my head on the railing. Now I'll have to wait for the next time everybody's on their feet and no one's paying attention to me. I try to blend into a post a few rows up from Alice.

A cheer goes out as the Panthers file back on to the field. The sight of Court in his white soccer uniform makes my stomach turn a clumsy cartwheel.

The cheerleaders spell out "Sawyer" letter by letter with their bodies. Soon everyone begins chanting his name, especially Alice, who pumps her pom-poms with every beat of the cheer. When the cheer ends, she stands up and looks around her.

The Bulldogs reenter the field, and soon the ball's bouncing around the pitch. Back and forth it goes, never quite making it to one end or the other. Court and Whit tag team, each dancing with the ball until the defenders force a pass to the other.

Court fakes one direction, then needles the ball through the path of two defenders. People jump to their feet, screaming for him to kick it. Now's my chance. I squeeze by the row of people directly above Alice, making myself very compact so I don't touch anyone. When I get to Alice, I nonchalantly overturn my vial on her head. She doesn't notice.

The crowd groans as Court's ball goes high, missing the goal. I nearly trip in my haste to exit the row before everyone sits down again. Finally, I make it back to the aisle. There, I wait while I gauge Alice's reaction, crossing my fingers and praying.

Nothing.

According to Mother, the PUF almost always works immediately, just like BBG. But Alice doesn't show any sign of being confused or in a daze. In fact, she's still shaking her pom-poms, even though another of Court's kicks misses.

Suddenly, she spots someone. It's the math teacher himself, leading an unsmiling old black woman past Alice's section. Maybe that's his mother, the one who wanted to see him hitched before she died. Alice yells and waves a pom-pom in their direction. I watch in horror as Mr. Frederics wiggles his fingers in salute. The mother forms her mouth into an O, then nods at Alice.

The teacher begins climbing the stairs, leading his mother by the hand. He and his mother stop at Alice's row then edge past people, including a scowling Melanie, until they reach Alice, who pulls the mother into a hug. Finally, they all sit down.

My eyeballs are dry from staring so hard. I jam my beret further over my head, wishing I was someone else. Someone who didn't wreak havoc in the lives of others. Someone whose nose still led the way.

TWENTY-NINE

"If people only spoke their hearts rather than their
minds, they would have no use for us."
—Willow, *Aromateur*, 1840

I COLLAPSE INTO the seat by Pascha and Lauren. All that
work for nothing. Who was I fooling? I knew it wouldn't work. A
blind person had better odds of fitting together a thousand-piece
puzzle than I had of creating an elixir without my nose.

Alice and Mr. Frederics lean toward each other as they chat,
with the math teacher's mother sitting in between them. At least
there will be no kissing across the old woman's lap.

I cringe, thinking of how angry Mother will be when she
finds out. If I tell her when she calls on Sunday, she might have
time to cool off before she socks it to me in person. When Mother
gets mad, it is a sight to smell. Once, I overwatered the ghost
orchids, and Mother released a cloud of burning tires so singeing,
I could taste the bitter vapors lingering at the back of my throat.

Court bats the ball through a defender's legs, then lithely
rushes by to receive it again on the other side. Witnessing his

mastery over his game reminds me of our conversation on the way to Playa del Rey. Court doesn't need soccer to define him; he loves the ocean, he wants to study whales. But I don't have anything but my nose. Without it, who am I now?

Pascha's mouth falls open and she gets to her feet, watching as Whit dribbles the ball down the field. A Bulldog interferes, and Pascha nervously chews a fingernail, her eyes round and unblinking.

One of our defenders snakes the ball from the Bulldog and sends it back to Whit.

Pascha starts fanning herself with her scarf. "He's so hot," she gushes to Lauren and me. "I mean, look at him. I heard he likes spicy food. *I* like spicy food. How perfect is that?"

Whit, right in front of us now, looks around for Court. Pascha starts screaming Whit's name. Her panther ears slide to one side of her head. Whit looks up for a split second at Pascha, but then his eyes shift to me and he gawks like he's caught a glimpse of the yeti. I step behind Pascha and out of his sight line. Court runs up for the ball, but instead of passing, Whit starts playing with the ball, bouncing it off his knees and chest.

Court screams for him to pass it, but Whit ignores him. Now he's doing some kind of scissor step with the ball between his legs, despite the Bulldogs rushing up to him. He's completely forgotten about the game. He looks up and points at me, grinning.

Pascha's jaw drops. "Oh. My. Allah. Is it me?" She steers her open mouth from me, to Lauren, to me again. Whit, who still hasn't broken eye contact with me, puts two fingers to his lips and blows me a kiss.

Court beelines to Whit, and with one quick movement of his foot, jimmies the ball from him. The crowd cheers as Court dribbles it away. Whit's face twists, and he hauls off after Court.

Pascha crosses her arms and frowns at me. "It's you."

"I'm sorry. It's a temporary situation." I hold out my gloved hands in apology, but she only lifts her nose.

Lauren talks excitedly, "He's totally into you, Mim. How do you do that? No, seriously. How do you do that?"

Failure to BBG is how. I shake my head in misery and stare at the scoreboard. Five minutes left in the game and no goals yet. I should leave now. Try to find Kali. Maybe she'll be ready to talk now. At least I can congratulate her.

But there are too many people crowding the aisles. There's no way I could get through without contaminating someone, even with my long sleeves and hat. I shrivel back into my seat, defeated.

Just before the clock runs out, Court lets his foot fly. The ball practically sears a hole through the net as it lands.

Panthers 1, Bulldogs 0. The crowd roars and stomps its feet, and it's as violent as a hurricane to a single, beleaguered dandelion.

Outside the stadium, the crowds dissipate and head for their cars. "Sure you don't want to join us?" asks Lauren. "Stan's is hosting free donuts for everyone. I'm working up the nerve to ask Drew."

Maybe I should tell her not to go to the party, or at least, not to get her hopes up. Then again, maybe I would do the world a favor by just minding my own business. "I'm sorry, I can't go. I'm expected home."

Pascha hasn't stopped scowling since Whit blew me the kiss, and doesn't look disappointed at my response.

"Okay, well, have a nice weekend." Lauren grabs Pascha's arm and begins to pull her toward the parking lot.

"Lauren?" I call out.

She turns around. "Yeah?"

"The wider open the heart, the easier it is for Cupid to shoot his arrows."

She cocks her head to one side, then gives me a baffled smile. "Okay, thanks."

Instead of the parking lot, I follow those ambling toward the street.

"Mim?" says a voice from behind me. Court, still wearing his uniform and bright with the flush of victory, steps into the fluorescent lighting.

There are no mood scents to guide me, but there's a bouncing energy around him, a liveliness like a puppy who has found its favorite kid. My insides spin with his nearness. "W-what, don't you have a debrief or something?"

"The debrief went something like this, "Nice footwork, you clowns. Don't be late to practice on Monday.""

"That was an amazing kick."

"Thanks, though you better spray Whit before I get jealous." From behind him, a couple of girls whisper and giggle.

I chew on my lip. I can't spray anybody until Mother returns and makes the BBG. Of course, by then, I won't need to because Mother will have exiled me to the far reaches of the Arctic Circle.

I need to tell him the truth at last. But before I can muster the words or the courage, he grabs my hand. "Let's get lost."

We dash back toward the stadium, through exiting stragglers, and over litter and pulled-down posters. A few fans try to stop us, but we run past them.

When I'm out of breath, Court pulls me to a dark spot underneath the bleachers.

"The PUF didn't work," I gasp.

"For sure?"

"Yeah, for sure."

He looks more surprised than worried. "So what's next?"

"My mother will be home soon. I'm in way over my head." I stare glumly at my shoes.

"Hey, don't feel bad. You know, it's not so bad, Mom being in love. She's been laughing a lot this week. And Mr. Frederics is kind of cool. He bought every one of her pies at the rally this morning. Maybe the PUF didn't work for a reason."

Yes, the loss of my nose.

He tucks me into his arms. "You don't have any excuse not to kiss me now that the game's over."

My resolve weakens with one glance into the still waters of his eyes. One little kiss. I already lost my nose, and I may as well enjoy myself while I can. It's his big night after all.

I draw back. No. I can't do that. A kiss would just dig me deeper in the hole, further strengthening a bond that should never have formed. I already made my choice—nose over love. If I can sever our tie, maybe Mother can make an elixir for me like she did for Aunt Bryony. I tear myself away. "I can't." The two words weigh heavy as cement blocks.

"What are you talking about?"

He comes close again, but I hold up my hands. "You don't like me that way. You think you do, but so do the rest of the people I infect."

His face is half-smiling, half-disbelieving, as if waiting for me to deliver a punch line. "What are you saying?"

"I'm saying you should forget about me."

A look of pain washes over his face, and then quickly disappears, leaving me with no clue as to what he's thinking. Straightening his throat, he focuses on a wad of neon-green gum on the pavement. I push the knife in further, so there is no going back. "I mean—it's been fun."

"Wow," he says, clearly not meaning the gum.

My heart feels like it's about to collapse into a black hole, pulling the rest of me along with it. Who knew heartbreak was a literal thing? Court's eyelashes dip toward my hands, which are wringing themselves dry.

A familiar laugh sounds from above, followed by voices growing louder with each footfall on the metal grating of the bleachers. We both look up. Vicky and Melanie pause just a few feet above Court's head. I freeze, though it's too dark for them to see us below them.

"Whit totally lost it. At least now everyone will know she puts spells on guys. Love witch," Vicky spits. "She's an attention-whore."

"I know," says Melanie.

"And you know what? I practically threw myself at Court yesterday and he completely ignored me. Like I was wallpaper. You sure you gave him the elixir?"

My heart screeches to a stop. Court quirks an eyebrow at me, and I want to seep into the earth.

"Of course I did," says Melanie, halting. "You were there. You saw me drop it in his drink."

I cringe. Court stares into the shadows, not looking at me.

"Why is it taking so damn long for him to fall back in love with me? The situation is making me crazy. I nearly asked Drew Reaver to the dance this morning. I mean, Drew Reaver?"

Reaver Fever. She definitely caught it.

Melanie doesn't answer. The sole of her shoes twists back and forth on the grate. Finally, she says in a voice so quiet it's nearly drowned out by the drone of the stadium stragglers, "Have you ever thought, maybe you and Court aren't meant to, you know . . ."

"No, I don't know. Please enlighten me." Vicky's voice turns icy.

"I'm sorry, Vicky. I just think when you have to try so hard, maybe it's not meant to be."

"I thought you believed in us. Why would you help me if you didn't believe in us?"

Melanie falls silent.

Court stands rigid and apart from me, his lips pressed into a hard line. I shake my head at him, trying to pass him the truth even though he's not looking at me. It's not what you think. The elixir was just water. I was trying to help you.

"You never believed it would work," comes Vicky's accusing tone.

"I thought you needed to see for yourself that he wasn't meant for you."

Vicky makes an indignant gasping noise. "Well, I guess you're not as bad an actress as my father thinks you are. But you can forget about a part in his movie. When you have to try so hard, maybe it's just not meant to be." At that last line, she makes her voice go high and overarticulated, like Melanie's.

Vicky gets to her feet. The bleachers rattle like thunder as she stomps off.

Court's breath escapes in a hiss. He looks up at Melanie, now by herself. Her stiletto pokes through the grated flooring of the bleachers and gets stuck. She twists her foot to free it, then runs in the opposite direction.

Court swears. "You fixed me with Vicky?"

"No, it's not like that. It was w-water. The elixir." My stammering makes my explanation sound even lamer.

He snorts. "So you charged her for water? That's a good one."

"Elixirs are free."

"Free?" His eyes flick to the side and he shakes his head. "So are private jets."

I cringe as I remember my boast to him about having a private jet. Why did I do that?

He walks away, then reverses course. "This is seriously jacked up. I thought you cared."

"I do."

"Right. You needed my help to fix your mistake." He rakes a hand through his hair and some of it remains sticking up. "You know, I would have done it anyway. She is my mother."

"It's not like that."

"Did you ever care about me?" His eyes plead with me to make it right.

"Not that way." My voice sounds raspy and dry. I swallow hard. "I told you, love witches can't love."

He coughs in disbelief and his head draws back. His hurt eyes linger for a moment on mine, then with a muttered curse, he strides off.

I waver between laughter and tears as I stumble away. BBG was never the answer. All I had to do was lie.

THIRTY

THE PIERCING WHOOSH of a plane like a Cloud Air jet rouses me from my slumber, and for a moment, a thrill of panic stabs through me. But it can't be Mother. She won't be here until Monday. I squint at the clock—almost eleven a.m. I haven't slept this late in weeks. Sunlight streams through my windows, but today it doesn't burn my eyes. Perhaps I am getting accustomed to my other senses. I sniff, but don't detect any olfactory improvement.

I try calling Kali. With every ring, I'm filled with hope that this time she'll answer. That she'll be ready to get our friendship back on track. When the call goes to voicemail, I say, "Hi. Your poem—what you did—was amazing." I stretch out the coil of my old-fashioned phone. "*You're* amazing. If you feel like talking, call me."

The bag of candy grams on the floor catches my eye. I shake myself free of my quilt and sort through the messages, one by one. The sight of Court's neat printing squeezes my chest, making it hard to breathe. Twenty of the twenty-one are written by the same hand.

I read one:

> I'm a veggie vampire,
> Who does not suck on necks,
> I only eat bean sprouts and peas,
> And other healthy snacks.

I snivel a few times but won't allow myself to cry. You're not supposed to cry if you're the cause of your own misery. Then it's just pathetic.

I should throw them away, but I can't. So I stick them in my nightstand drawer. The Rulebook falls over when I close the drawer. I pick it up and flip through the pages once again. Maybe there's something about recovering your nose.

The book opens to Rule Eighteen, the rule on PUFs, probably because I've been reading that page a lot lately. My eyes stick on the Last Word penned at the top of the page: *Love is revealed through sacrifice. —Shayla, Aromateur, 1633.*

Shayla was Layla's daughter, the one for whom Layla gave her life. Is there a reason her Last Word appears on this particular page? Last Words appear throughout the Rulebook in no particular order, though most aromateurs put them in the blank pages at the end.

My mind drifts back to the day I asked Mother about PUFs. She said, *Sniff-matching. It wasn't December, you know.*

I grip the book too hard and leave a wrinkle on the page. Mother had said those words when describing how to make a PUF for Aunt Bryony. December is when Layla's Sacrifice is in bloom, the plant with the scent so complex—over ten thousand notes—a single orchid can substitute for an elixir. Could it also substitute for a PUF?

I snap my fingers. That's it. Even if I'm wrong, I have to try. I don't know for sure if Alice and Mr. Frederics kissed, but maybe not, given his mother's presence at the game. I pull on leggings and a tunic, and bobby pin my hair into submission.

Outside, I hurry to the workshop.

The twin buds of Layla's Sacrifice are big as my thumbs and still closed. Harvesting the petals early kills the whole plant. My breath fogs up the glass as I wonder what Mother would do.

Pointless. Mother would never be in this situation. I'm toast whether I kill Layla or not. Alice might as well benefit.

I lift off the glass cover, and stroke one of the buds with my finger. This particular specimen has been growing in this case for twenty-odd years. When they were teens, Mother and Aunt Bryony spent three months in the Brazilian jungle sniffing it out. To end it now while it's still in its prime sends a needle of pain through my heart. But it's either Alice's future happiness, or the plant. To me, the choice is clear. I can always sniff out another orchid. At least, Mother can.

I swab my sharpest clippers with ethanol. Flowers start disintegrating within minutes of cutting, which is why we put them in carrier oil right away. But an enfleurage will take days to reach usable concentrations. I'll need to cut and run. I'll have an hour, two, tops to swipe the fresh cut flower directly onto her skin before it starts to go rancid.

Holding a bud with two fingers, I snip it at the base. Then I wrap it in gauze and place it in a six-pack cooler along with an ice pack. Back outside I go. I stop at a hyacinth bush. Like the rest of the garden, the hyacinth is crying out for a trim, but I clip only a single stalk. Hyacinth means, "Please forgive me."

Moments later, I'm on my bike, working out how to PUF Alice without her knowing. All she needs to do is touch the bud, which should be easy enough.

A pile of debris sweeps over me, kicked up by an easterly draft. I wipe dust from my eyes and nearly knock off my bucket hat. It's the same one I was wearing that day at Arastradero when I first met Court. I should've grabbed a different one. Maybe Court will be sleeping. He was the star last night, and no doubt there was plenty of celebrating. With luck, he won't wake until noon. Then again, the aspen shadows have started to seep eastward, which means its well past one.

I'm tempted to turn back and wallow under my covers.

I pass Main Street and approach the turnoff into the hills of Cypress Estates with its griffin fountain. A black compact whizzes by me. The driver's head cranes around, and I swear she looks like Mother. Of course not, Mother's not back until Monday. But—?

I whip my head around, remembering the jet that woke me up. The black compact slows and makes a U-turn.

It is her. Mother's back early.

I veer into the rumble strip, nearly colliding with a side rail. The cooler jostles in my basket. What am I going to tell her? I'll have to make it snappy. Layla's Sacrifice will go to waste if I don't swipe Alice soon.

I'm a heaving, sweaty mess by the time Mother pulls up to me.

The passenger side window lowers. I rub my eyes, not sure I'm seeing right. A vibrant-hued gypsy dress swathes her petite frame, topped with a triple strand of iridescent beads. And is that makeup? Mother got a makeover?

She tilts her head and smiles. Her expression is half-amazed, half- . . . tearful. "Well. She must've put something in the soil. You're as tall as a sunflower!"

"Mother?"

"Honey, I'm not your mother. I'm your aunt Bryony."

THIRTY-ONE

"IT IS NOT A COINCIDENCE THAT CLIMBING
BITTERSWEET REPRESENTS TRUTH."
—*Jonquil, Aromateur, 1699*

I TRY SPEAKING twice before I can form a sentence. Except for the gray streak on the left side of her hairline—Mother's is on the right—my aunt is an exact physical replica of Mother. "Y-you're, h-how did you know it was me?"

"You look like her. Which means, you look like me." She covers her mouth with her hand as we stare at each other. Cars collect in back of us. Some of them honk. Aunt Bryony motions them to go around. "Where are you headed?"

"I have to PUF someone." I yell to be heard.

Her thin eyebrows lift. "Impressive. Made it yourself?"

"No, I cut Layla's Sacrifice." I show her the cooler.

"Ah, well then, time's wasting. Get in!"

"But, my bike . . ."

"Leave it."

Abandoning my trusty steed is almost as painful as cutting

Layla's Sacrifice. With a sigh, I dismount and prop my bike against the fountain. I lift my hyacinth and my cooler from the basket, then slide into the passenger seat, still not quite believing my aunt is here in the flesh.

She places her hands around my cheeks and kisses me on the forehead. "Look at you. Prettier than we were at your age. You didn't get those eyelashes from our side of the family." She taps me on the jaw. "Or that disappearing chin."

She motors off, and the backlog of questions waterfall off my tongue. "So when—how did you get my message?"

"Bryony Suzuki got your message and she passed it to me. News travels fast when you live on an island and your name is Bryony. I couldn't reach you yesterday so I decided to come find out what the heck is going on. Thank the lilies for the private jet."

"You have a Cloud Air card, too?"

"Naturally. Where next?"

"Um, make a left at the top."

She steers the car up the hill. "Tell me she's okay."

"Mother? She's fine, I think. She's in Oman, and won't be back until Monday."

"Oh, that's good." She blows out her breath. "Now tell me who we're PUF'ing."

"Mrs. Alice Sawyer. I accidentally fixed her a week ago."

"A week? You got her written permission to PUF her, I assume?"

"There's a good chance she hasn't kissed him yet."

"What are the signs?"

In a few sentences, I explain about the cake and the seating arrangement at the homecoming game.

I don't notice we passed the cul-de-sac until we're halfway down the hill. "Oh, turn back!"

My aunt executes a five-point turn. Driving isn't Mother's forte either. "Mimsy, why do you think we have a Rule Eighteen?"

She still remembers the rule numbers. "To give us an out in case we screw up?"

"No, it's to give us a *fair* out in case we screw up. If you PUF before a party falls in love, no harm is done, no one is the wiser. But once a party falls in love, PUF'ing would take away one of life's greatest treasures. You must disclose."

My heart sinks to my feet. Somehow, I knew that, I just didn't want to admit it.

I point to the Sawyer residence and my aunt parks in the driveway. The sight of the familiar Jeep parked out front makes my adrenaline spike.

Aunt Bryony squeezes my arm. "Let's do this."

Moments later, I'm shuffling up the driveway after my aunt, cooler and hyacinth in hand.

As I muster the nerve to ring the doorbell, a motor roars behind us. A sporty yellow two-seater pulls into the driveway next to the rental car, rumbling loudly. Trees reflect off the glossy windows, obscuring my view of the occupants, but as the car inches closer, then stops, I make out the driver and her corkscrew red hair. It's Cassandra, and next to her is Court.

The engine fades to a purr. Court's aviators hide his expression. He says something to Cassandra that makes her smile.

So he wasn't sleeping. Boy, I got it wrong. My insides churn with emotion—resignation, regret, and even a little outrage. Court hops out of the car. He's wearing a rumpled shirt, dark jeans, and a military-style jacket, the kind of outfit for a Friday night, not a Saturday morning.

To my surprise, Cassandra's window slides down. A series of white bangles adorn her tan arm. "Hey, Mim. What'd you think of the performance?"

"You were great," I say with more enthusiasm than I feel.

"Thanks. Kali rocked that house, too. She's awesome!"

"Yeah, she is."

"See you!" She backs out and roars off.

Court treads up, his mouth tight. He pulls off his sunglasses and squints at my cooler, like the sunlight hurts his eyes. "What are you doing here?"

His words are so curt, they rob me of my reply. My aunt's nose wiggles like Mother's when she's trying to read the situation. She bends her gaze toward me, then chirps, "Good morning. We're here to talk to your mother. We want to make things right for her."

Court sweeps aside a purple blossom with his foot. Then, with a dark look at me, he pulls out his keys. "Fine."

The house is bright, but quiet, and smells faintly of lemons.

Court heads down a hallway. "Mom!"

Aunt Bryony and I remain in the entryway with Melanie's vases. Closing her eyes, my aunt points her nose to the ceiling and inhales.

Court returns down the hall, followed by his mom. Even in yoga pants and sandals, Alice walks carefully, with poise, just like one would expect from a Miss California. She rolled the sleeves of her Go Panthers! T-shirt past her freckled shoulders, and her smiling face is clean of makeup. "What a delightful surprise."

"I'm sorry to disturb you, Alice. This is my aunt Bryony."

"How lovely." Alice squeezes Aunt Bryony's hand. "I see the family resemblance."

I hand the woman my stalk of hyacinth. "This is for you."

"Thank you." Her eyes squeeze shut as she buries her nose in the periwinkle blossoms. "How I do love your visits."

I have to keep myself from making tracks out the door, down the hill, and maybe to Alaska.

She places the stalk into one of Melanie's vases, this time, one of the earlier, clunkier pieces, then sweeps her hand toward her prairie chic living room. "Come, sit down."

The tiled entryway spills into thick carpets. A ukulele rests on one of two overstuffed chairs. Court removes the ukulele and leans it against the coffee table.

Aunt Bryony and I each take a chair, and I set the cooler on the carpet. My chair engulfs me like a cloud, too fluffy, too suffocating. I scoot to the edge. Alice settles on a matching couch opposite my aunt and I, and Court sits beside her. He leans his chin on his hand and glares into the carpet.

"We'll get right to the point," says Aunt Bryony. "Mim?"

All three pairs of eyes draw to me, one encouraging, the other confused, and the last unforgiving. I squeeze the armrests and a trickle of sweat escapes the hatband of my bucket hat.

Alice turns her fine-boned face toward me.

"Alice, I very accidentally gave you an elixir meant for someone else. I am very, very sorry." I try to keep my voice steady, but it trembles at the end. I keep my gaze trained on Alice.

"An elixir?" Alice's mouth, still smiling, hasn't caught up with her disbelief. "Is that one of your love potions?"

"Yes." I let the news sink in. A gust of hot air blows on me as the heater turns on. It's hot enough in here.

Slowly, Alice shakes her head, causing her ponytail to wag. "Who?"

I let her figure it out herself.

"Franklin." The sight of her perfect nose turning red stabs me in the heart. I try not to throw myself in front of her and beg her forgiveness. Aunt Bryony's chin bobs up and down.

Court curses. Alice grimaces at him, then she returns her gaze to me. "How did it happen?"

I can't tell her about the espresso otherwise she'll figure out it was meant for Ms. DiCarlo. "You touched something that had elixir on it."

"But who was supposed to get it?"

Aunt Bryony gently adds, "We're not at liberty to say."

Alice presses her hand to her mouth. Then she shakes her head. "I don't believe it. I'm sorry. I know how I feel and it can't be because of some love potion. It's just impossible." Her knuckles go white as she interlaces her fingers. She looks to Court for help.

"Mom, it's true."

"You knew about this?"

"Yeah. We spent the last few days on a scavenger hunt for plants to puff you with." He glances at me. "Explain."

Alice hugs herself. "Puff?"

I toy with the hem of my shirt. "A PUF is an elixir to rid you of your feelings—"

"I don't understand. Are you saying my feelings aren't . . . real?"

Aunt Bryony twists her gold wedding band. "The elixir just opened your eyes to Mr. Frederics. Your feelings are genuine."

Court's mom doesn't have a single filling as far as I can see.

I show her the cooler. "The PUF can also be a special kind of flower. It's painless. Just a swipe on your skin."

Aunt Bryony's iridescent beads clack together as she leans forward. "It won't erase your memories of Mr. Frederics. It just makes you less attached to them. The heart is like a balloon. The PUF just tugs it back to earth."

"A balloon? No, no." Alice shakes her head.

Court rouses himself out of his black mood and puts his arm around his mom. "It's going to be okay."

She wiggles out from under his arm. "I'm sorry, Mim, I just can't believe it. I like Franklin, and I think he likes me, too." Tears collect in her eyes and she wipes them with her palms. Court passes her the tissue box.

The sound of someone shuffling down the hallway causes all of us to lift our heads. Melanie, clad in sweats, glares at me. Her face is puffy like she's been crying. She asks, "What's going on?"

Alice waves her hand distractedly at her daughter. "We have visitors."

Melanie locks her arms in front of her and glowers at me.

Alice switches back to us. "I mean, we've had a great time this week, when I wasn't yard sailing, and I just don't see how that can be fake." Her pitch goes high and she places a hand over her chest. After she collects her composure she reaches for the ukulele resting against the table.

"It's not fake." I do my best to ignore the frost coming from Melanie's side of the room. "You really do like him, but he came to us originally for help with someone else."

"Ah. What if I don't want to be puffed?"

Court squeezes his eyes shut and I can't help wondering if he's remembering when he asked me a similar question.

"It's your choice. A PUF will take away the hurt, though."

Court glances up at me, then returns his head to his hands.

Placing the ukulele on her lap, Alice tentatively plucks each string. "It's just so embarrassing. I baked him a cake. And a pie."

Aunt Bryony opens her hands. Her nails are buffed to a high

shine. "The embarrassment is all ours."

Alice starts strumming a series of minor chords.

Court rubs at his jaw and looks at his sister. Shaking her head, Melanie stomps away. Alice stares through the distressed finish of the table as her fingers pick out a slow, depressive tune.

"Will you be telling him?" Alice doesn't break her rhythm.

"Only to the extent that we failed to fix the correct target," says Aunt Bryony.

Mr. Frederics has to know? I hide my surprise by staring at the crystals dripping from the chandelier.

"He would never know that you received the elixir, unless of course you wish us to tell him." Aunt Bryony leans back, absent-mindedly twisting the gold band around her finger.

"Why would I do that?"

"To put your actions in the right context."

"Right. D-do most people in my situation choose to undo it?"

"It's only happened twice, and in both cases, the parties elected not to be PUF'ed. As Lord Tennyson observed, 'tis better to have loved and lost, than never to have loved at all."

The strumming stops. Alice passes her gaze over all of us, her face faraway. Then she starts up with her uke again.

Aunt Bryony rises. "Take as long as you need to decide. We'll see ourselves out."

I linger, looking for my feet in the fluffy Sherpa carpets.

"Court." His gaze snaps to me, but I can barely meet his eyes. "It could work on you, too."

He scoffs, a sharp exhale of breath, and shakes his head.

I back away, a smaller, more wilted version of myself. "Again, I'm really sorry." Head down, I follow my aunt. Once the carpets end, our footsteps clack noticeably on the home stretch of tiles to the front door.

As we reach the front door of the great hacienda, the ukulele stops midsong, and the notes hang in the air.

"Stop," says Alice, pushing off against Court's knee to standing.

"I'll do it."

"Mom." Court lets out a frustrated groan. "Are you sure?"

Alice pads to us, shoulders straight and head lifted. "Yes. I have already loved and lost. I'd rather not do it a second time."

Court moves reluctantly behind his mother.

"As for Franklin, if there's someone else he loves, I don't want to interfere."

Aunt Bryony opens the cooler. The bud transformed into a papery white bloom with three petals, bursting with golden marmalade hues. "Your mother would be proud of you," she whispers in my ear.

Alice squeezes her eyes shut and bares her wrist, as if this were a blood transfusion and not a simple swipe of the skin.

Court, who has ceased making eye contact with me, watches

my fingers pluck a petal to injure the plant. I slide the torn petal across Alice's skin. She sighs, a breathy *hmm*. The PUF will reverse my erroneous fixing, but I cannot put things back the way they were.

For anyone.

THIRTY-TWO

"'Why do the plants smell like us?' you ask.
Why not? We drink the same water, we breathe the
same air. We share a history on this earth."
—*Ruza, Aromateur, 1818*

BACK IN AUNT Bryony's rental car, we glide to the fountain. Thankfully nobody has pinched my bike. "What if Mr. Frederics really does like Alice? Is there an exception to the no-rekindling rule?"

The emergency brake makes a ripping sound as she steps on it. "No, we can't fix her again. It would be unfair."

A vision of an old and feeble Mr. Frederics seated in front of a TV tray flashes in my mind. He stares at a pink bakery box, sun-bleached white after decades of decorating the mantel.

"You're a worrier, like your mother. Here's a secret for you." She leans closer to me. "We're not as powerful as we think." Her amber eyes glitter. "Sometimes things happen that have nothing to do with our flowers, and the best we can do is the best we can do."

I hop out of the car to fetch my bike.

She rolls down her window. "Meet you back at home."

Home.

Afternoon sunshine makes the garden glow by the time I drop my bike in our courtyard. The light catches the droplets from our water misters and turns them into fireworks. I shuffle into the kitchen, where Aunt Bryony's dropping vegetables into a pot of heating water.

She smiles at me. "You're back just in time. Sit down."

I pour myself onto a chair.

"What possessed her to paint all the cupboards blue? It's damn depressing."

"They've always been blue." Like her clothes. Like her.

"Not always. They used to be buttercup yellow." She plucks the seven spices from the cabinet used to make Seven-Spice Soup. I watch her moving about the kitchen with ease. She knows where everything is.

"Your mother still keeps them all separate, I see. She could save a lot of time by putting all seven in the same bottle, but no shortcuts for your mother." She taps one of the containers with her fingernail. "Still even using the same rusty tins."

A bubble of defensiveness rises up, even though I know she means no offense. "We need to live frugally."

She hooks an eyebrow. "Please. She could sell these for a hundred times what we bought them for. The vintage look is very popular right now. The more banged up, the better."

"Maybe she doesn't know."

She shakes her head. "Dahli did always have trouble letting things go."

My gaze travels from the old spice tins to the chipped bowl we use for guacamole. Mother should've thrown that ugly thing out after she cut her thumb on the broken edge, but somehow, there it still squats in its usual spot on the counter. I never thought of Mother as sentimental, but I'm beginning to realize there's a lot I didn't know about her.

Aunt Bryony positions a bell pepper on the cutting board, then starts chopping with a few slow strokes. The chopping increases in tempo until the very last slice, which she pops into her mouth.

"Mother chops the exact same way."

She smiles at me, lost in a thought she doesn't share. After adding the pepper to the soup pot, she rejoins me at the table and places her still-damp hand over mine. "So, are you ready to tell me why you called?"

For a split second, I forget. Then the ugly truth pours down on me. I needed advice on how to fall out of love. But now it's too late.

I tap my nose, a nose whose only purpose now is to generate stuff for me to wipe. "I lost my nose."

Her eyebrows go crooked. "I figured. You smell like boiled beets."

My knee knocks into the table leg. Boiled beets—the telltale sign of desperation. "H-how? You can smell?"

"Didn't your mother tell you? It came back."

"Your smell came *back?*" I press my hands on the table to keep me steady.

She nods. "The salt killed off all the old nose receptors and it took about four years to grow them back, but now they're stronger than ever, just like how agapanthus becomes more hardy when you cut them down to their crowns. Aromateurs have always been good at adaptation."

"But sometimes, if you cut the agapanthus down too severely, it just dies."

"No, no. You can still smell this soup, can't you?" I nod. "Your agapanthus didn't die. And you'll be able to go into the ocean whenever you want now."

"The ocean?"

She looks at the wagon-wheel lamp that hangs from the ceiling. "What exactly did your mother tell you about me?"

"She said you almost drowned. And then you lost your nose because you fell in love."

She leans her forearms against the table ledge. "You do know what a lie smells like, don't you?"

"Of course. She wasn't lying."

"But I made it very clear in my letter."

Letter? Mother mentioned that Aunt Bryony had written her a letter, but she threw it away. *If it was something important, she could have told me in person. She never came, of course.* "I don't think she read it."

A gasp rattles my aunt's throat and she's back to staring at the wagon-wheel lamp. "Someone yelled 'Whales!' and Dahli wouldn't hand over the damn binoculars. So there I was, craning my neck to see the sights, and the next thing I know, I *am* the sights. I must have drunk half the sea by the time Michael hauled me out."

I press my finger to a throbbing point on my temple as the coincidences line up. We both nearly drowned. We both lost our nose. "So the ocean—?"

"It's all the salt in it. The seawater literally shocks the nasal passages out of commission. That's why aromateurs are not supposed to swim."

"Then it's not because I kissed Court Sawyer."

She smiles. "Nope. Michael and I will soon be celebrating twenty years of marriage, and my nose works better than ever, probably even better than Dahli's. She was always the better nose growing up. I can even eat salty foods now."

"But Larkspur's Last Word says not to fall in love."

"Larkspur was a bit of a drama queen. How can anyone prohibit an act that is as natural as breathing? She just wanted us to watch out for conflicts of interest."

"So there's no jinx."

"Nope. Besides, if she was going to jinx us, don't you think she would've mentioned it?"

It all sounds so reasonable, the way she explains it. A knocking starts up between my ears, like the beginning of a headache. I grip the edge of my seat and feel the soft wood give under my fingernails. So I could have had a relationship with Court, assuming I hadn't botched it up so royally by lying to him.

"Did you try to contact Mother again after the letter?"

Aunt Bryony snorts and sets an elbow on the table. "I called her, but she never picked up. I figured she was still mad, and so I left her alone."

"How long ago was the phone call?"

"Seventeen years."

My tea goes down the wrong pipe.

She sniffs. "The ball was in her court." She sucks in her bottom lip, the way Mother does when she's brooding. "Forgiveness is a gift you give yourself. Obviously, she didn't want the gift."

So if Mother had just read the letter, I might have grown up with an aunt. Why had Mother never reached out to her sister in the years following? Wasn't she concerned, or at least curious? Perhaps there are some injuries for which even the greatest aromateurs cannot self-heal. My heart sags in my chest, and for the first time since Mother left for Oman, I miss her.

Not long after eating Aunt Bryony's soup, I go limp as an unwatered Gerbera daisy and can't stop yawning. Aunt Bryony follows me into my bedroom. The bright colors of the quilt kaleidoscope together in my tired mind. She regards the quilt a moment, then pulls it back.

I drop down into bed. "Thanks for letting me borrow it."

"It's yours, Mimsy. I have no one to pass it down to. Just think, you might have twins one day."

"You don't have children?"

"We weren't so blessed." A smile passes over her lips, then disappears.

"Are you an aromateur now?"

"Yes. I do a pretty good business out there. Wish I had a daughter like you to help me." She combs her fingers through my hair and I suddenly remember Mother doing the same when I was still small enough to sit in her lap.

I yawn again. "Did you put something in the soup?"

"I put in a whole lot of things. And a few extras winks of sleep every night will help you recover your nose sooner."

Valerian root, probably.

"But I don't want to go to sleep yet. I want to hear about your life," I murmur.

"All right. Where should I start?"

"At the beginning."

THIRTY-THREE

"Unlike morning glories, love can bloom
twenty-four hours a day."
—*Lavender, Aromateur, 1949*

I MISS THE rooster crowing, and sleep until past noon. I take my time dressing, feeling more at peace than I have in a long time. My aunt's presence calms me like chamomile tea. Mother is more like triple espresso. Mirror-image gray streaks. Identical, yet opposite.

Once outfitted in my favorite gypsy skirt and oversize sweatshirt, I hunt for Aunt Bryony. Overnight, order has been restored to the garden, leaves swept, branches trimmed, dead flowers picked off. She must have worked all night and all morning.

I find her in the workshop, vigorously shaking a fist-size mixing flask. Spider plants have been placed at strategic locations, one near the lavender stain and a few on the worktable. A line of test tubes stand in traditional arc formation at the table.

She wipes the sweat from her brow onto her apron and smiles. "Good morning."

"Good morning. Thanks for cleaning up. You should've let me help."

"Oh, we saved the mud tubers for you. Neither Kali nor I wanted to get our nails dirty."

"Kali was here?" Something bright and effervescent bubbles up inside me.

"I like her. She smells wholesome."

Aunt Bryony smiles at me, probably detecting the bright mandarin I must be giving off—the childhood scent of hope. If Kali came to help with the garden, maybe she's over being disappointed in me. Maybe things can go back to the way they were. "Why didn't she stay?" We always have lunch together on Sunday.

"She said she had things to do."

"Oh." The mandarin must be fading. It's strange not to smell my own emotions anymore.

"I see your mother never joined the twenty-first century." Aunt Bryony nods to Mother's antique beam scale. "Still doing everything the long way. They even have machines that will shake the vials for you, did you know?"

"She doesn't trust them."

"Naturally." She holds the mixing flask up to the light and swirls the liquid, which is the same dark amber of her eyes. She unstoppers the flask and sniffs. "Perfect, as always."

"Thanks."

She fills the sink with soapy water. I collect glass vials in a tub and bring them to her. "Actually, the last batch didn't work so well."

She hoists an eyebrow at me and an owl-like seriousness descends upon her features. "Neutralizing mist always works."

"But—"

"But nothing. Now, tell your Mother her spurge weed's going mushy."

I nearly drop one of the vials. "Wait, you're not going to see her?"

"No, honey."

"It was so long ago. I'm sure if you explain to Mother what you wrote in the letter, she'll understand."

"We drifted too far apart on our own boats. And you know swimming was never our strong suit." Aunt Bryony returns Mother's apron to its hook. "Come, walk me to my car."

Thanks to Aunt Bryony and Kali, the main garden and the house are up to Mother's standard of cleanliness. Still, I can't help but frown.

Aunt Bryony takes my cold hand in her hot one. "Cheer up, honey. Your mother will always be on your side. You know, between the two of us, your mother is actually the nicer twin."

"Mother?"

"Whenever we argued, Dahli was the one who gave in. Even that time with Edward."

"Who is Edward?"

"The boy who was sweet on Dahli." She cuts her eyes to me, gaping as I walk alongside her. "We heard him bragging about his 'parts' and so we spied on him and his friends by the creek. Dahli goes, 'Zucchini, my foot. More like zuke-teenie.'" Aunt Bryony grins, and her cheekbones bunch up like crab apples. "Anyway, the boys chased us to the road, but couldn't go farther because they weren't wearing clothes. Next day, Edward's bringing her violets."

Her grin fades. "I didn't realize she was pressing the violets in the telephone book, and I used it to whack in a nail. The flowers were fine, but we still got into it."

Mother's favorite bookmark has violets in it.

"The groundskeeper, William, locked us into the workshop and wouldn't let us out until we settled our differences."

"Did you?"

"First, we tried to escape out of the skylight. Nearly killed myself when the chair fell off the table."

"So *that's* what caused that dent in the hardwood." Grandmother didn't fix it because she wanted to remind her daughters not to play on chairs.

"Yes. Dahli gave in that time, too, or we would still be in there." She bends to pick up a fallen leaf and drops it in the nearest composter. "Maybe she was just tired of giving in."

The Mother I know rarely gives in, at least to me. Maybe losing her sister hardened her in ways I never knew. "It's been nearly twenty years. Surely she's ready to talk to you."

She snorts. I don't even sound convincing. "What happened to Edward?" I ask.

"Our mother found out and forbade Dahli from seeing him." She stares ahead of her, eyes unfocused. "Last I heard, he'd become a mathematician."

The winds of chance blow a chilly breath down my back. That would explain Mother's aversion to algebra. "So Mother caught her falling heart."

She stops walking and gives me half a smile. "*Though cowslips line thy mapled cart, the wise will catch a falling heart.* That's another one of those Last Words that's subject to interpretation."

"Wh-what do you mean?"

"I mean, our ancestor Carmelita was a poet, not a historian." The black rental stands in the driveway. Aunt Bryony opens the driver side, setting off a warning chime.

"But, I'm not ready for you to leave."

She hands me a business card from her purse. It simply says "Bryony, Aromateur," followed by an address and phone number. "Call me anytime."

My nose begins to run, and I frown to keep my emotions in check.

The car door continues to chime annoyingly. I want to slam it closed, as if that could prevent her from leaving. "Maybe if Mother saw you, she'd realize how much she misses you. I mean, people might disappoint each other, but that doesn't

314

mean it's over." At least, I hope so.

A pained expression crosses her face, and she touches my cheek. "Oh, Mimsy. You and your mother are going to be okay. And if you ever need an escape, you will always be welcome at my home." With that, she scoots into the rental and blows away with the wind.

I stand there long after she has gone, breathing in exhaust fumes and missing her already.

I wonder how much Mother argued with Grandmother Narcissa over Edward, and how much it had hurt to let him go. Probably a lot. Love is never easy, even for people like us. All this time, I thought she knew the tail end of the chicken from the head, but turns out there were a whole lot of feathers in between for her, too.

What did Aunt Bryony mean about Carmelita's Last Word? Cowslip, or primrose, grows in clusters and was a key ingredient in medieval love spells. Mother interpreted the Last Word to mean our matchmaking required us to keep our own hearts tightly cloistered, but maybe there is another way to read it. Cowslip can symbolize many things, like pensiveness, womanly grace.

The faint ring of the telephone sends me rushing back into the house.

"Good morning, dear," says Mother's voice. "I'm at Muscat International. Traffic was horrible, now they're calling us. How are you?"

My tongue stalls, and my brain stretches taut as a rope

between equally matched emotions of relief and anxiety. I cover the mouthpiece and exhale before answering. "Fine. The emergency line doesn't work."

"Really? Is there an emergency?"

Should I tell her now? If I do, she'll just stew on the way home. If I don't, she might be even madder when she learns I lied. But after all the other lies, maybe this one won't even register. "Emergency solved." For now.

"Mim?" she asks sternly.

"I'll tell you all about it when you get home."

"Okay. Well, see you tomorrow after school."

"Good-bye, Mother."

I dial Kali. I no longer expect her to pick up, but the act of calling her is strangely soothing. Maybe when she sees my call come in, she'll remember that someone cares. This time, her phone goes straight to voicemail.

I pour myself into a chair, suddenly weary, though I haven't done so much as pull a weed all day. It's as if all the people I've let down in the past week are standing on my shoulders. Mr. Frederics. Alice. Ms. DiCarlo. Kali. Drew. Mother. And of course, the one who smells like campfire, Court.

THIRTY-FOUR

"THE MARIGOLDS ARE HARDY SOULS. IN RAIN,
DROUGHT, EVEN SNOWFALL, THEY FLOURISH, POKING
THEIR HEADS OUT, LIKE TINY TORCHES OF TRUTH."
—*Privet, Aromateur, 1703*

THE NEXT MORNING, I pedal to school, filled with an acute awareness that this might be the last time I make this trek. Mother will be home in a matter of hours. I try to appreciate the sights rushing by—a screen of Texas privet with its tiny, dark berries, a wooden gate that Frankensteins into an iron one, then chain link, then back to wood again. The iris I wrapped in silk hops in my basket when I roll over a speed bump.

Today, the ever-changing signage on the school facade says, "Cheeseburger Monday! Today at Noon!" Another homecoming tradition. If somebody buys you a burger, that's an invitation to the dance. Eat it and accept the invitation.

A crowd collects around a bulletin board outside the school office. Beside pictures of the SS *Argonaut*, the venue for the homecoming dance, are photos of court nominees. I give the board a cursory glance from under my fedora as I stroll by with my bike. Not surprisingly, Court and Whit are up there, along with Vicky and Melanie and other A-listers. What causes me to nearly crash into a trash can is the sight of Kali's brown face, smiling right alongside Vicky's.

Kali's nominated for homecoming queen.

"I'm so voting for Kali," one girl says to her friend. "It's about time someone besides a mean girl won."

The friend's head pumps up and down. "It's about time a Latina won."

"Vicky *is* Latina, stupid," says the first girl. "Kali's black."

"Actually, she's Samoan," I inform them.

I can't help worrying about what will happen if Kali beats the odds and wins. That will be another pin in Vicky's cushion. Then again, what more can Vicky do? She's done her best, and Kali's still standing. No, she's outstanding.

Ms. DiCarlo, sitting behind her computer monitor, sneezes as I enter the library.

"Good morning. I was thinking about your allergies." I take out the Post-it on which I had written the name and office number for Dr. Lipinsky, the junior. "He's an otolaryngologist."

She studies the paper, her nose draped by a tissue. "That's kind of you. But I'm beginning to think I know what I'm allergic to."

"What?"

"Actually, you."

My mouth opens and closes.

She chuckles. "It must be all those flowers you work with."

I grab the edges of my hat, as if that will contain the pollen. "I'm sorry. I should stop coming in."

"It's okay. I enjoy our visits. And anyway, I might be moving soon."

"Moving?"

"Yes, one of the inquiries worked out."

"But it's only been a few days."

"I know, isn't it great? The University of Oxford's library was very excited to get my résumé. They've been looking for a medieval collections specialist." She smiles, lowering her eyes modestly to her keyboard.

Her résumé. Here I had thought she was on a manhunt, not a job hunt. "That's great." I rock forward on my toes and back again, marveling at how just when you think you've found the answer, it turns out you were asking the wrong question. Whether Ms. DiCarlo finds love, or moves into an English castle hemmed in with coralbells, I hope she enjoys her journey. Isn't that why I went to high school, despite knowing I'd be an aromateur in the end? To experience everyday life on the other side of the briar. I didn't realize I could foul it up so completely. But if I could do it all over, I might not change a thing. Mostly.

In algebra, the sight of a substitute teacher at Mr. Frederics's desk launches new worries in my head. Is Mr. Frederics's absence due to Alice? My pencil draws zigzags in my notebook. Maybe it's good that he's absent, as I still haven't figured out the best way to tell him about the elixir-gone-wrong.

The substitute teacher knits while we do independent study, which for Drew and Vicky means passing each other folded-up pieces of paper—probably love notes.

I pass Drew a note of my own. "Meet me by the drinking fountain."

Then I take one of two hall passes and hurry around the corner to the designated place. Moments later, Drew appears. He peers through a curtain of his greasy blond locks, blue eyes bright with curiosity. "What's up?"

"Do you, um, like Vicky?"

"Yeah, why?" He lowers his freshly scrubbed face closer to mine.

"Sometimes love isn't what it's cracked up to be." I rub my arms, which have gone rubbery.

"You brought me out of class to tell me that?"

"Yes."

"Well, thanks." Unlike mine, his laugh sounds genuine. He cocks a blond eyebrow at me and leans in again. "Actually, it's not like that between us. She doesn't like me. Like a boyfriend, I mean. I asked her to the homecoming dance, and she said no."

My jaw rolls open. "She did?"

"Yeah. And it's okay, because I don't like her that way either. I mean, I thought I did. But hanging out with her is just like, fun, you know?"

"It is?" Fun? Vicky?

"Yeah."

But the elixir worked, I saw it with my own eyes. Everyone saw it. My aunt's words echo in my head. *We're not as powerful as we think.* Elixirs, after all, only open the eyes to the possibility of love. The individuals, both target and client, still have a choice on whether to act on those feelings. Sometimes romantic love isn't the end point, only the beginning.

Drew's still looking at me expectantly as he scratches his back with the hall pass. "You're kinda weird, but I like you."

"Thanks, I, er, I feel the same."

The lunch bell rings an hour early to give everyone a chance to get his or her cheeseburgers, which are sold by an outside vendor. With the cafeteria closed today, Kali should be on the field with the rest of the school.

After I stuff my things into my locker, I remove the iris I stored there. Irises say, "Your friendship means so much." Things might not be the same between us anymore, but I want Kali to know I will always be there for her.

I head into the cluster of students buying cheeseburgers in the parking lot from one of two Cowboy Cheeseburgers food trucks, each shaped like a cowboy hat with a brown awning for the brim.

Something's different today. The sea doesn't part when I walk through it. Either people are too excited about Cheeseburger

Monday, or they're getting used to me.

Cassandra's soprano catches my attention. From somewhere nearby, she's singing "Cheeseburger in Paradise." Craning my neck, I spot her, sitting thirty feet away. As she sings her last note, she stretches her arm toward Kali, sporting her Twice Loved Vans, and munching a cheeseburger. Who bought her that?

Stunned, I think back to the drive home from Meyer. Court had said, *Cass is just a friend, you know. I mean, obviously.* At the time, I thought he meant, of course he wouldn't have a girlfriend if he liked me. He meant something else. Something obvious to everyone but the love witch. If falling in love had a smell, Mother never mentioned it. It occurs to me that we can detect heartache, a crush, admiration, and a hundred other love-related scents, so why not falling in love? Perhaps the note of a heart in free fall is too fleeting to notice.

Cassandra pulls out a pickle from her burger, and Kali opens her own bun to receive it. Her expression is happy, relaxed, the way I will always remember her.

A group of passing girls yell, "We voted for you, Kali!"

I blink, wondering how and when Kali developed such a following. Though her surge in popularity cheers me, I can't help feeling a little like bread crust—left behind. She nods at them. "Cool."

Catching sight of me, she waves me over with her burger. I brighten by a factor of at least sixteen.

She hands Cassandra her burger, then climbs to her feet and meets me halfway. Her expression is even, almost wry, though my inability to pinpoint her exact mood without my nose unsettles me. She neatly rolled her sweats to midcalf. Her hair looks different, no longer in braids, but neatly tucked into a bun. "There's gonna be a lot of heartburn here today," she drops casually, as if nothing was ever amiss.

I grin. "Thanks for coming by yesterday."

She nods. "Your aunt's a trip. Almost fell over my slippers when I saw her. Thought she was your mom."

"You're not the only one."

"She told me what happened with Alice. Too bad about poor Layla, but it was for a good cause."

"Right." Guilt starts to creep in, but I push it away, feeling Kali's eyes upon me. "I meant what I said on your voicemail. You were amazing."

"Thanks. My mom didn't think so. Made me see a shrink on Saturday and our pastor on Sunday."

So that's why Kali didn't stay for lunch yesterday. No, the world does not revolve around Planet Mim. "I'm sorry. How is she now?"

"We're still working on it."

"And . . . how are you?"

"Good. It felt like I had all this lint clogging up my trap, and now it's cleaned out. Doesn't mean I won't catch more lint, but for now I'm running smoothly." She pops her neck from side to side.

I hand her the iris. "I should've trusted you to handle your own business."

"Thanks." She takes the flower and puts its frilly petals to her nose. "But that wasn't why I got mad." She frowns into the yellow center of the bulb, her lips a tight rosebud. Then her dark eyes probe mine. "Look, why do you think I like hanging out with you?"

"Lifetime all-you-can-eat salad?"

She gives an emphatic shake of her head.

"You're trying to steal my dance moves?"

Her eyes flick to the sky. "Definitely no. When I got suspended back in eighth grade, Dad gave me a choice—take that weeding job with your mom or highway cleanup. It was a close call, believe me."

I remember that day Kali's father brought her to us. She barely spoke a word and smelled so blue and lost.

"It was the best thing I ever did." She opens a hand large as a catcher's mitt, moving it gracefully to accentuate her points. I feel a rush of love for her. "You and your mother are true to yourselves, even if it means not getting paid, or spending half of your day up to your ears in dirt, just like those earthworms. Made me think I could be an earthworm, too. My poetry started flying after that."

I swallow hard. Kali had never told me that before.

"I needed you to stand up to Vicky, so *I* could stand up. I needed to see you wouldn't cave."

"I'm sorry I disappointed you."

"You didn't disappoint me." She points the toe of one slip-on, then the other. "The thing about you is that, even when you're wrong, you're still trying to do right, even when most people would've punched out, called it a day. It's like you have to take the hardest route possible or it doesn't count."

"It's a survival instinct. We hail from a long line of women who don't want to face our mothers."

"It's more than that." She cocks an eyebrow at me. "You're honest as a Sunday shirt. I guess I never expected to see the shirt get wrinkled."

That chafes a little. "All shirts get wrinkled, even the polyester ones. *I* was trying to be there for you." I can hear the injury in my own voice.

Kali's mouth bunches up. She's either thinking, or about to clobber me. Then her face relaxes. "I'm sorry, Nosey. I should've been there for you, too. I guess I have a lot of wrinkles of my own to iron out."

I nod.

"How can I make it up to you? You need me to be there when your mom comes home?"

An image of Mother's angry face springs to mind. I consider. Mother can't explode with Kali present, but maybe she would just store up more anger for later. "It's okay. I like to make it as hard as possible for myself, remember?"

"Your mom's not so bad. She's got a big heart, though she

doesn't like to show it. I guess it's just her way."

"It's not just her way. It's the aromateur way. We have a say-ing, *Though cowslips line thy mapled cart, the wise will catch a falling heart.*"

"Cows' *lips?*" A smile lurks behind her lips.

"Cow *slips.*" We share a chuckle. "They were used in love potions. It means, though we deal in love, we must keep our own feelings in check. Aromateurs have never been the life of the party."

She wedges her chin between her thumb and forefinger. "But you're not like that—restrained. Neither is your aunt. You don't push people away. I think you like them a lot more than I do."

"Guess I should work on that," I mutter.

She paces in a circle then faces me square on, arms crossed. "I think you're reading it wrong. It doesn't say catch *your* falling heart; it says catch *a* falling heart, meaning anyone's. It's like the saying, 'catch a falling star.' Just like love, stars don't fall too often, and if you see one, you don't close your eyes. You don't let the love go splat."

I squint at the Jupiter grass, wondering if she's right. Kali is a poet. If anyone can untangle a verse, it's her. Larkspur was wrong about romantic relationships, so perhaps there's room for this new reading of Carmelita's Last Word, too. If she's right, life just got a lot more interesting. Still. "Mother won't believe it."

"Tell her it makes sense from a business perspective. You

can't sell the product if you don't use it yourself."

Cassandra starts singing again, holding her hands out to Kali. We watch her a moment.

"You better finish your cheeseburger. Thanks, Kali."

She bumps me with her elbow. "Good luck." She starts off toward Cassandra, then turns around again. "Hey, Nosey, if you get sacked, can I still keep my job?"

I make a face. She laughs as she treads away, arms swinging easy and free.

I pick my way through the grass, around the cheeseburger crowd and toward the school.

"Mim!" Lauren trots up to me, pulling Pascha behind her. "Help us. Pascha's dad said she could go to the dance and she wants to ask Whit, but she's wussing out."

Pascha clutches an unwrapped cheeseburger to her chest. Oil from the burger seeps through its papery envelope. "I'll just dog myself. He likes Mim, not me." She sniffs loudly and wipes her nose with her headscarf.

"Where is he?" I ask.

"Over there." Lauren points to a cluster of guys tossing around a Frisbee. Whit leaps, his hair whipping in all directions, and plucks the disc out of the air.

Not seeing Court anywhere in the vicinity, I square my fedora on my head and pull my sleeves down to my knuckles. "Follow me."

327

We troop across the field to the target. When Whit sees me, a goofy smile spreads across his face, and he opens his arms wide enough to hug one of the huge recycling bins set nearby. This time, I'm ready for him.

THIRTY-FIVE

"Even the toughest philodendron can go into shock if the weather drops suddenly. I wrapped mine in a wool sweater and it did just fine."
—Hazel, *Aromateur*, 1901

"HELLO," I TELL Whit brightly. "This is Pascha."

Pascha's gone as white and still as a saltshaker. While Whit takes in the girl resisting Lauren's efforts to push her forward, I hit him with a double serving of BBG from behind. Whit's goofy grin disappears. He takes off his sunglasses and squints at all of us.

"Pascha likes spicy food," I say.

Lauren gives her friend a final push. "I slipped a jalapeño in her smoothie once and she didn't even notice."

Whit switches to me again and a smile creeps up his cheeks. My mouth goes dry. Don't tell me Aunt Bryony's batch is defective, too. Maybe something's wrong with the formula. Now I'll have to make another disclosure and—

"Do you have a library card? Because I am checking you out." Whit beams at Pascha.

Pascha blushes, and Lauren claps her hands together.

I let out a held breath, then back away slowly. The only person who notices me leave is Lauren, who gives me a thumbs-up.

I take a shortcut around the crowd back to the library to grab my bike. After lunch, instead of regular afternoon classes, the whole school does "school-spirit-building exercises on the field, like tug-of-war and three-legged races. I might as well go home and talk to Mother. No use putting off the inevitable. Plus, then I can stop worrying about running into Court.

On my way to the library racks, I pass an equipment shed, wincing at the acrid smell of cigarette smoke. That odor could seep through a brick wall. A figure leans against the back of the shed, looking out toward the street. Melanie's cigarette's short enough to burn her fingers. When she sees me, she chuckles, then throws her stub to the ground. "Well, hello, witch."

I don't remember smelling tobacco on her before. Must be a new habit. Maybe she was sick of getting hand-me-down fumes from Vicky and decided to make her own. I'm tempted to throw something back, but then I notice her knees, both skinned and bleeding.

She snorts. "I *tripped*."

I think about asking her if she's okay, but she would just ignore me. Her trembling fingers reach into her purse and pull out a lighter and a fresh cigarette. I hike my messenger bag more securely over my shoulder. I should just leave her alone. But I can't, either because I'm genetically predisposed to meddle in the lives of others or because I feel like she has earned the right to a few punches in my direction. "I can find you some aloe."

"You think plants can fix everything." Her face is blotchy with dry patches above her mouth.

"Not everything. We're still looking for the cure for the common cold."

She fumbles with her lighter but manages to light her cigarette. "Why couldn't you just leave it alone?"

"What do you mean?"

"Mom and Mr. Frederics were good together."

I swallow my surprise and lick my dried lips. "I thought you didn't want them to be together."

"At first. But they're like, made for each other. Anyone with half a brain could see that. It would've been easier on everyone." Spittle flecks her mouth.

I lift my chin. "Easier doesn't make it right."

"Harder doesn't make it right, either."

Touché.

"You live up there in your fairy-tale garden, thinking you're so special because you bring love to the world." She draws out the word *love* as if it's a disease. "But what happens after you make those matches? What happens if Prince Charming turns out to be more like Prince Loser? Life is not all roses for the rest of us. Sometimes the right thing is the wrong thing." Smoke curls out her nostrils.

I shift from clog to clog. She has a point. The Rulebook

prescribes one course, but it's not always the most humane.

When did the path grow so crooked? At first, undoing my mistake seemed all important. Then things changed, relationships changed.

The blood is starting to clot on Melanie's skinned knee. I suddenly remember the business card in my bag. The words "Evelyn Salzmann, Sculptor to the Stars" are printed in typewriter font with a phone number. I hold the card out to Melanie.

She barely glances at the name and doesn't take it. "Yeah, so?"

"She's looking for an intern." I stick the card in the hedge right where she can see it. Then I leave. If she decides to keep the card or burn it, I don't want to know. I have enough Sawyers on my mind at the moment.

I collect my bike and walk it through the courtyard. Students lounge around a flagpole, eating lunch. Once I reach the parking lot, I hop on my bike.

Court's Jeep is toward the back. The sight pours a giddy kind of poison into me. I think back to our kiss in Neptune's court, knowing that the smell of the ocean, the miso scent of bladder wrack, the California lilac, even the Styrofoam smell of neoprene will always remind me of the pain and the joy of knowing Court.

A Volkswagen brakes hard right next to me and I stumble off my bike, but catch myself before I go splat.

Through the open window, the driver, a girl in a drill-team

uniform, yells something at me. I hardly hear the obscenity when I recognize her passenger.

The sight punches me in the gut.

Court Sawyer, his face stricken, is holding a cheeseburger.

Everything goes cold inside me. It's like someone poured in ice cubes and shook me up, and I can hardly make sense of which way's up. The door opens, but I push off, hurtling away like a meteor in search of her orbit.

My chest shakes when I inhale, and I press one arm into my stomach to cage my sob. Somehow, it hurts to breathe even worse than when I was underwater, drowning. If this is how love feels, it makes you wonder why everyone's so obsessed with finding it. Maybe our elixirs should come with a warning label: product comes with serious risk of total meltdown.

I wanted him to get over me. I should be happy he moved on.

I wipe my eyes with the back of my hand. It's better this way. Relationships just distract us from our life's work. Grandmother Narcissa only became great through devotion to her craft. Assuming I can get my nose back, think of all the matches I can make, undistracted by other people. Undistracted by the one commodity in which we trade.

My legs feel shaky and tired even before I get to Parrot Hill.

Should I tell Mother straight out, or come into it sideways once she's had a chance to tell me about her trip?

As I round the curve toward the home stretch, a singular

sight makes me slam on the brakes. A bamboo-green hybrid with a Honk If You Love Math bumper sticker sits in the driveway.

Mr. Frederics is here.

Mother already knows.

THIRTY-SIX

MOTHER AND MR. Frederics sit outside the workshop under the nutmeg tree and its buddy, the ylang-ylang. Their backs are to me, with the tops of their heads peeking out above the shrub line. As I approach, Mother calls out my name without turning around. She can smell me from a hundred yards away.

Mother's still in her traveling clothes—blue pullover, loose-fitting pants, and a scarf knitted by a client. She stands to give me a perfunctory hug, not smiling. Her nose wrinkles, catching a scent of something it doesn't like. It could be a dozen things, Aunt Bryony, the stink of deception, unwashed hair. But a single word causes a chill to snake up my spine: "Blueberries."

I forgot about that one. Of course she smells my heartbreak.

Mr. Frederics nods at me. "Afternoon, Mim."

"Hi, Mr. Frederics."

"Mr. Frederics was sharing with me something very interesting." A muscle in her cheek twitches.

"Oh?" I sink onto the bench opposite them. My big eyes don't fool Mother for a second.

Mr. Frederics laughs sheepishly. "Well, Sofia, Ms. DiCarlo, isn't interested in me after all. You were there at the Puddle Jumpers event. I was trying to teach the children mathematics with the grapes. She told me to give it a rest, not everyone likes math. Imagine that." He scoots back on our teakwood bench and matches his fingertips together. "Anyway, no matter. Turns out, I'm in love with someone else."

Mother's nostrils flare and she twists around and peers at our solid wooden gate. "Seems we have another visitor."

Who does she smell?

"Hello?" calls the familiar voice of a former Miss California.

Mr. Frederics hops to his feet and shades his eyes. "It's her. Now what could she be doing here? Allow me." He starts toward the gate.

Mother fixes me with an unblinking stare. "How long was Bryony here?"

She smells the remains of my aunt's presence. "Two days."

"Why'd she come?"

"I called her."

The blood drains out of her face. "You *called* her? Whatever for?"

"I lost my nose."

"I know. You smell like boiled beets." Her voice becomes a whisper.

Mr. Frederics trails after Alice, his face animated as he speaks to her. Alice picks her way toward us without looking back at him.

"But the good news is, I still have the rest of me." I laugh shakily.

She blows out an irritated breath. Something catches her nose, and she sniffs. Her eyes snap to mine. "Is that bladder wrack? And thirty-two-thousand-year-old narrow-leaf campion from Siberia. What have you done?"

My words trip out. "About the bladder wrack, that's the one I told you about, the one with the silvery finish, like miso soup. I found it, er, in the ocean, and as for the campion, it was bushy. Meyer won't even notice—"

"You *stole* it?"

Our visitors reach us. A film of hospitality barely conceals Mother's anger. We both stand to greet Alice.

Alice holds out her hand. "Hello. It's nice to see you again."

Mother's eyes grow round, but Alice doesn't notice. She's distracted by Mr. Frederics behind her, who's furtively pressing a handkerchief to the damp spots of his head.

I better pipe up. "Oh, this is actually not my aunt—"

Mother swipes a finger in the air toward me, telling me to shut up. She recovers herself. "How nice to see you, too." She slides me a questioning look.

"Mrs. *Sawyer*, won't you have a seat?" I help Mother out, still puzzling over why she doesn't want me to tell Alice of her real identity.

"Please, it's Alice."

"Alice." Even Mother's heard of the infamous Sawyers. Her nose twitches as she inhales sharply, trying to figure out the situation.

"I think I hear the kettle boiling," I fib.

"Sit down, Mimosa." Mother shifts her gaze between Alice and Mr. Frederics. "Mr. Frederics, would you be so kind as to fetch the tea tray from the kitchen?"

"My pleasure." Mr. Frederics hurries away.

Alice gives Mother a grateful smile that turns panicked. "It's not working," she hisses.

"Oh?" says Mother, steering her raised eyebrows to me.

I marvel at the power of a single uttered vowel. My insides wring out and sweat pools on my back and neck.

"Why do you think the PUF isn't working?" I ask.

Mother straightens up like an arrow shot her in the back. "The PUF."

"You know, the orchid we swiped on her wrist."

Another invisible arrow shoots Mother, this time in the front, and her breath sweeps out of her. She grabs her palm and begins kneading it with her knuckle. Her mouth flattens into a grim line.

Alice glances toward the kitchen. "You said it would be

immediate, but I can't stop thinking about him. I mean, I started to make an omelet this morning, and before I knew it, I was making cake batter." She presses her hand to her heart.

Mother stops kneading her palm and folds her hands in front of her, back in charge of the situation. "The heart remembers. It's perfectly possible to fall back in love with Mr. Frederics again, all by yourself." She slits her eyes at me. "Or have I mentioned that?"

"You said the heart was like a balloon," Alice volunteers.

"Ah, yes, I did." Mother sends me a withering glance.

Tabitha the chicken flies under the teakwood table and starts pecking at my shoes. "As, er, you explained, a PUF just tugs the balloon back to earth. Maybe Alice just let go of the string?" I glance at Mother for confirmation.

Her sigh is loud enough to have its own echo. "Yes, it's very possible for you to fall in love with him again on your own. I should have mentioned that."

Alice pats a stray hair back in place. "But I didn't even see him after you puffed me."

"Something must have reminded you of your feelings for him," says Mother. "The PUF doesn't take away memories."

Alice wraps her cashmere sweater more snugly around her. "He let me borrow his coat during the homecoming game. It's still hanging on my coatrack. And it smells like him." Her worried eyes follow a trail of scarlet runner beans. "So I *am* in love with him. For real."

"Seems that way," says Mother. "Let me add, and hopefully

I've mentioned this before"—another glare at me—"how sorry I am that this happened."

Alice shakes her head and studies the ground.

"I'm sorry, Alice," I say. "Is there anything I can do?"

She looks up, and I realize she's not frowning, but smiling. "Honestly, I wasn't that surprised to learn I had been fixed. I didn't think I could love anyone again. But now that I know my balloon can still float away, I think I'll be fine, even though I'm not the one Franklin wants."

Mr. Frederics suddenly appears from behind the shrubs, bearing a tray. The china clinks.

"Let me take that from you." I set the tray on the table.

He rubs his hands together as if trying to get them warm. "Alice, I know it's none of my business why you're here, but I pray you're not ordering an elixir."

Alice drops her gaze demurely to her hands, twisting at a ruby ring around her finger. "It isn't easy for an old divorcée like myself. Why are you concerned?"

He blushes and straightens his tie, the same way he does before he explains corollaries. "You see, well, I bought two tickets to see the Austrian Ukulele Orchestra." His crinkly brown eyes lock on her mascaraed blue ones.

"You did?"

"I sure did. Had to snap 'em up before they sold out."

"But, but how would your lady friend feel about that?"

"Lady friend?" His eyes uncrinkle. "I don't have a lady friend."

"Then why are *you* here?"

Both Alice and Mr. Frederics look at Mother, who in turn passes them to me. Everyone's wondering what the heck everyone else knows and only I can enlighten them.

I straighten my throat. "I, uh—" My voice comes out too high. Tabitha continues pecking my leg. "I accidentally—very accidentally—put your elixir, Mr. Frederics, in Alice's Starbucks. Ms.—er, the *target* was never fixed."

Mother's shoulders slump, even though she probably figured out most of it.

"Well, I'll be," says Mr. Frederics.

I hang my head. "I'm really sorry."

Tabitha starts clucking. When I look up, I realize it's not my chicken, but Mr. Frederics laughing. "I'd say that's your best mistake ever, and you know I've seen a few of them."

A dimple appears in Alice's cheek, the same spot as her son's. She glances up at Mr. Frederics, still standing beside her bench. "Oh, Franklin."

The two gaze at each other, and the moment sparkles with electricity.

Mother quickly rises from her spot next to Alice and waves her hand at the vacancy. "Please, Mr. Frederics, sit here." She grabs a handful of ylang-ylang blossoms that fell from the tree and crushes them in her palm, releasing the aphrodisiacal scent.

"Mim, pour the tea." She's all business now. There's love at hand. I wouldn't be surprised if she clapped her hands and a rainbow appeared.

"We shall let you two talk privately. Please enjoy our garden as long as you wish."

Who knows if they hear her. They're still staring at each other.

I trot after Mother who surely has her own private talk in store for me, and it won't be nearly as pleasant.

THIRTY-SEVEN

"A HOT TEMPER CAN WILT PETUNIAS."
—*Kohana, Aromateur, 1728*

"WHAT WERE YOU thinking? You must always witness the fixing." Mother slaps one hand against the other. Her unopened suitcase lies upon her bed. "Always. Now you understand why we have the rules? They're to keep us from making life-altering blunders."

"Okay, I'm sorry," I say for the tenth time. I push aside the antique lace curtains of the turret and stare down at Mr. Frederics, helping Alice into her car one story below. "Their lives turned out okay."

"You lost your smell! And you should never have called your aunt."

"Who should I have called?"

"Me."

"I did try calling you. The circuits were busy."

She sucks in her breath, then groans. "Well, you wouldn't

have needed to call anyone had you focused on your task, instead of, what's his name?"

"Court." Just saying it stabs my heart.

"Yes, him. Is it over between you two?"

I nod.

"Good. Then maybe we can do something about this *problem*. Do you know how long it took me to make that elixir for Bryony? I had to go to forty-seven countries. *Countries*, Mim. By the time I got everything together, it was too late."

I should tell her about Aunt Bryony's nose returning, but I don't want to yet.

The Merengue roses and chicory wave good-bye to our clients as their cars ease down the long driveway to the street. Maybe it's a road all must walk, this margin between bitter and sweet, not just in love, but in life. The driveway tiles form a stony rainbow, which flow into the sweetbriar hedges. Inside the sweetbriar, sprightly dogbane forms an even row, followed by goldenrod, lavender, and so forth. Layers wrapping us tight as an onion.

"What if it's too late for me, too?" I finally say.

She pulls her hair. "If that's the case, then all of this"—she opens her hands and sweeps them around the room—"and the garden? A waste."

"Maybe there's more to life than just smelling plants."

"Like what?" Her lips form a tight line.

"Who was Edward?"

She throws her arms to her sides. "She told you about him?"

I rub my finger over one of the bench's velvet-covered buttons.

"Did you like him?"

"Of course not."

"Then why do you carry around that bookmark? You must have sort of liked him."

Her lips unstick. "I may have been curious about certain things that it is natural to be curious over, but I never veered from the course predestined for me."

I may not have my nose, but I'm discovering there are other ways to tell if someone is uncomfortable, like the drift in the eyes, or the way bare toes can grip at the floorboards. "And anyway, you should be more worried about your nose than my bookmark." She throws her hands at me. "You're barely fifteen. Barely even used it. Do you realize you might *never* smell again. You'd be utterly . . ."

"What?" My throat has gone dry, but I push out the word. "Useless?"

I'm seven years old again, wandering the warehouse of spider plants. Does my mother love me? I didn't know the answer then, and I was afraid to ask.

Mother lifts her nose a fraction and squints at a spot on the wall. Her silence punctures me like a dart to the heart.

The rumble of car engines fades, and the lovebirds leave us to our strange jungle.

The rounded windows of the turret squeeze around me more tightly than I remember. No longer does the cramped space strike me as a space capsule, but a time capsule, where nothing inside ever changes.

At least for Mother.

She doesn't say a word as I leave her room, compounding the ache in my heart.

I hike to the farthest reaches of our property, where the plants grow wild and rabbits hop through mushroom rings wide as Hula-Hoops. A cluster of Italian cypresses solemnly commune. I flop down on the ground and stare up at their elfin-hat treetops, rising at least thirty feet.

My dream of going to high school was hatched in this very spot, a dream that I could live more than the odd, hermetical life of an aromateur. Never did I imagine those dreams would cost me so dearly.

Useless.

My mother doesn't love me. I am like one of her garden tools, and now that I am broken, she no longer has a need for me. For her, an aromateur only becomes great by forsaking all personal attachments, not just romantic ones. Even one's own flesh and blood.

I pick up a pinecone, and begin to count all the spiral patterns whirling in one direction—thirteen, and then the other—eight. Both Fibonacci numbers. A bitter laugh stalls in my throat.

Well, now I have all the time to study as much math as I want. But that isn't what I want. Suddenly, I'm sniffing, then snuffling, and then the spider thread of my resolve breaks, and I'm weeping into my sleeves.

I will live with Aunt Bryony. Mother can find someone else. My presence will just remind her of my failure, or her failure as she might see it, to safeguard my nose. I nearly laugh out loud. I thought I *was* choosing my nose, lying to Court about not liking him. But love fell into my path, and I tried, but I couldn't get out of the way fast enough.

I hike back to the house, passing the workshop. Mother's form is framed by the window. The sight of her, already back to work, puts a hot stone in my sandal. She's still young; she could have another daughter if she wanted. Maybe the next one will be a keeper.

The sun has already set. I'm still so keyed up, I hardly feel the drop in temperature. I stomp into the house, and dial Aunt Bryony's number. She's probably still in the air, but I'll leave her a message. Then I'll start packing.

The phone rings, and then I hear a click. But instead of going to voicemail, someone answers. "Hello?"

"Aunt Bryony?"

"Hi, dear."

"I really need to speak with you."

"In person or on the phone?"

"Er, aren't you in Hawaii?"

"I'm at the bottom of Parrot Hill. I didn't want your mother to smell me before I could decide whether I wanted to come back."

She never left. "I'll see you in five minutes then."

THIRTY-EIGHT

"Whether a plant feels pain when cut is open to debate. What is not, is that pruning is necessary if the plant is to thrive."
—*Champa, Aromateur, 1778*

AS SOON AS Aunt Bryony hauls herself out of the car, I hug her close. "You didn't leave."

"I rescheduled the jet for tomorrow. Decided to visit Meyer Botanical. I haven't been there in years." She glances at our rounded front door. "And I figured it wasn't going so well here, but, well, I didn't want to interfere."

The door opens and Mother marches out, wearing her dark woolen jacket from Mongolia with the embroidered edging. "You."

"Good to see you, too, sister."

They're so alike, even I would have a hard time telling them apart were it not for the clothes and the opposing gray streaks.

Mother crosses her arms in front of her, as tightly closed as an iris bud. My aunt looks her up and down. "Well, I have a few pounds on you. But a few less wrinkles, too. You haven't been using the cornflower, I can tell."

"I'm sorry you had to come all this way to tell me that. Now go back to your tropical paradise and your boatman with the bad hair. I've already covered for you with Alice Sawyer, just like I always do, though God knows why. Good-bye."

"Mother!"

Mother pivots around, but instead of going back inside the house, she marches through the gate to the garden.

Aunt Bryony runs her hand down my bare arm, which has started to goose bump. "You smell like you've been hit by a truck of swamp mud and sour strawberries."

I almost miss the smell of my own anxiety. My throat begins to stick again and I can't answer.

She puts an arm around my shoulders. "Let's go talk to her."

Mother's wearing her *Thursday* gloves, even though it's Monday, and pruning a rosebush.

"Put the clippers down, Dahli. I trimmed it yesterday."

"I can see that. This is not a forty-five-degree angle." Mother points at one of the clipped branches.

"You're welcome."

"For what? For sticking your nose where it doesn't belong?"

Aunt Bryony folds her arms. "I have every right to be here. Mother left the garden to us both."

"How convenient of you to reclaim your interest now, after I've spent the last twenty years working this soil by myself." Mother doesn't find anywhere to prune so she repockets her clippers. "Where were you that spring when the garden flooded and I had to replant everything? My fingers bled every night for a year."

I've never seen Mother so mad. She's almost spitting. She sways slightly as she glares through the rosebush. Cursing, she storms over to a basket of tools and removes a shovel. We follow her as she marches twenty paces in another direction.

Mother sinks to her knees, and dirt starts flying.

"I'm sorry," says Aunt Bryony in a gentler voice.

"You abandoned me."

"You told me I was useless. I lost my smell, remember?" Aunt Bryony slides her eyes to me. Then she kneels down beside Mother, who's still flinging dirt.

"I needed my sister," huffs Mother. "Not a nose. I have one of those, remember?"

"What about your daughter?" My voice comes out small and unsure.

Mother notices me, holding my elbows. "Of course I—" She pulls her shovel out of the dirt and gestures with it at my nose. "Don't try to sidetrack me. What happened between your aunt and me has nothing to do with you and me. You withheld vital information."

"Maybe she wouldn't have if she wasn't so scared you'd seal her in a cave."

"And you're the Miss Nose-It-All now. Seal her in a cave, my foot." Her eyes slide to me. "For heaven's sake. I would've understood the error."

"Yes, because you're a fount of blue thistle," mutters Aunt Bryony, referring to that foggy note of empathy.

"Oh, you're one to talk about blue thistle. You weren't exactly brimming with blue thistle yourself when you left me BY MYSELF."

"It's not just that." I hear myself say. My ears ring with the noise of their dispute.

"What is it, then?" Mother snaps.

I gather the fibers of my courage before they fly away. "Sometimes it feels like the only thing you care about is my nose. Like, you never ask me about how school is going. You didn't even know I aced my Spanish test. Or that I fell on my face in Cardio the first day. It's like you forget I'm a human being."

Mother's nose reddens and her face looks on the verge of crumpling. "Is that what you think, Mim?" Her small hands grip the edges of the shovel.

Aunt Bryony tries to take it from her. "I dug up the oca tubers yesterday."

Mother won't let go of the shovel, and the two wrestle with it. "How did you know I planted oca tubers here?"

"I smelled them, of course."

"*Smelled* them?"

My aunt flexes a thin eyebrow at me, and I hug myself tighter. "Aunt Bryony's smell came back. It was the seawater. There is no jinx." I almost tell her about the falling hearts, too, but decide she's had enough surprises for one day.

Mother's grip on the shovel weakens. "I don't believe it."

"Fine, don't." Aunt Bryony gets to her feet, and her nostrils twitch. "But you might want to take care of that spurge weed growing in section D. It's going to sprout soon."

Mother also gets to her feet. She sniffs, then her mouth splits open. "How did you . . ." Her voice grows weak. "It can't be."

"I always told you our mother loved William."

My skin tingles. "The groundskeeper?"

Aunt Bryony gives me a solemn nod. "He was your grandfather. They loved each other for fifteen years before our mother sent him away, and her nose was legendary."

Mother snorts. "Then why would he leave?"

"Because even love witches have love problems." She slips her hands into the pockets of her red traveling cloak. "Of course you wouldn't understand that."

Mother points the shovel at my aunt. "You sure waited a long time to tell me."

"You would've known earlier if you'd read my letter." Aunt Bryony's earrings swing.

"I threw it away."

"Why?"

"Some things can't be fixed with pen and paper." Mother's voice is getting hoarse. "Anyway, something so important, why couldn't you tell me in person? You have a Cloud Air card, too. At least, let your fingers do the walking." She makes a phone with her hand and holds it to her ear.

"I did call you after *you* threw away my letter, but you never answered. And anyway, don't take your anger out on poor Mimsy."

"*Mimosa* is none of your business."

"I called *her*," I pipe up. "Aunt Bryony came to help me."

Mother throws down her trowel and climbs to her feet. "I don't believe this. Was she here to help when you were born?" Yanking off her scarf, she shakes the bundle at my aunt. "Imagine nursing a baby and weeding at the same time." Back to me. "Did she watch you take your first smells? Nope. Send any birthday cards? Ha! It's not like she forgot the address."

"I didn't know about Mimsy until I read the 'Living Miracles' article in the *Times*."

"She was five when they wrote that! What have you been doing for the last ten years?"

"Waiting for you to respond to my letter." Aunt Bryony pulls the edges of her cloak more snugly around her. Two bright spots of pink appear on her cheeks. "Anyway, I already said I'm sorry. Now it's your turn to apologize to Mimsy."

"For what? And will you please stop calling her that?" She reties her scarf around her neck with exaggerated movements, but it comes undone again.

Bryony stares up at the palm fronds. "For having your nose so deep in the soil you don't know if it's raining on your ass." She prods Mother with the double barrel of her amber eyes.

"You were always the crude one." Mother stuffs her hands into her pockets. She looks like she belongs somewhere on the Asian steppes, with the woolly jacket, the scarf, and the two bright spots of red on her cheeks. "And I have no idea what you mean."

"She asked you a question that you still have not answered."

My head throbs and my throat feels swollen, as if I swallowed a fig whole.

"What question?"

"She wants to know if you love her."

Every plant in the garden seems to hold its breath. Even the papaya trees seem to clutch their fruits tighter, as if afraid they might drop them and ruin the silence.

Mother lets out an exasperated breath. "Of course I do! You're my daughter, aren't you?" Her eyes flood with emotion, and she holds herself so tightly, her body trembles. Some invisible wall keeps us apart. I fear if I reach out to her, she might break or I might, and I won't know how to put back the pieces.

An evening breeze stings my cheeks. I didn't even know they were wet.

Abruptly, Mother flings one end of her scarf behind her, nearly whipping my aunt in the face. "You may take your quilt. After that, I hope you have a nice trip back to your own life." She retreats to the house, a solitary majorette.

This time we don't follow her. She doesn't even bother to remove her clogs before entering the kitchen.

My aunt pulls a handkerchief from her pocket and hands it to me. "Well. You know about the giant sequoias, right?"

"They need fire to grow."

"Yes. But unlike us, sequoias only need one fire. We go through several in the course of our lives. It's the human condition. We never stop growing."

"I have a lot to learn still, I know."

"Not just you." Her mouth softens into a smile. Then she tucks her arm under mine and tugs me toward the courtyard. "As I said, the quilt is yours, but keep your mother out of the oca tubers. In her mood, she'll dig herself back to Oman if you let her."

"You can't leave like this."

"I can't stay here, dear. Not after that."

"But you have to stay somewhere." I have to get them talking again, for Mother, for all of us, but that won't happen if my aunt leaves. "It's getting late, and—"

"There's a motel—"

"Please. Just this one thing."

She clamps her lips and one eyebrow hitches. She shifts her gaze from the gate to the house.

Before she can protest, I say, "You can have your old room. I'll stay in the guest room." We keep it for out-of-town clients, but since we have enough local clients to keep us busy, we haven't used the room in years.

Mother's door is closed and her room is dark when we return

to the house. I fix my aunt squash soup, then she retires, too.

After everything that has happened today, I want to crawl under the covers and not wake until spring. But instead of going to our tomb-like guest room, I fetch the key from our kitchen cupboard and head to the workshop.

THIRTY-NINE

"Larkspur's Last Word is for the parrots. Just stay out of the salt water. (But if you don't, your nose will come back, don't worry!)"
—Bryony, *Aromateur, 2017*

THE GARDEN IS dark, but not quiet. The lights I spent a winter stringing around the cherry trees resemble giant clouds of fireflies, and hum in a way I never noticed before. Gravel scrapes and crunches under my feet as I head to the workshop.

I insert the business end of the key, worn smooth after so many years of service. William—my grandfather—used this same key. I turn the heart-shaped end. The lock fights me, then with a screech, gives way.

Standing in the threshold, I notice particles floating in front of me, illuminated by our old-fashioned hurricane sconces. I never noticed how my own breath makes the dust motes dance. I imagine the way that dust used to smell, like old books, sluggish on the liftoff and mellowing into dried leaves. The memory is so vivid, I can almost . . . but not quite.

Instead, my head fills with the symphony of chirping crickets playing in counterpoint to a hooting owl.

I hang up the key, and get to work.

The alarm wakes me before the rooster crows. After dressing, I pack a basket full of food and other supplies, then hurry to the workshop.

Everything's in order here. Last night, I cleaned the bathroom, stocked fresh towels and blankets. I even brought a crossword book, which I thought was a nice touch.

My breath lifts in white plumes, but I'm too pumped to feel the chill in the air. I set water to boil on a hot plate. Then I fetch Layla's Sacrifice, which has shriveled into a crispy nest. The second bud looks like a corn nut.

I set the terrarium atop the workshop table. Using a hooked pole, I budge open the skylight.

I strike a single match against our workshop table and flames dance before me. The dried leaves of Layla's Sacrifice ignite as soon as I touch it with the fire. Soon, the whole plant is a burning mass. Smoke lifts in gray tendrils toward the skylight, the marmalade scent now dusky and bitter. When enough smoke has escaped, I replace the glass lid over the burning plant and the flames die. The glass cage fills with gray smoke and ash.

Any moment they'll come running. The smell of burned Layla's Sacrifice is strong enough to awaken any aromateur.

As I wait, I prepare tea. I haven't felt so calm in weeks. Mother and Aunt Bryony just need a chance to work out their problems. It's like the old key to our workshop—with the right amount of jiggling, I feel sure their problems can be worked out.

Aunt Bryony arrives first. She waves the silk sleeves of her pajamas. "What happened here?" She crosses to the table and squints at the sacrificial terrarium. "You *burned* Layla?"

Mother bursts into the workshop next. Her blue flannel pants stick out from under her terry-cloth robe. A wavy line from her sleep mask runs across her forehead. "What the blazes is going on?"

"Please, make yourself comfortable." Into the two cups, I pour perfectly steeped Ceylon. "Honey? Cream?"

Mother doesn't sit. "What are you doing?"

Aunt Bryony pushes her teacup and saucer at me. "I'll take both."

Mother wilts Aunt Bryony with her gaze. "Mim, tell me what you are doing NOW."

I serve my elders, placing Mother's teacup on the workshop table next to where she stands, brittle, holding her arms and observing me.

Aunt Bryony slurps her tea.

I cross back to the blue door. Dawn peeks through when I open it. "Aunt Bryony said William locked you in here once to sort out your differences. Please don't use the skylight."

"Mim." Mother starts toward me. "This is not funny."

I shut the door behind me. As I jam in the key, I feel Mother trying to pull the door back open. She's faster than I thought.

Quickly, I twist the key, and for a panic-stricken moment, I wonder if it will fail me.

But this time, the lock clicks easily into place.

"Mim!" Mother wails.

"I have a plane to catch in two hours," Aunt Bryony calls loudly.

"Well then, you'd better get talking," I call back. I wait patiently outside the door.

"You go climb out the window," Aunt Bryony says in a fainter voice.

"I most certainly will not do that. You do it."

"I'd get stuck. You weigh less. You'll make it. I'll push."

"No."

After a pause, Aunt Bryony calls through the door. "Are you bribable?"

"No."

"Come on, honey. How about a new car?"

"She doesn't know how to drive," snaps Mother.

"No? What kind of teenager lives in California and doesn't know how to drive?"

"She's only fifteen."

"And next year she'll be sixteen. Better start teaching her now."

"Now you're the expert on raising teenagers." I can already see the dent between Mother's eyebrows deepen. Probably Aunt Bryony has the same groove.

"It doesn't take an expert to realize when a young lady is growing up. You never even told her about Edward and the No Mister."

Silence. I stick my ear to the door. When no one speaks further, I say, "What's the No Mister?"

"It's 'No, Mr.' Get it?" says Aunt Bryony.

I choke on my own spit. They have a nickname for BBG, too.

"Your mother hit him with No Mister seven times before she believed me."

"I will explain, if you don't *mind*." Mother spends a moment clearing her throat. "Well, Mim, you're a young lady now. Boys will be calling for you."

My cheeks warm. "I'm not six."

"Up the G-rating, Dahli."

Mother grunts in indignation and footsteps thud, as if my aunt pushed her aside. Aunt Bryony takes over. "Mimsy, you're more lovable than you think. If you need to remist, our aromateur's pollen is not the reason someone likes you."

"Meaning—?"

"Your boo is into you."

Mother snorts loudly.

I stare at the wood grain of the door, slow to make sense of what she's saying. Court liked me for me, not because of being infected by aromateur's pollen. The ground seems to pitch, and I put my hands on the rough door to steady myself.

"Does falling in love have a scent?"

"Theoretically—" Mother begins just as Aunt Bryony says, "Butterscotch pudding."

I stare through the peeling blue paint. Court told me I smelled like butterscotch pudding when we first met.

"You can't detect it because all aromateurs smell like butterscotch pudding," my aunt continues. "Work with love, and eventually it gets into the bloodstream. Our olfaction adapts to no longer notice it."

"But I can smell my other heart notes."

"Not all of them. Some are too small to be detectable by our brains, well, your brains, though your noses know."

"And makes your brain so special?" comes Mother's incredulous voice.

"I'm telling you, a good dunk in salt water does wonders. You should try it."

"So, what do I do about someone who is, er, into me?" I ask quietly.

No one speaks and I'm not sure if anyone heard me.

But then Mother's voice replies, "You'll have to let him get over you the old-fashioned way."

"Or not," adds Aunt Bryony brightly.

I rest my forehead against the door. Court already got over me the old-fashioned way, if by old-fashioned Mother meant "hopped the bullet train to recovery."

"Mim, you better open this door before we kill each other."

"Sorry. I have school now."

They protest loudly. I try to ignore them as I tread back to the house. Locking them up could be a disaster. We might be in for a very frosty winter at Sweetbriar Perfumes. On the bright side, at least I won't be treated to the scent of all those burning tires. As for Aunt Bryony, I haven't felt the force of her anger yet, but something tells me I want to stay far away. Extreme measures were necessary, though. After all, what are the chances they'd ever be in the same slice of the world again, let alone the same room?

They do have a phone. If Mother got desperate enough, she could call a locksmith, though I bet the thought of a stranger tromping through our garden would put her off calling for a little while. At least Aunt Bryony could cancel her flight.

I don't really go to school, so I can keep an eye on them, though I do leave a message with the school secretary, citing a "family emergency." Time to gather eggs, a task Mother usually takes care of. The chickens have already flown the coop, and I collect an even dozen. Using the front of my skirt as a basket, I carry them to the kitchen.

As I cross our bull's-eye courtyard, a heavy thud followed by scraping sounds carry from the front of the house. I listen to the silence being scratched, grateful to my ears for sticking by me all these years, despite my inattention.

Still holding the eggs, I stand on my toes and peep over the gate.

The back of Court's shirt pulls out from his jeans as he

squats, positioning a box onto a dolly.

I gasp. "What are you doing?"

He freezes, then slowly straightens up. A lock has pulled away from the rest of his neatly combed hair, but his part is ruler straight. "Delivering bricks." He rests an arm on the top of the dolly. "I guess I couldn't wait to patch things up."

I fall back onto my heels and say through the gate, "Our wishing well?"

"Among other things." His footsteps draw near. "Mel told me about Kali's journal."

It takes me a few moments to process what he's saying. Melanie told him?

He peers over the gate and reaches for the latch. "May I?"

Before I can answer, the gate opens and suddenly we're standing face-to-face, with only a skirt full of eggs between us.

Amusement flits across his face when he takes in my makeshift apron. But then he's back to being serious. "I'm an ass for believing you would actually fix me, even with a fake—"

"Forget it."

"Why didn't you say anything?"

"I was afraid it'd get back to Vicky. Then, when I lost my smell—"

"You lost your smell?"

"It's only temporary, I think."

He winces. "How?"

My wrist cramps, and I shift position, causing the eggs to

roll around. "I thought it was because I fell in love with you, but it was because of the salt water."

"What did you say?"

"It was the salt water. Love witches don't mix well with salt. Sort of like garden snails."

His eyes soften. "I meant the other thing."

I retrace my sentence and gulp. I can't *say* things like that, especially now that there's a new girl in his life. My lips have suddenly gone dry. I step back. "Doesn't matter anymore. It was nice of you to bring us bricks." The eggs start to tremble.

"Let me help you." He takes the corners of my skirt before I drop them. Thank the lilies for leggings.

I knead my numb hands together. Court gazes at me, his face full of longing, and the memory of a campfire springs to my mind. Closer, he tugs my dazed self by the skirt.

Then the chatter of familiar voices breaks the silence.

"They got out!" I jerk back.

Thankfully, he doesn't drop my skirt. "Who?"

"Mother and Aunt Bryony. They'll put me in the cold press. You have to go."

It's too late. They've already seen us. I collect my skirt and grit my teeth.

"Which one's your mom?"

"The one who's not smiling. Just don't look her in the eye."

Mother strides up, and it strikes me that even though she's not smiling, neither is she frowning. But Aunt Bryony, holding a pie pan with a chunk of frankincense on it, looks like she discovered gold. She give me a thumbs-up from beneath the plate, though I don't know if that's for Mother or Court or her nugget.

The twins appraise me through the same hooded cat eyes, magnified in the case of Aunt Bryony, who's wearing Mother's reading glasses. They even have the same prescription.

"Nice to see you again, Court," says Aunt Bryony.

"Likewise." His brow creases as his gaze shifts between Mother and Aunt Bryony.

"Have I met you, too?" Mother asks dryly. She picks up an empty flowerpot.

I recover my breath. "How'd you get out?"

Mother transfers my eggs into her pot. "That shall remain a secret in the event we decide to lock you up."

Aunt Bryony leans in. "It was a snap."

I sniff out of reflex for burnt tires, but all I get is soil and lavender from the closest bushes. "So . . . you're not mad anymore?"

Aunt Bryony lifts her plate. "I will be if she doesn't share this."

"Get your own frankincense. You have a Cloud Air card." Mother pushes her flowerpot of eggs into Court's midsection. "Do you know how to boil water?"

Aunt Bryony tsks her tongue. "Don't mind her." She steers Court by the elbow toward the kitchen. "She gets cranky every time she's incarcerated."

Mother doesn't release her mask of control until they

disappear into the house. Then she heaves a long sigh and reaches for me. "Honey, I'm sorry."

She hugs me tight with her bony but stalwart arms, and tears spring to my eyes.

"I shouldn't have tried so hard to keep you from the world." Mother's voice trembles and she caps her words with a loud sniff. It turns up the waterworks happening in my own eyes. "Though you can't blame me for wanting to save you from a curse."

A laugh escapes me and that sets her to laughing, too. But then she turns serious again. "You see, I just didn't want, want to—" She claps a hand to her mouth.

"You won't lose me, Mother. We're a family." An odd one, but is there any other kind? "And I *want* to be an aromateur. One day."

"As great as your grandmother Narcissa?"

I slip my warm hand into her cool one. "No, as great as you."

FORTY

"THERE IS NO FLOWER QUITE SO EXQUISITE,

AS SHE WHO ANSWERS TO 'DAUGHTER.'"

—*Rosie, Aromateur, 1672*

KALI'S EYES HOP from Aunt Bryony to Mother. "Dang. Which one's witch?"

The four of us stand in the garden near the well, which overflows with gardenia.

"Aunt Bryony is the one with the earrings."

My best friend looks like a Polynesian princess in her homecoming attire—white lavalava, styled with flip-flops and a gold bracelet. For me, she procured a dress of blush-colored silk from Twice Loved with balloon sleeves that my aunt snipped off with the sewing scissors. I float my arms above my head, reveling in the freedom of my strapless gown. According to Aunt Bryony, the dramatic decrease in the number of botanicals going in through my nose means a proportionate reduction in aromateur pollen. In other words, I'm no longer so contagious. For the time being.

Aunt Bryony places a tuberose lei around Kali's neck, while

Mother produces a corsage from a box. I gasp when I see it. It's the second bud from Layla's Sacrifice. It's no longer shriveled like a dried corn nut, but a white bud edged with pink, like the head of a brush dragged through paint. Mother wrapped it with tiny loops of pearls.

"How? I burned it."

Mother fusses with its placement. "Some things never die. It's useless for elixirs now, but it'll still smell sweet." Then she sprays BBG on my hair like a beautician. "Just in case."

Aunt Bryony swats her arm. "She hardly needs No Mister anymore, I told you. And that stuff is expensive."

"I know that. You used half my jasmine to make it." She stops spraying and fiddles with one of my hairpins. "How would you like to spend the summer with Aunt Bryony in Hawaii?"

I pull away from her to see if she's serious. She clamps a hairpin between her lips.

Kali clasps her hands together. "Say yes, Nosey."

"Yes! But, who's going to help you?"

She removes the hairpin from her mouth. "I decided it's time to modernize."

Aunt Bryony snorts. "It was that time twenty years ago." She removes the lens cover from an expensive-looking camera and aims it at Kali. "More attitude. Come on, work it!"

Kali unleashes a supermodel pout, and Aunt Bryony snaps away.

"Your aunt's going to order some new equipment for me. But

I'm keeping my beam scale." She throws Aunt Bryony a warning look.

Loud squawking from overhead halts further conversation. A swarm of birds with bright-green feathers swoops down out of nowhere and dives into our palm trees.

Aunt Bryony shades her eyes with her hand. "Well, isn't that something? I haven't seen them since Mother died."

"Neither have I. They haven't been back for twenty years."

"Those are the parrots?" I stretch my eyes open as wide as they can go.

Kali covers her ears. "They sure make a lot of noise."

The parrots leave the trees and start circling above us. "That's not all they make." Mother covers her head with her arms. "Let's go inside before they ruin your finery."

From the minute I lay eyes on my tuxedoed escort aboard the SS *Argonaut*, I'm floating. Even when Kali is crowned homecoming queen to the squeals of her date, Cassandra, I'm still so starry-eyed that I almost forget to snap their picture.

One table over, I hear Vicky boast, "I knew Kali was a lesbian all along."

Everyone's too busy cheering to notice. After a nod from his date, Lauren, a freshly shampooed Drew coaxes the sour-faced Vicky onto the dance floor.

Though I will never be chummy with Vicky, the sight of her giggling gives me a weirdly warm feeling. All it took was a cheerful heart like the one inside Drew to break through the ice. Did I ever think in a million years the most popular girl at school could be BFF with the gamer nerd? No. Then again, I never dreamed that the soccer star would be holding my hand.

A Michael Jackson mash-up hits the airwaves, and that's my cue. I pull Court to the dance floor and he shows me just how light he is on his feet. Behind him, Kali desperately tries to feed me dance moves, like always. But I've found my own groove, and even though it makes me look like a whirling dervish, I don't fall once. If people wonder why Warrior Sawyer is getting down with the school love witch, no one says anything. Turns out, people care less about me than they care about not tripping on the dance floor.

When the song ends, Court leads me by the hand to the upper deck. The ship lurches as we climb the narrow staircase, passing by the newly crowned homecoming king, Whit, who is snuggling with Pascha. They don't even notice us pass.

Stars, like sequins, scatter the black cloak of the sky. We find a secluded spot near the bow. The ocean's so black, it's invisible, only felt through the *shushing* of the waves against the hull of the ship. I revel in the velvety sounds, in the way they echo in my ear.

My orchid corsage is open now, its scent so honey-sweet, it even sings to my ordinary nose. Freesia on the front end and muscat on the back. That's all I can do for now, but with luck, one day I shall smell the hundreds of notes in between.

Mother said some things never die. Inhaling again, I finally see. Layla's Sacrifice smells exactly like a mother's love, honed by fire, tested through time.

Paper crackles as Court pulls something out of his jacket pocket. He holds up a brown packet. "When I asked you what three things you would do if you couldn't smell, you said eat movie snacks and float. M&M's were easier to fit in my pocket than the Dead Sea."

He pulls the M&M's just out of my reach. "You never told me what the third one was."

My heart begins to applaud in my chest, growing more urgent as the moment stretches out. I tilt my face up to his and just before I kiss him, I whisper, "This."

ACKNOWLEDGMENTS

"LET US BE GRATEFUL TO PEOPLE WHO MAKE US HAPPY.
THEY ARE THE CHARMING GARDENERS WHO MAKE
OUR SOULS BLOSSOM."
—*Marcel Proust*

I have several people to thank for helping me nurture Mim's story to full bloom: my intrepid agent, Kristin Nelson, and the Nelson Literary Agency, and my publisher, Katherine Tegen, and her vibrant team—in particular my scent-sational editor, Maria Barbo, and her whip-smart assistant, Rebecca Schwarz. A full field of beaming sunflowers for you in gratitude.

To several key plants in my garden: stargazer lilies for Stephanie Garber, purple freesia for Mónica Bustamante Wagner, Creamsicle tulips for Jeanne Schriel, Zahara zinnias for Caitin Swift, and edelweiss for Evelyn Skye. Thank you also to all the people who blow their magic flower dust my way: Anna Shinoda, Beth Hull, Janice Hardy, Kat Brauer, Marieke Nijkamp, Jodi Meadows, I. W. Gregorio, Kelly Loy Gilbert, Virginia Boecker, Alice Chen, Ana Inglis, Adlai Coronel, Sabaa Tahir, Abigail Hing Wen, Parker Peevyhouse, Jessica Taylor, Amie Kaufman, MacKenzie Van Engelenhoven, Dahlia Adler, Rachel

Evangelista, Angela Mann, Eric Elfman, Bijal Vakil, Susan Repo, Angela Hum, Jennifer Fan, Ariele Wildwind, and Vasanthi Suresh. May heirloom Damask rose petals ever be strewn in your path.

To my amazing family, Laura Ly, Alyssa Cheng, Dolores and Wai Lee, Evelyn and Carl Leong, and to my sweet peas, Avalon, Bennett, and Jonathan: You are the rare flowers that make my life beautiful.